MEDICINE FOR THE BLUES
a trilogy of novels

Based on extensive period research, *Medicine for the Blues* explores the complexities of gender and sexuality through the historical lens of the early 1920s.

Book 1 *Acquaintance*

As a young surgeon, Carl Holman has experienced the horrors of World War I and the death of his lover, a fellow officer. Back home after the War, he befriends a young jazz musician who he hopes will become a companion he can share his life with. But this is Oregon: the Ku Klux Klan is gaining influence, homosexual acts are illegal, and such a relationship will jeopardize Carl's promising medical career. Musician Jimmy Harper has his own dreams for the future and his own obstacles to overcome before he will allow himself to accept Carl's love. Published in Fall 2017.

Book 2, *Chicago Blues*, tells the story of Jimmy Harper's adventures in Chicago where he becomes entangled with an array of underworld characters. Available Spring 2018.

Book 3: *Dangerous Medicine* returns to Portland where Carl Holman struggles to navigate his medical career in the face of social and personal obstacles from the KKK, society, and other dangers. Available Fall 2018.

CHICAGO BLUES

Book 2:
MEDICINE FOR THE BLUES
trilogy

by
Jeff Stookey

PictoGraph Publishing
Portland, Oregon 2018

Medicine for the Blues trilogy
Book 2: Chicago Blues

PictoGraph Publishing
©2018 by Jeff Stookey

Book and Cover Design
Amy Livingstone, Sacred Art Studio
sacredartstudio.net

ISBN: 978-1-7326036-1-5

Library of Congress Control Number:
2018908708

PERMISSIONS PAGE

DEDICATION

from "For the young who want to,"

Talent is what they say
you have after the novel
is published and favorably
reviewed. Beforehand what
you have is a tedious
delusion, a hobby like knitting.

—Marge Piercy

For Ken:
When you first began learning to knit, you unraveled
the yarn of that sweater over and over, only to start again.
Where would I be without your fine example?
If the sweater fits, wear it.

After his death in 1983, Dr. Carl Holman's memoirs were found in a desk drawer. The estate sale manager donated the document to the local historical society. This quotation was paperclipped to the front of the manuscript:

"I've held nothing back of the bad, added nothing extra of the good, and if it happens that I've used some small embellishment, it's only because of the gap in my memory; I may have supposed something to be true that could well have been so but never something that I knew to be false."

—Jean-Jacques Rousseau, *Confessions*

Facsimile of the title page from Carl Holman's manuscript.

Memories of Jimmy

by Carl Travis Holman, MD

completed 1981

"Oh, let me, true in love, but truly write."
-William Shakespeare, Sonnet 21

From time to time, I forget the self-pity I've fallen into: he will make me strong, we will travel, we will hunt in the desert, we will sleep on the cobblestones of strange cities, carefree, carefree.

—Arthur Rimbaud, "Delirium I: The Foolish Virgin, The Infernal Bridegroom," *A Season in Hell*

ONE

October 1923

As Jimmy Harper rode out of Portland, Oregon, with the Diggs Monroe Jazz Orchestra headed for Chicago, he felt something tugging at him to stay. He was leaving Carl Holman behind. But he disregarded the feeling and watched the road ahead, never looking back.

It was a fair October morning, and the six young men in the two automobiles stuffed with luggage and musical instruments were off on an adventure. Their first destination was a small town in eastern Washington that was home to the state college. Diggs had belonged to a fraternity during his truncated college career in southern California, and he had arranged for the band to stay the night with brothers of his chapter on campus. The Greek brothers coaxed them into playing some tunes the afternoon they arrived and were so impressed that they quickly organized an informal dance that night. So the band got paid for an unanticipated booking.

From there the band drove east for many days. They were delayed by a flat tire while crossing a bridge over an Idaho river. They got stuck in snow in the heavens of the Rockies. They were caught in a windstorm in eastern Montana. Crossing the vast godforsaken prairies of North Dakota, they took a wrong turn and got lost, winding up with both cars stuck in mud on a reservation. An Indian family passing by in a horse-drawn wagon pulled them out of the wallow. The driver told them they should get a horse and said his uncle had one for sale. The band of musicians declined the horse, but they did buy a bottle of bootleg whiskey from him, and before driving on they paid him extra for the tow. Outside of a small Minnesota border town, they ran out of gas and had to spend the night in their cars when a rain storm caught them by surprise. At long last, they arrived in Minneapolis.

Diggs had lined up a date playing for a homecoming at the University of Minnesota, where a fraternity brother of his was now teaching. The frat brothers put the band members up on couches and cots in nooks and crannies of the fraternity house. The band was so well-received that they were asked to play at a Sunday tea dance the following afternoon. Next, they drove on to Madison for another date at the university there. When Diggs and the band left on the last leg of their trip to Chicago, they were flush with cash.

At a roadhouse where they'd stopped for lunch, the band members began talking about what they would do first in the Windy City. Chuck, the trombone player, was a big bear of a fellow who rarely talked, preferring to let his horn speak for him. He surprised them when he volunteered, "I want to see the Loop first." Everyone turned toward him. "What about you, Diggs?" he said.

The band leader and business manager of the group scrunched up his freckled face and ran a hand over his red hair. "I'm going to be pretty busy hustling up play dates for you fellas. I don't think I'll have much time for sightseeing. I'll be lucky if I can find time to practice my cornet."

Jimmy's old college friend Howard Henderson, the clarinet player, repeated his intention to go to a high-toned brothel. He had a reputation as a womanizer and his looks helped him out in that department. Because of his suave demeanor and air of worldly knowledge, the other band members tended to look up to him.

Larry, the banjo player, smirked at Howard. His long, thin face and pointed nose always reminded Jimmy of a weasel, and Jimmy often had second thoughts about Larry's judgment.

"Hey, I'm with you," Larry said. "I haven't been able to get close to a girl this whole trip." The remark was no surprise and the others laughed. Larry was so brazen with girls that he usually offended them. He affected a bravado but lacked Howard's cool finesse. "What do you say, Jimmy?"

"I don't know." Jimmy hesitated. "I'd like to hang onto my money until we see how things work out in the big city."

"Oh-ho. I bet you're just chicken." Larry elbowed Jimmy.

"Aw, get outta here." Jimmy elbowed him back.

Bill, the drummer, who spent a lot of his time with Larry, chimed in. "Why, I bet Jimmy hasn't gotten any since he broke up with his girl this summer." There was a dumb grin on Bill's face. He had bad acne, bad table manners, and a bad habit of making thoughtless remarks intended as jokes. The band members all knew that Jimmy's break-up was still a sore spot.

Jimmy shot Bill a piercing glance.

Larry caught Jimmy's look and said, "That is, unless Jimmy's turned fairy on us and he's been getting it from that doctor fella." Amused with himself, Larry let out a horselaugh, and Bill joined in.

"You haven't turned pansy on us, have you?" Bill called out. The remark could be heard across the cafe over the murmur of the other diners.

A sudden rage flooded Jimmy and before he knew what he was doing, he jumped up, and with more force than he intended, yelled, "Oh, go to hell, you bastards." A silence fell over the cafe. As Jimmy turned to walk away, his coat caught on his chair and it fell to the floor with a clatter. He stormed out the door.

When he got hold of his emotions, he was a quarter mile up

the road. Something told Jimmy he should just keep on walking and never turn back.

The sound of a stream running alongside the road murmured to him through the trees. He remembered talking to Carl by a stream at the Grange dance not long after they first met. He missed Carl with a deep ache that surprised him.

He stopped and took a deep breath. Carl had listened with concern when Jimmy described his disastrous engagement to his girlfriend Mary. Jimmy had wanted to prove his manhood after Carl made that pass at him, so he proposed to the girl and persuaded her to have sex. She had seemed so willing and passionate, but then Jimmy wasn't able to perform. His wounded pride resisted the memory.

To hell with Larry and his insinuations, Jimmy thought, maybe I should just forget about Chicago—and the band, too.

Deep in thought, he walked on. Up ahead through the trees, the stream babbled along below the roadway, and across the water an embankment with railroad tracks rose above it. In a clearing farther on, the smoke from a small campfire caught his attention. There sat two hobos, one was about 30 with a full dark beard, the other, a youngster. A passing fantasy about taking up the life of a hobo flickered across Jimmy's mind. Maybe he could befriend these knights of the road and they would teach him how to hop a freight back to Oregon and Carl.

Then doubts overwhelmed him. What would he do without the band? Jimmy slowed his pace. What if they left without him?

Jimmy wanted a musical career and he thought that he could have that with the band. Besides, he had been with them the better part of a year, and now he felt somehow bound to them. He might be able to find another band or make it on his own, but he knew he was not prepared to do that now. Standing there, teetering on the cusp of the past and the future, he had no idea what tomorrow would bring, and it seemed safer to cling to something he knew than to strike out into the unknown all by himself.

Jimmy stopped and fumbled for a cigarette. As he struck a

match, he noticed that his hands were still trembling. He knew he had to calm down and think this through.

Maybe the band could make it big in Chicago, and he wanted to be there with them to make it happen. Maybe he could even learn to change and be like the fellows in the band, after all. Maybe he could go to the cat house and prove himself to them, prove his manhood, prove to himself that he could still desire women. He was willing to try. He decided he had to. Maybe he could arrange to see Mary again in Chicago and even patch things up with her after their ill-fated engagement.

He turned and headed back toward the cafe, collecting his thoughts and planning what to say to the band members, trying to think of a way to smooth over his outburst.

When he got back to the roadhouse, the band members were standing around the two cars, some leaning on the fenders, Howard with his foot up on the running board smoking. Jimmy mustered his courage and looked straight at them as he approached.

"Hey, Jimmy," Larry began, but Jimmy held up both palms to stop him.

"Fellas, look, I'm sorry about that. I didn't mean to fly off the handle. It's just that Dr. Holman has been so good to me, letting me leave my stuff at his house and all. He's been a real pal and I—I'm sorry, Larry, I know you were only kidding me."

"He didn't mean anything by it, Jimmy," Diggs stepped in. The others voiced their agreement.

"I know, I know," Jimmy raised his hands again in surrender. "I guess I'm just tired from all this traveling. I don't know what came over me. Just forget it. Let's go to Chicago. I'll ride with Larry and Howard for a while." Jimmy squeezed into the back seat of Howard's car next to the luggage and the others piled in with Diggs.

Larry settled into the passenger seat, then half-turned to look at Jimmy. As Howard pulled out, Jimmy leaned into the front seat and put one hand on Howard's shoulder and the other on Larry's and said, "Say, look, I've never even seen a whorehouse. No kidding. Let me come with you when we get to Chicago. What do you say?"

Howard shrugged and said, "It's your call." He eased the car into first gear and headed off. Larry let out a whoop and called out, "Wicked, windy city, here we come!"

TWO

The band approached Chicago as the afternoon faded. First, more small towns appeared along the road, and the open farmland gave way to the city's outskirts. More houses, more automobiles, then workshops and warehouses crowded together along the streets. Factories, monstrous operations, loomed up along the road, spewing out smoke and steam and soot. Dense truck and auto traffic slowed the band to a standstill, and people and bicycles and handcarts darted past. Smells assaulted them, a stench of animal manure and putrid flesh, burnt hair and hide, all mixing in with gasoline and diesel exhaust. The night descended as the band steadily wound their way through the congested streets and across railroad tracks, occasionally blinded by the headlights of passing locomotives. Tall buildings sprang up, surrounding them. They were engulfed by the din of trains rumbling by overhead on the tangle of black steel girders and freight whistles screaming past on nearby rails.

It was dark when at last they found their way to the Firestone Hotel, an inexpensive place where Diggs had booked rooms. As they piled out of the cars, they were hit by blasts of icy wind off the lake. It was as cold as Hades.

They checked into the hotel and moved into two rooms with twin beds, arranging for an extra bed to be brought to each room. Before anything else, Howard went to the lobby and telephoned his cousin to find out the address of the brothel. Jimmy and Chuck and Howard moved their things into one room, while Diggs took the other with Bill and Larry. After stowing their luggage and musical instruments, they went out to a nearby diner.

Diggs had already lined up two college dances through fraternity connections and he planned to drum up more work as he became familiar with the Chicago scene. While they ate, Diggs reminded everyone that they had to play for the sorority ball the next evening. In order to arrive at the ballroom in plenty of time to set up, they would be leaving the hotel at 7 sharp. "I'll give you each a hundred dollars of your earnings back at the hotel after dinner, but that's all you'll get until we've finished playing tomorrow night. That ball is going to be a high-toned affair and I want you all in good shape to play. We've got to make a good impression. So whatever you do tonight, get some rest before tomorrow evening. And I don't want any of you winding up in jail your first night in town." Diggs eyed Howard and winked. "I know where your hundred bucks is going."

Diggs went on. He wanted the band to go to a photo studio at 4 the next afternoon. They were to take their instruments with them and have some publicity pictures taken to hand out while they looked for work. Tonight he had to go meet with some people he knew, but he suggested a couple of dance halls they could check out and listen to the bands and find out what was popular. Clearly Diggs had a good sense of business, but Jimmy was no longer so sure how much Diggs cared about making great music. And at that moment, hot jazz was what Jimmy cared about most.

Back at the hotel, Diggs paid each of the band members and left for his appointment. The band members cleaned up and changed, getting ready for a night on the town.

Jimmy showered in the bathroom down the hall and studied himself in the mirror as he dried off. He thought of Carl, sleeping naked next to him—the way Jimmy's slim, hairless body fit against Carl, feeling the dark hair of Carl's chest against his back.

He dried his sand-colored hair and leaned into the mirror to see if he needed a shave. His beard was thin and pale and wouldn't need a shave till the next day. By contrast, Carl's beard began to darken his chin late each afternoon.

Jimmy evaluated himself. Not a bad face. Carl liked it. He had admired Jimmy's blue-gray eyes. Maybe he could attract a female—although, he guessed, at a whorehouse that wasn't the way things worked. As he dried himself, he looked at his penis, so different in appearance from Carl's which was uncircumcised. Jimmy hoped that he would be able to get it up for a prostitute.

Back in his room, he oiled and combed his hair, parting it carefully down the middle and slicking it back. He pictured Valentino and considered moving the part over a bit, then decided to leave it. He put on his best suit and met the rest of the band in the hotel lobby.

"Come on, lover boy," Larry said as Jimmy joined them.

They all headed off in Howard's car for a dance hall called the Avalon Gardens. It turned out to be the largest and most elegant dance palace any of them had ever seen. A band of ten white musicians, including a couple of violins, played what Jimmy judged as routine popular music. He told the others that he was hankering to see some hot Negro jazz bands. They listened to the music for a couple of hours, and Howard kept trying to meet girls and get their phone numbers. But he didn't have much success. About 11 Howard announced that he was ready to try his luck with the *filles de joie*.

"With the what?" Larry asked. Howard leaned in close to be heard over the music and said, "The ladies of the evening."

"Oh. Yeah, of course," Larry said.

"But you can all stay here and listen to the music if you want," Howard said. "I noticed some taxis out front when we came in. You can catch a ride back to the hotel with one of them."

"Hell, no, I'm sticking with you, Howard," Larry said. No one else wanted to be left out of Howard's adventures of the flesh, least of all Jimmy after the incident at the roadhouse. So they made their way out of the dance hall and back to the side street where Howard's car was parked.

The wind from earlier had let up, but the air was still chill and damp.

Howard couldn't get his car engine started, and after numerous attempts and spells of angry cursing, he gave up and suggested catching a cab. Howard's cousin had given him the address of the brothel with directions to another part of the city.

"This pleasure palace may be easier to find by cab anyway," Howard said. "Cabbies always know where the cat houses are located."

They walked back toward the dance hall, and Howard stopped at the first taxi he came to. He leaned in to ask the driver if he knew the address and to negotiate a fare. Then he turned and said, "Pile in, boys. This fellow is going to ferry us over Jordan to the Promised Land."

As they started off, they discussed the band they had just heard and argued about whether the music was any good. After a time the cab driver turned and said, "Sounds like you boys are musicians."

"Yeah," Bill answered. "We try to be."

"I'll make you a deal. I know where you boys are headin' and it ain't no cheap dive. You're gonna need all the dollars you got. Now, if you can sing me something while I drive, I'll take you across the river for free. What do you say?"

"That's mighty sportin' of you," Howard said. "What do you say, fellas?"

"Jimmy's got the best singing voice," Chuck said. "What should we do, Jimmy?"

"How about some blues for this gentleman?" Jimmy said. "Let's do 'Graveyard Blues.' You fellas can vocalize your instrumental parts and I'll take the melody in the lyrics. Okay?"

The others all agreed and Chuck took out a pocket comb and some tissue to improvise a kazoo. Jimmy counted out a rhythm and said, "Hit it." After a short musical intro, he began to sing.

"Blues on my mind and blues all around my head.
Blues on my mind and blues all around my head.
I dreamed last night
that the man that I love was dead.

I went to the graveyard, fell down on my knees.
I went to the graveyard, fell down on my knees.
And I asked the graveyard digger
to give me back my real good man, please.

The gravedigger looked me in the eye.
The gravedigger looked me in the eye.
Said, "I'm sorry, lady,
but your man has said his last good-bye."

I wrung my hands, and I wanted to scream.
I wrung my hands, and I wanted to scream.
But when I woke up,
    I found it was only a dream."

As Jimmy crooned the lyrics, the others wove their parts around the words. Loosened up from drinks at the dance hall, the band fell into this musical exercise with an uninhibited enthusiasm. The driver tapped his fingers on the steering wheel in time with the music. The black Ford glided over the dark pavement of a bridge, and the lights of the city glistened on the inky river.

With the last notes of the song, the cabby let out a laugh and a hoot. "Man, you fellas sure do know a thing or two about music. Where'd you learn that stuff?"

"We listen to phonograph records," Jimmy said. "But we came to Chicago to hear the real thing. Tell us where can we go to hear some good Negro jazz?"

The driver named a couple of clubs and their house bands. Jimmy made a mental note.

Before long the taxi drove up in front of a three-story Victorian mansion. Both the house and the neighborhood looked like they had seen better days. The lights were on and there were girls in the front window. Larry rolled down the car window and waved, and the girls blew kisses back.

"Looks like we've found the party," Howard said with a grin. He asked the cabby to drive around the corner to let them off. The band members got out and thanked the cabby for the bargain fare. Jimmy went over to the window of the cab and thanked the driver for the advice about bands and clubs and slipped him some money. As an afterthought, the cabby added, "Oh, by the way, you should be sure to catch the band at the Checker Club too. They're hot."

"The Checker Club?" Jimmy repeated. "Okay. Thanks for the tip."

As the taxi pulled away, Howard said, "I'd keep some of my money in my stocking if I were you," and he bent down to pull up his pant cuff. Jimmy had left half his money at the hotel, and he was wearing the money belt Carl had given him with the $200, but he transferred his billfold to the front pocket of his pants.

The sky had cleared a bit and a sliver of the waning moon showed between the clouds, pointing its horns to the West. The cold breeze stirred again as the men started for the front of the house.

Waves of butterflies fluttered in the pit of Jimmy's stomach, but it was different from the stage fright he felt before a musical performance. He stifled the chattering of his teeth, caused as much by nervous anticipation as by the cold wind.

But Jimmy felt better when he heard ragtime coming from inside as they mounted the front porch. The beveled glass door was opened for them by a stocky black man in a tuxedo, admitting them into a large entry hall dominated by a broad curving stairway. A laughing woman in a blue kimono was leading a man up the red carpeted steps.

The newel post at the bottom of the stairway was embellished with a bronze statue of a woman dressed in a Greek gown, unfastened at one shoulder so that her breast was exposed. In one hand she held aloft a red glass torch with an electric light and in the other hand she carried a basket containing grapes and sheaves of grain.

Three women waved down from the banister as the young men entered. A well-groomed older woman in an elegant black evening gown came forward to welcome them and introduced herself as Miss Eva. She led Howard and his friends into a plush carpeted salon, dimly lit by glittering chandeliers. Just inside the room, under the stairway, sat a heavyset older Negro man, also in a tuxedo, playing a grand piano. While the music was ragtime, it had something else to it that Jimmy couldn't name, and his attention was drawn to the piano rhythms, in spite of the many distractions that filled the room.

Some women, lounging on the overstuffed furniture, smiled and winked at the boys. A heavily rouged redhead sat in the lap of an older man in full evening dress and fed him from a brandy snifter with a spoon. Other gentlemen danced with girls in various stages of undress. At an ornate bar at the side of the room, a bartender in a tuxedo served two men in evening dress who were being fussed over by a couple of the girls. A roar of laughter burst in through an archway at the far end of the room where well-dressed men were gambling. Miss Eva invited the band members to have drinks at the bar and make themselves comfortable. When Jimmy paid for his gin cocktail, he was shocked at the charge.

As he took a seat at a table with the others, Jimmy leaned close to Howard and said, "Looks like we won't be getting drunk tonight. Now I understand what they mean by whorehouse prices."

"We didn't come here to get drunk," Howard said and turned, raising his glass in a toast. "To love and life," he said.

Larry leaned in to Howard and asked in a low voice, "How does this work? Do we pay Miss Eva or what?"

Howard said he had asked the bartender, who told him to

choose a girl. "She'll show you to a room, and then you can pay your thirty-five dollars to her."

Miss Eva approached, escorting two young women in loose attire that revealed their undergarments. "Boys, this is Lily and Rose. I'll send some more girls round for you to meet. Have another drink and enjoy yourselves."

Howard winked at the dark-haired Lily and she sauntered over to him and ruffled his hair with her fingers. He reached out and slid his hand across her posterior, then moved his arm around her waist and invited her to sit in his lap.

"Do you find me beautiful, love?" she said in a British accent as she eased onto his thigh.

"Well, beauty is one thing," Howard said, eyeing her cleavage. "And love is another thing." He reached his other arm around her and gave her a squeeze. "And sex is something else," he whispered as he nuzzled her neck.

Rose, a short blonde, asked where they were all from. Jimmy took another swallow of his drink and started to relax. He sat back and listened to the old black musician at the piano, who was now in the middle of a ragtime tune like nothing Jimmy had ever heard. He began tapping his hand on the table to the beat of the music.

Two other girls approached the table and began asking their names. A pretty blonde strolled over from the bar with a languid gait. Something about her struck Jimmy as familiar but he couldn't quite place it. He smiled at her and she introduced herself as Elsa. He told her his name and she asked if Jimmy liked dancing. He told her that he did, and she pulled him up from his seat to dance with her. They did the fox trot and got better acquainted.

"You boys part of a football team?" she asked. Jimmy told her no and explained who they were. He said he was interested in Chicago race music and asked Elsa if she would introduce him to the piano player.

"Oh, sure," she said. "He's great, ol' Mr. Keys." She told Jimmy that Mr. Keys had played piano in Storyville down in New Orleans. When the Navy shut down Storyville, he had come north to find work and ended up working as a night watchman. One night he found a piano in a room in the building he was guarding and he started playing a little every night. About a week later, one of Elsa's regulars, who was working late in the building, heard Mr. Keys playing and confronted him.

"Poor Mr. Keys was afraid he was going to lose his job," Elsa said.

The man told him that he could earn a lot more money playing piano than working as a night watchman.

"Mr. Keys has been working here ever since," she said. "That's why they call him Mr. Keys, because of all those keys he used to carry as a night watchman."

The tune came to an end and Elsa and Jimmy joined in the smattering of applause.

"Come on, sweetie, I'll introduce you." Elsa laced an arm around his waist and led him to the piano.

"I understand you used to play piano in Storyville," Jimmy said.

The piano player nodded. Jimmy complimented him on his playing and asked about the ragtime tune that he just finished.

"Well, son, I just sort of feel my way as I go along. It's easier like that and it comes out sounding better."

"It sure sounds great," Jimmy said. Mr. Keys adjusted his bulk and began to play another piece.

"I'm honored to meet you," Jimmy said. The Negro nodded to him.

Jimmy turned to Elsa, and she indicated a large brandy snifter on the piano. It had a few bills in it. Jimmy pulled out a dollar and dropped it in the container. Mr. Keys nodded to him again.

When Jimmy and Elsa returned to the table, the other fellows seemed to be enjoying themselves with the women who surrounded them. Howard was nibbling the earlobe of a short redhead in his lap. Larry was arm wrestling with a blonde. An odd-looking brunette was lighting a cigarette for Chuck. A girl in a black corset was playing a game called "waterfall" with Bill the drummer, pouring his drink into his open mouth in a thin stream from high above his head to see how high she could go.

Elsa asked Jimmy if she could fetch him another drink from the bar. He leaned close to her ear and said, "How about plain ginger ale? I don't want to get too drunk." Then he surprised himself by kissing her on the cheek. He felt a moment of genuine affection for her and then it dawned on him that something about her reminded him of Carl's friend, Charlene Devereaux. It may have been Charlie's blonde hair, but it was more than just her appearance. He couldn't define it. Maybe it was because back in Portland Charlie served as part of the ruse that Carl and Gwen were one couple and he and Charlie were another. Now Jimmy saw Elsa as a partner in his deception of the band. She would help him prove his manhood to them, and, for that, he felt a wave of gratitude towards her.

Elsa laughed as he handed her money for the bartender. Perhaps she sensed his sudden gratitude or his momentary feeling of genuine affection, but she looked at him openly for an instant, then turned and walked toward the bar. In that moment, Jimmy sensed she had let down her guard for the blink of an eye, and he had caught a glimpse inside her. Her laughter was almost convincing, but it faded a bit too fast. Her smiles seemed a little too forced.

The odd-looking brunette was telling a story about a man in a runaway automobile that had lost its brakes, and the boys were all laughing. Larry kept giving her the eye, and she went over to him. Jimmy could see Elsa across the room talking with the bartender, who poured her a shot. She tossed it back in one swallow, while the barkeep poured Jimmy's drink.

Howard stood up and asked the redhead, "Can you show me the way to the gents' room?"

"I'll do better than that," she said. "I'll show you to a private bedroom."

Howard laughed and put his arm around her. "You're a girl after my own heart."

"Well, it's not your heart I'm after, lover boy," she said as Howard kissed the side of her neck.

Larry piped up, "Yeah, Howard, it's your wallet she's after." He sounded a bit drunk.

The brunette next to him put her arm around his shoulder and cooed, "Now you be nice. This is an honorable establishment here. We just want you boys to have a good time so you'll come back and see us again. We like well-mannered young fellas like you."

Something about the girl struck Jimmy as peculiar. She kissed Larry's cheek and he pulled her down into his lap. She giggled and kissed Larry on the lips. His hand wandered down to her crotch and began exploring.

"Shit!" he cried out and shoved her off onto the floor. He jumped up, yelling, "God damn it, she's a boy!" There was a chorus of laughter from around the table. Larry's face turned bright red, and he screamed, "He's a fucking fairy!" The little blonde, Rose, came around the table and put her arms around Larry.

"Now don't get angry at our little Sylvia," she said. "She thought you knew what you were getting. Come on, Larry, sweetie, let me get you a free drink." Rose pulled Larry away toward the bar.

Elsa returned with Jimmy's drink. She handed it to him and turned to help Sylvia up from the floor, where she sat rubbing her knee and pouting.

"Oh, men are such beasts," Sylvia said.

"Get up, now, dearie," Elsa said, "and don't be theatrical. Some of our other patrons appreciate you."

Sylvia stood up. "Well, some boys have no sense of humor."

As he watched all this, Jimmy realized that Sylvia was a boy of no more than 15 or 16. Elsa gave her a squeeze and Sylvia sauntered off across the room toward the piano where she stood with her hands on Mr. Keys' shoulders and swayed to the music. Mr. Keys turned his head and said something to her. She laughed and gave him a quick hug before she headed for the curving stairway.

Elsa returned to Jimmy and placed an arm around his shoulder.

Jimmy could see that if he wanted to make a show of his manhood, he had to make a move soon before the party broke up into couples. He glanced around the table.

"Well, if you boys will excuse us…" Jimmy stood up and put his arm around Elsa's waist. She leaned into him and he nuzzled her ear. He glanced over at Bill, who gave him a knowing smile. "Let's find someplace private," Jimmy said in a voice that could be heard across the table. Elsa drew him toward the stairway. He felt an urge to glance back toward the band, but he resisted. As they passed the end of the bar, he saw Larry and Rose raising a toast, and Jimmy called out, "Take it easy, Larry. I'll see you later." Larry raised his glass to him and winked.

Elsa led Jimmy up the grand staircase. He was hoping that he could find some way to desire her.

As they climbed the stairs, a baritone voice began singing softly several steps behind them. Jimmy recognized the tune that had gotten him into trouble at the Bisby Grange. "It's right here for ya, If you don't get it…" The voice struck Jimmy as unusually melodious and sexual. He was tempted to turn back to see who it was, but Elsa recognized the voice and spoke up.

"Don't look now but we're being followed," she said in a way that was directed to the person behind them. Jimmy glanced back. A strikingly handsome young man with dark hair was a few steps below them. He was carrying the coat of his tuxedo over his arm and pulling the black bow tie from his collar. He eyed Jimmy as he finished singing the next line, "It ain't no fault of mine," then began unfastening the front of his shirt. He seemed to know that Jimmy found him attractive, and Jimmy felt embarrassed and diverted his eyes.

"Hi, Freddy," Elsa said.

"Hey, Elsa," he said and caught up with them. He reached into his coat and slipped something to Elsa. She pocketed it in a flash.

"I expected you earlier," she said under her breath.

"Aw, something came up," he said.

At the top of the stairs, Elsa led Jimmy across an expanse of red carpet toward a second floor bar, where she greeted the bartender. "Hi, Harry, how did the football game go?"

He remarked on the game, and she asked what room she could use.

"Number 5 is vacant."

During this exchange, Jimmy couldn't take his eyes off Freddy, who crossed behind them to stand in the archway of an alcove beyond the bar. Something about Freddy's face and dark hair made Jimmy think of Carl. Freddy leaned against an alcove pillar with his profile to Jimmy as he finished removing the studs from his shirt. Even though Jimmy could only see the side of Freddy's face, he felt that Freddy was still watching him. Inside the alcove, Sylvia sat on a sofa smoking cigarettes with a muscular young blond fellow dressed only in an undershirt and tuxedo slacks. Freddy greeted them, laid his coat on the arm of the sofa, and took a glass of beer the blond fellow offered him. When he settled back in a chair facing the bar, Freddy's shirt fell open, revealing a chest tattoo—a scorpion with its foreleg pincers surrounding his nipple. Freddy looked up and saw that Jimmy was staring at him. Freddy smiled and raised his glass, then took a sip, never once losing eye contact.

Elsa leaned into Jimmy drawing him away from the bar.

Freddy called out, "Hey, Elsa, you're stealing my business."

She glanced at Jimmy with a soft laugh, and turning back to Freddy, she asked, "Got an appointment tonight, Freddy?"

"My one o'clock regular," he answered, keeping his eyes on Jimmy, who looked away.

Elsa led Jimmy down a hallway to a room at the end and opened the door. Jimmy felt a quiver of nervousness as he stepped into the dimly lighted room. It was hung with heavy gold curtains and had a large angled, gilt-framed mirror at the head of the wooden bedstead.

"Do you like a girl to leave some article of clothing on?" Elsa asked taking a seat on the edge of the bed and slipping off her shoes. Jimmy was still puzzling over Freddy and he had to think a moment to understand her question.

"Uh, no. Just undress." He sat in a chair opposite Elsa and began removing his tie.

"You know it's thirty-five dollars," she said, pulling off a stocking. "You can just leave the money here on the bedside table."

He took out the cash and placed it on the table.

"Who was that fella out there?" Jimmy asked, trying to make the question sound off-handed.

"A friend," she answered.

"A regular patron?" he asked, removing a shoe.

"No," she said and laughed her strange disconnected laugh. "He works here."

Jimmy's expression must have betrayed his confusion. "It's not uncommon," she said. Jimmy's confusion turned to disbelief. She added, "Some of our patrons prefer boys instead of girls."

Jimmy was astounded. He had never heard of a male prostitute. Sylvia may have been a boy, but she looked and acted like a girl. Freddy, however, was every bit a man. The idea of Freddy selling himself slowly set off explosions in his imagination. By the time he finished undressing, he was beginning to be aroused.

Elsa lay back on the bed and beckoned to him. Jimmy went to her and began to kiss and embrace her. He moved his hands over her body, perfect and beautiful and white, but to him somehow cold as porcelain.

While his hands fondled her body, Jimmy remembered the sound of Freddy's voice humming that tune behind him as they climbed the stairs. Jimmy began to hum the tune quietly to himself as he nuzzled Elsa's neck and held her body against his. So Freddy was Elsa's friend—and a prostitute? He remembered that fiery glint in Freddy's dark eyes. Had she and Freddy had sex together? Had Freddy done what Jimmy was doing now? His mind focused on the image of Freddy's tattoo and the thought of touching his chest, then the thick, dark hair on Carl's chest and smell of Carl's body.

And so it was by a trick, by a sleight of hand, that Jimmy's member became erect.

While he was conjuring up images of Freddy and Carl in one corner of his mind, Jimmy became aware of an odd physical detachment in Elsa's lovemaking, as if she were not there. She seemed to be just going through the motions. He was struck by the sharp contrast between Elsa's lifelessness and the eager passion that Mary had exhibited in his only other sexual encounter with a female. This confused him. He sensed that Elsa was emotionally wounded somewhere and she carried that deep in her soul like a disfigurement. It occurred to him that she was willing to be used. In the midst of these vague intuitions, the image of Charlie unexpectedly floated across Jimmy's consciousness again and then was gone. He dismissed it as an effect of the strangeness of the brothel. Jimmy focused on the movements of his body and imagined Freddy.

When they finished, Elsa indicated a door in the corner, which opened into a small bathroom. "If you want to clean up…" she said. He went in and used the facilities. As Jimmy washed himself, he realized that he had forgotten all about the condoms Carl had given him before he left Portland. Well, there was nothing to be done about that now.

After a short time, he came out toweling himself off. Elsa sat at the bedside table sniffing a white powder from the lid of a small brass box. She looked up. "Want some?" she said. "I can give you a bargain."

"Uh…no," he said shaking his head. "Thanks." He began to dress. Elsa closed the little box and went into the bathroom.

The world's oldest profession, Jimmy thought as he put on his clothes and mused about the ancient temple prostitutes he'd heard about. He was feeling good about his performance. He wondered if the fellows in the band would be able to see that he had made love to a woman. Maybe he was normal after all. Maybe he could win Mary back. He would telephone her at her parents' home the first chance he had. He spontaneously began singing under his breath. "It's right here for ya, If you don't get it…" Elsa came out of the bath. Hearing him sing, she laughed and said, "That old song."

Jimmy finished tying his shoe laces. "Yeah, we do that number in the band. I noticed your friend Freddy was singing it earlier."

As she pulled on a stocking, she asked, "Are you interested in Freddy?"

Jimmy paused, tying his tie, and turned to her.

"For a little more money, I can show you to a place where you can watch him at work."

Again Jimmy was astonished and at the same time a fire ignited somewhere down inside him. His throat felt dry and he had trouble speaking. "How much?" he asked. His voice trembled unexpectedly and he tried to steady it.

"Twenty."

"Fifteen is all I've got," he lied. He knew there was more in his wallet. He wasn't counting the $200 in the money belt, but he didn't intend for anyone to know about that.

"Okay, fifteen then."

All over again, Jimmy felt a wave of nervous excitement sweep through his body. I can't believe this is happening to me, he kept thinking to himself, and he had difficulty tying his tie, his fingers had begun to tremble so.

When they were both dressed, Elsa said, "I've got to tell Harry at the bar that we're through with the room. Wait here." She was back in a minute. "Harry says they're in their regular room. I'll show you the way, but you've got to pretend like you're falling down drunk. Now put your arm around my shoulder and keep your mouth shut. And once we get to the basement, don't make a sound."

At the word "basement," Jimmy began to feel apprehensive about what he was getting himself into. Was he being set up for a robbery? Well, he didn't have much cash left on him, except in the money belt and that would be hard for a robber to find.

"Are you sure about all this?" Jimmy asked.

"It's okay." she laughed her peculiar hollow laugh. "If you can't trust a whore, who can you trust?"

Jimmy laughed too and put his arm over Elsa's shoulders. They stumbled out. She led him to a back hallway and down a servant staircase. At the bottom of the stairs, cool air from a rear entrance wafted in. A tall man stood outside a screen door smoking a cigarette. "Hi, Elsa," the man said, "need any help?"

"No, Gus, thanks. He's just one of my regulars. Had one too many. He'll be okay once I get him to the kitchen for a bite to eat." They passed through a steaming kitchen filled with food smells, to another staircase that descended into a dim, cool basement hallway.

Jimmy heard a woman weeping and the sound of slapping. There was a flash of light as a door opened and a man hurried past them up the hall. "Murray, this damn girl ain't cooperating," the man called out and disappeared into another room.

Elsa guided Jimmy into a room near the end of the hall. She closed the door behind them. The small room was lit only by a red-tinted lamp. Jimmy could just make out a small bed and another door. Elsa stood Jimmy up straight and removed his arm from her neck. She put her index finger against her lips as a signal for silence and opened the other door, which appeared to be an empty closet. She held the door open and motioned him in.

As Jimmy stepped into the small enclosure, he was overcome with doubt. Was this a trap? Regardless of the money belt, Jimmy was concerned for his safety. He turned back and looked at Elsa.

There was no danger. She stood there holding the door in the dim light, just a worn-out whore in a tawdry gown. She was not attractive to him. But the prospect of seeing Freddy at work seared Jimmy's mind.

Elsa stepped inside and reached to the back of the closet, silently unhooking a heavy curtain to reveal an eye-level slit in the wall, which let in a dim strip of light from the adjoining room. She ushered him up to the wall, and then she was gone. He heard the closet door quietly closing behind him and he was left alone in the darkness.

Jimmy peered through the opening into another room. As his eyes adjusted to the dim light, he made out the shape of the room and a bright light spilling in from an adjoining bath where the end of a claw-foot tub was just visible. There was the sound of running water.

After a time the water sounds stopped and soon three figures entered from the bathroom. Jimmy felt an internal electricity as he recognized Freddy and the muscular blond boy from the alcove by the mezzanine bar. They were naked, except for the third man who was a stranger to Jimmy. He had very light hair and wore only a white dress shirt, the collar open. The stranger had Freddy stand on a chair and he told the blond boy to start sucking on Freddy. The stranger fondled himself under the tail of his dress shirt as he watched.

"Careful, there, Roscoe. I don't want him going off half-cocked," the stranger said and laughed.

"It's okay, Mr. Felton," Freddy said. "I've got it under control."

"Sure, Freddy, I know you do. You're my best boy. Just a little joke."

Then he produced two condoms, handing one to the blond and then reaching under the shirttail to work one onto himself. After the blond had worked the condom onto Freddy's erect member, the stranger told the muscular blond to get down on his hands and knees.

"Okay, get him ready," the stranger said, handing a tube to Freddy. Freddy knelt down behind the blond and began applying something between the boy's buttocks.

The stranger watched for a bit, continuing to fondle himself, before he came forward and pushed Freddy out of the way. He stood behind the blond boy for a moment, reached down to place one hand on the boy's shoulder and the other went under his shirt. With a quick thrust he mounted the boy dog style. A groan sounded. The stranger held his position for several moments, his head shaking with spasmodic movements.

Freddy used the tube to grease his own member. Then the stranger called to Freddy who approached him from behind and lubricated deep between the man's buttocks. At another command from him, Freddy began slapping the stranger's backside. The slapping increased in harshness. "Now, now," the man breathed. Freddy lifted the dress shirt and mounted the stranger from behind and, in turn, placed his hands on the man's shoulders. Gradually the three began to move in rhythm and the heavy breathing turned into grunts and moans from which Jimmy could not distinguish between pain and pleasure. Jimmy reached down and unfastened his trousers.

The threesome writhed with more intensity and their groans became more staccato and sharp until they appeared to be a ferocious barking three-headed beast.

Jimmy couldn't believe what he was seeing. The stranger was sexually giving and receiving at the same time, both male and female at once. It was a paradox that Jimmy could not fathom. He couldn't believe that men performed such acts, that places like this existed, that he was there in such a place observing the spectacle. Jimmy experienced his second orgasm that night.

After a time the threesome subsided into exhausted panting and began uncoupling. Before long, the stranger in the shirt stood up and ran his hand through Freddy's hair. "You do that real good, Freddy," he said. "You're a good boy. You deserve a special favor after that. Take a look in my briefcase."

Then the stranger went off into the adjoining bathroom and there was the sound of running water. Jimmy watched until Freddy and the other boy began to dress. Before Freddy put his shirt on, just as Jimmy was about to turn away, Freddy took the belt off his trousers and walked over to a black valise on the bed, only a few feet from Jimmy's hiding place. Freddy took out a gold case, the size of a small book, turned on a bedside lamp, and sat down on the bed.

"You want any?" he asked the blond boy, who shook his head no and continued to dress.

From inside the gold case, Freddy took out a syringe with a hypodermic needle and a small vial. He filled the syringe from the vial, then wound his belt around his biceps, held it tight with his teeth, and gave himself a shot in the arm. Then he pulled out the needle and lay back onto the bed.

Although Jimmy had heard of musicians using needles, he had never seen this kind of drug activity, and it was almost as shocking to him as the sex acts he had just witnessed.

Jimmy turned away. He fastened his fly and slipped noiselessly out of the closet. He made his way out of the room, checking first to see that no one was in the hall, then retreated toward the stairs. As he passed the room where he'd heard the weeping, a woman's voice said, "Now I'll ask you again. Are you gonna do what the gentleman asked you to do?" and there was a crack of leather against flesh.

Passing through the upstairs kitchen, Jimmy found an old Negro woman cooking at the stove. She flashed a gold-toothed grin at him and he asked the way to the front room. She directed him through a china pantry that led into a dining room set with white linens. The far door of the dining room opened onto the bar where Jimmy had first met Elsa.

The room was nearly empty now but for a few men and women at the bar. A white-haired gentleman in evening clothes was sitting in one of the overstuffed chairs sipping from a brandy snifter and laughing with the dark-haired girl Lily. The gamblers in the back room were still hunched over their cards. The grand piano stood silent under the stairway. Jimmy approached the bartender and asked if the other men in his party were still there. The bartender hadn't seen them come down yet. Jimmy was about to order a drink when he remembered he didn't have much money left, so he wandered over to the piano.

He hesitated a moment, then sat down at the piano bench and began playing a few chords, which soon became a full improvisation. He didn't know how long he'd been playing when he felt the presence of someone standing behind him watching. At first something told Jimmy he shouldn't turn to look but keep on playing, yet he felt the attention so keenly that he brought the improvisation to a close and looked around. Behind him stood the stranger from the basement room. He was clothed now in full evening dress with white tie and tails. The man might have been in his 30s or 40s, but he was one of those men whose age was impossible to guess. You wouldn't have picked him out of a crowd. His face was nondescript. However, his hair was ash blond, or was it white? He had pale eyebrows and eyelashes, and his skin was white, like something that had crawled out from under a rock and never seen the light of the sun. The intense gaze of his blue eyes and something indefinable about his presence sent a combination of thrill and dread through Jimmy.

The stranger smiled at Jimmy and said, "You're exceptionally eloquent with that instrument. I'm impressed." He looked Jimmy up and down. "What's your name, kid?"

For a split second, Jimmy wondered if the man somehow knew that he had been watching from the basement closet. Maybe Elsa had told him. Jimmy was on his guard. He stood up from the piano. "I'm Jimmy Harper."

"A pleasure to meet you, Jimmy Harper. Danny Felton." The man extended his arm, and as Jimmy shook the cold hand, Felton asked, "You new around here? I haven't seen you before."

"I just got into town from Oregon."

"Oregon. What brings you to Chicago?"

"I...uh...came here to find something I lost."

"I hope it wasn't your virginity you lost. You're not likely to find that here at Miss Eva's. Or anywhere else in Chicago."

Jimmy blushed, feeling foolish.

Felton laughed and studied Jimmy's face.

"Actually," Jimmy said, trying to regain his composure, "I've come here looking for musical work."

"You've made a long journey. Maybe I can help you out."

Felton took out a gold business card case and an expensive fountain pen, and he began writing on the back of one of the cards. A signet ring with a black onyx surrounded by four small diamonds flashed on his left hand as he wrote.

He had an air about him that made you think you were talking to the most important man in the world. It went deeper than his dress and grooming, deeper than the shining gold accessories. Felton's whole demeanor was slick. It was as if all the rough edges had been sanded off and he was as smooth as a polished sapphire, but behind the gleaming surface there was something dark and threatening. The contrast between this refined stranger and the astonishing scene that Jimmy had witnessed in the basement captivated him.

"We could use a good piano player. If you're interested, go to this address some night this week and ask for Eric. Tell him Danny Felton sent you." He handed the card to Jimmy, watching him. "Hey, Arnie," he called to the bartender without shifting his eyes. "Give this kid anything he wants. Put it on my tab." He took out a gold cigarette case inlaid with diamonds and tapped a cigarette on the lid of the case. He continued to look Jimmy over. Once more the signet ring flashed as Felton lit his cigarette.

Jimmy began to feel uncomfortable again, and he glanced toward the staircase.

The muscular blond boy, now dressed in a tuxedo, walked down the stairs. He looked over at them and stood waiting nearby. This was the first time Jimmy had gotten a good look at the fellow and he was struck by his cherub-like features.

Felton said, "Well, you'll have to excuse me, I've got an appointment. It's always nice to meet a fresh young face." He extended his hand and placed it on Jimmy's shoulder, next to the collar almost touching the skin of his neck. A small shiver went through Jimmy. "Give me a call if I can be of assistance." He smiled slowly and for a long moment scrutinized Jimmy's face. Then with an abrupt turn he walked to the entry hall, a distinctive limp impairing his gait. Felton asked the Negro at the front if his car was ready. The blond boy followed Felton to the door.

Jimmy stood for a moment trying to make sense of the encounter. He read the business card in his hand. One side read "Daniel N. Felton, property manager" with an address and telephone number printed in dark red lettering. On the back, written with elegant penmanship in blue ink were the words "Pluto's Lair" with another address and telephone number and the name "Eric." Jimmy glanced up just in time to see Felton and the blond fellow disappear down the porch steps. Slipping the card in his breast pocket, Jimmy turned to the piano. He sat down and picked out a chord.

He had just begun to play a melody when Mr. Keys approached. Jimmy felt like a commoner caught sitting upon the royal throne. A wave of self-consciousness came over him. His playing trailed off and he jumped up from the piano bench.

"So, have you come to replace old Mr. Keys?" the Negro asked him, laughing.

Jimmy blushed and stepped back away from the piano, bowing his head. "No, Mr. Keys," he said and went down on one knee, his head still bowed. "Sir, I could never replace the likes of you."

Mr. Keys took his arm pulling him up. "Son, keep your self-respect," he said in a low voice that only Jimmy could hear. "You play good. And you don't need to bow down to nobody—least of all an old Negro who plays piano in a whorehouse."

Jimmy raised his bowed head.

"Just you remember." Mr. Keys eyed Jimmy. "Music is a gift you've been blessed with. It comes out of the deep—and what you play belongs to everybody."

Jimmy nodded and gave a shy smile. A burst of laughter came from the gamblers in the far room.

"Please. Play us a tune," Jimmy said.

Mr. Keys settled his heavy body at the keyboard and began to play. Jimmy studied the movement of his thick hands for a long time. At one point, when Mr. Keys paused between tunes, Jimmy asked a question about his use of a strange modulation into the minor key at the end of the piece. Mr. Keys glanced up at him, and as he began to play again, he said, "I wouldn't know about all that. I just—you know—play."

"You never use any sheet music," Jimmy observed.

"No sir, I don't read. I just learn it all by ear and then I keep it all right here in my head."

Jimmy felt he was asking too many questions. He watched for a moment longer and then drifted over to the bar, where he stood listening.

"What will you have? It's on Mr. Felton," the bartender said.

"Uh," he turned to the bar, "how about a gin?"

When the bartender handed him his drink, Jimmy asked, "Is it okay if I wait upstairs for my buddies? They'll be coming down by this stairway, won't they?"

"More than likely. Make yourself at home," the bartender replied.

As he climbed the stairs with his drink in hand, Jimmy caught sight of Freddy, now dressed in a tuxedo and watching him from above. When he reached the top of the stairway, Jimmy looked around and saw that the upstairs bar was empty but for the barkeep. Feeling some trepidation, he walked up to where Freddy stood at the railing.

"Did you change your mind and decide to give me a try?" Freddy said with a smile.

Jimmy stared at him in disbelief.

"Oh, I knew the minute I saw you," Freddy continued. "It's the aroma of desire. After you've been in this business for a while, you get so you can smell it at a distance. Earlier this evening I caught the scent of your desire, even before you spotted me following you and Elsa up the stairs here. You just haven't figured out where to direct it yet."

Jimmy was taken by surprise and became confused. "No. I, uh… I've got to ask you something. Your name's Freddy, right? Elsa told me you're a friend of hers. My name is Jimmy."

"Yeah. Hi, Jimmy. Hey, I heard you playing the piano. You're good. You're a man with a gift."

"Thanks." Jimmy glanced down at the floor. "Say, tell me, who is that Danny Felton fellow?"

"You're not from around here, are you?"

"Is he really a big shot?"

"That depends on who you talk to," Freddy said. "The blue blood society types will tell you that he's just a lowlife no-account."

"Well, what do you say?"

"I can tell you this. He grew up in the slums around poor immigrants and poor Negroes and he wanted to get ahead, just like the next fella. He wanted respect. But he was a dark-blooded Sicilian, even though his skin doesn't show it. So the Sicilians didn't like him and the blacks didn't accept him, and the whites knew where he came from and wouldn't let him play their game. He tried to go into the meat-packing business, but they had that all sewed up. He tried to go into manufacturing, but they blocked him there. He wanted to go into real estate or banking or any other legitimate business, but there was no room for him. So what did he do? He got into the only thing that was left open to him. Vice. Prostitution, gambling, drugs. All that lucrative vice trade."

A gentleman in formal dress crossed the mezzanine and descended the curving staircase.

"But is that so different than anything else? Isn't it just a matter of who's eating who? Everybody's outside the law in one way or another? I mean the politicians, the city officials, the police? And especially the wealthy, the society crowd. They just hide their crimes behind jewelry and furs and fancy clothes. But here, Danny Felton is king. And he smiles and welcomes them all down here, the wealthy and the powerful, at night—when it's dark—to play his game. And everyone plays the vice game. It's as inevitable as Death. Down here he mixes that upper glittering world of high society with the dark lower world of the common street walker."

An old black woman in a maid's uniform wandered through the entry hall below, emptying the ashtrays.

"But the society set, they keep pretending that they're all clean white linen and perfume. But they're the same as everyone else, with the same private needs and desires as the next fella. So they come down here and take what they want, what they need, and then go back to their ivory towers. But they're no different from Felton. Everyone's just trying to keep his head above water in this sewer."

"Boy, you are a silver-tongued demon," Jimmy said.

"Yeah, and I know when to hold my tongue too."

The bartender called to Freddy from across the mezzanine and said they were ready in number 12. Freddy turned to Jimmy and said, "I've got to go."

"Wait. Felton says he has a job for me playing piano. Can I trust him?"

"Yeah, he probably does have a job for you. But it might not be what you think." Freddy paused. "Be careful not to turn your back when he's around. But if you do, don't be too quick to turn and check your backside with him." Freddy took a step away toward the bar.

"Hey, what about this Pluto's Lair?" Jimmy showed him the card. A smile broke over Freddy's face.

"Oh, that's an out-of-the-way speak, way down on the southwest side. It's…let's just say, it's got a flavor all its own. But it's a hot joint. Check it out."

"Hey…uh…thanks. Thanks, Freddy."

"Come and see me sometime." He winked. "I'm here every Thursday night." Freddy walked past the bar and disappeared behind a far door.

Jimmy was left sexually stirred up, befuddled, and confused. He wasn't sure what was happening. Could he trust what Freddy had told him? Could he trust Felton's offer?

He took a seat at a nearby table and lit a cigarette as he mulled things over. Had all this actually happened tonight? What was going on? As he sipped his drink he looked around and noticed cigarette burns on the edge of the table and the chair next to his had a rip in the upholstery where the cotton stuffing showed. A stain on the carpet caught his eye, and then he noticed that patches of the carpet were threadbare. Maybe Miss Eva's was not the high-toned place that Howard had made it out to be. But what sort of place was it that Jimmy had stumbled into?

Before long, Bill the drummer came down the hall and joined Jimmy. Soon Chuck showed up. They got a pack of cards from the bartender and were just getting a hand of rummy underway when Larry joined them.

Larry wore a self-satisfied smirk as he arranged his cards. He looked up at the others and said, "I tell you, that was some gal I had. Boy, oh, boy, she bucked like a snake." He peered around the table. Bill glanced at Larry and gave a little laugh. No one else said anything. Larry stared at Jimmy and said, "That blonde of yours was a hot number. How was she, Jimmy boy? Did you jazz her?"

A silence fell over the table. Jimmy looked up from his cards and stared his opponent down. "What do you think?"

"Hey, it's your play, Larry," Chuck interrupted. They played cards for a time and no one said anything.

After a while, Howard finally walked up to their table and suggested they all go out for breakfast. They had the doorman call a cab and they piled in to go home. All the way back, Jimmy kept thinking about Freddy and remembering the things that he had said.

The sun was just coming up when they got to the diner by their hotel.

THREE

Jimmy slept until 3 the next afternoon. He would have gone on sleeping, but a persistent knocking on the door got him stumbling out of bed. It was Diggs reminding him that they were meeting in the hotel lobby at 4 to go to the photo studio. Jimmy reassured him that he would be there, and Diggs reminded him to wear his tuxedo.

At the photo studio, there was a lot of joking around. They tried some wacky poses, but Diggs insisted on some more formal ones too. He said he would have two photo postcards made for each of them to send home to family and friends, but it was the quantity of publicity photos Diggs was most interested in. That would all be paid for out of their collective earnings. If they wanted to buy extra photos, they could make arrangements with the studio individually. After they were finished, they went to dinner and gathered at 7 in the hotel lobby.

Just as Diggs had said, their Chicago debut at the Grand Ballroom of the Redfield Hotel was a high-toned affair. The lobby of the Redfield was one of the most elegant Jimmy had ever seen, and the college crowd assembled beneath the opulent chandeliers in the rooftop ballroom was the cream of the society set. Jimmy felt ill-dressed in his tuxedo when he saw the frat boys in their white ties and swallowtails and the sorority girls in their evening gowns. He was intimidated at first by the grand piano on the stage, but it had a great sound and he soon got used to it.

Diggs had the band start out with a few popular titles that they had worked up. Jimmy didn't like this music, but there was nothing he could say. As the evening progressed, the band got requests for a number of tunes they didn't know, and Jimmy could sense Diggs' growing discomfort. After a while, Jimmy was feeling loosened up and he wanted to try to jazz things up a bit. One of the pieces they played had some possibilities, he thought, so he tried a variation on the piano part.

At their first break, Diggs cornered Jimmy at the piano.

"Look, Jimmy," he said, his voice quiet but emphatic, "just play the arrangement the way it's written." He stared hard at Jimmy.

"Oh, I was just improving on it a little," Jimmy said with a laugh.

"When you publish your version, you can write it any way you want to, but for now just play it the way it appears on the page." Diggs was serious.

"Okay, Diggs. Don't worry, I'll play it straight," Jimmy said. "Anything you say."

Diggs gave him a stern look and walked away.

Jimmy left the bandstand and went over to one of the refreshment tables to get a glass of water. A nearby set of French doors let in the night air from a terrace that looked out over the city. Jimmy walked outside and lit a cigarette.

A number of couples had migrated out for the view. Jimmy strolled to the balustrade where a potted cypress stood next to the side of the building. He stared out at the city lights, trying to distract himself from Diggs' criticism. Diggs is just a little nervous tonight, Jimmy thought, and it's only natural, this is a big deal. He tried to laugh it off. Finishing his cigarette he turned to go in just as a young blond man with a pretty brown-haired girl on his arm stepped out through the French doors. They were preoccupied in an intimate conversation, their faces turned toward each other as they walked off to the far end of the terrace. Jimmy thought that, from the side, the young man's face looked familiar, but the couple was too far away to get a good look. Just then Diggs came out from the ballroom and walked up to Jimmy.

"Looks like you've got your eye on a real cutie-pie there," Diggs said, his voice friendly now. He put a hand on Jimmy's shoulder. For a split second, Jimmy feared that Diggs had caught him staring at the blond fellow, then realized he was referring to the pretty girl. It became obvious to Jimmy that Diggs was trying to smooth any ruffled feathers from earlier, and he was glad to make peace.

"Yes, she's a looker, isn't she?"

"But she seems to be taken. Well, you've got good taste, anyway, Jimmy. You know who she is?"

"Tell me."

"She's Mary Lou Rawlins. Her father is one of the biggest manufacturers in Chicago. Let me tell you, that's some big money you're lookin' at."

"You don't say. Well, that's a lucky fellow with her, then."

"Yes, siree. I wouldn't mind being in his shoes." Diggs nodded toward the French doors. "I think we're seeing the whole social register represented here tonight. You see that redhead in the purple dress? Her father owns a big chunk of real estate in the Loop."

They watched the crowd inside the ballroom for a moment longer, and then Diggs said, "Well, it looks like it's time for us to make some more music." He clapped Jimmy on the back and walked back indoors.

Diggs isn't such a bad fellow, Jimmy reassured himself. He sure seems to have the goods on this crowd. I guess he's got all the right connections.

During the first number after the break, Jimmy again spotted the blond fellow as he danced past, close to the bandstand, with the same girl. Jimmy almost dropped the beat when he recognized him as the muscular fellow who had been with Freddy and Danny Felton in the basement room at the brothel. What was he doing at this fancy dress ball with a lovely young woman on his arm? And an heiress to boot. This was just what Freddy had described but in reverse—the lowlife of the brothels coming to mix with high society. Jimmy was perplexed and intrigued. He kept an eye out for the couple the rest of the night.

fOUR

The next day when Diggs rounded up the band in the afternoon, he was in a stew. He was disturbed because the band didn't know some of the popular songs that had been requested the night before. He said he would buy sheet music and arrange for a rehearsal space.

"We all have to get out and listen to the popular bands around town and report back on what tunes they're playing. This is Saturday night. If we all go to different joints, we can cover more territory. Now, I'm going to be tied up at a frat dance tonight, making some contacts. One of you go to the Starlight Ballroom. Someone else check out the Harlequin Club."

Chuck and Bill volunteered. The other fellows threw in names of places they'd heard about. Jimmy remembered the cab driver's tip about the Checker Club and said, "I got a good tip from a cabby the other night. I'll check it out." But the club he had in mind was the one that Danny Felton had written on his card. Pluto's Lair.

"Now I sewed up the deal for that rich bitch party tomorrow afternoon," Diggs continued. "We'll be playing at a mansion on the Gold Coast at 3. This do is very top drawer. That's spelled High Society with a capital dollar sign. I want you all to be in the hotel lobby and ready to go at 2." Then to refresh everyone's memory, he repeated that they had a fraternity dance on Tuesday evening, and he said he might also have a job for them the following weekend. He was hopeful about their prospects and even suggested that if things went well for them in Chicago, he might be able to arrange for them to go all the way to New York.

Since the boys were all to go their separate ways that night, Jimmy had resolved that he would telephone Carl before he left the hotel. He had been so busy since he arrived in Chicago, and always surrounded by band members, that he hadn't had a moment to himself. Jimmy wanted to talk to Carl, but he didn't want any of the band members to hear him make the call. He took his time getting ready to go out, so that he would be the last one to leave the hotel. After a long hot shower, he gave himself a close shave. He wanted to look especially sharp tonight. Meanwhile, the others hurried to get ready and left. Once he was alone, Jimmy looked at his clothes and considered what to wear to Pluto's Lair. Danny Felton had been in white tie and tails at Miss Eva's. Maybe this occasion called for his tuxedo—it was the best he could do. Jimmy dressed, attending to every detail of his grooming. After one last look in the mirror, he took some more cash out of his luggage and went down to the hotel desk to get a handful of coins for the phone. While he waited for the clerk to make change, he caught the headlines on a stack of evening papers. "Two Dead in Gangland War, Italians and Irish out for Blood." He remembered Freddy saying that Felton was Sicilian and he wondered if there was any connection. With coins in hand he went to the lobby phone booths.

Since it was early on Saturday evening, even allowing for the time difference, Jimmy figured Carl would be home. When Carl's voice came through the line, Jimmy was flooded with relief. He was reassured by Carl's enthusiasm at hearing from him, and Jimmy became excited describing what Chicago was like and how high-toned the sorority dance at the Redfield had been. Even if there had been time, so many other things remained that Jimmy couldn't tell Carl about—not now.

"Gwen and Charlie send their greetings."

"I miss them. Tell them both hello."

"I keep wondering." Carl paused. "I have to ask. Have you

contacted Mary?"

"I haven't had time, we've all been so busy. But I plan on it."

"Jimmy, you know I miss you."

"Yeah, I miss you too."

"Well, I wish we could talk all night, but you'd better save your money and get off that pay phone."

"Yeah, I guess," Jimmy said.

"Call me collect next time."

"Okay. I'm glad we got to talk." There was a pause. He didn't want to end the call.

"I'm glad you called."

"Well…good night."

Carl seemed to hesitate. Then he said, "Good night."

Jimmy hung up.

Afterward, Jimmy stood in the booth and savored the conversation for a long time. Then the thought of catching the next train back to Oregon arose. He remembered Danny Felton saying what a long journey Jimmy had come. He remembered the brothel, his success with Elsa, and then Mary came to mind. Maybe he would call her. No. He didn't want to be reminded of their devastating engagement night when he couldn't get an erection and…. He didn't want to think about all that right now. He'd call her later. He started across the lobby.

The image of the muscular blond boy dancing with the lovely society girl at the Redfield floated through his thoughts. If that fellow could win a beautiful society girl, maybe Jimmy could too. Mary's family also had some society connections. And things were going good for the band. What if Diggs got the band a permanent job? Diggs was such a busy bee, he was bound to succeed. Maybe things would turn out all right. Maybe, when Mary saw how successful the band was, Jimmy could win her back. He imagined himself dancing with Mary at a society ball. Maybe life could be the way Jimmy had always thought it would be.

Yes, he decided, he would go back and call Mary. It was early. If she were going out, she would still be home getting ready.

Jimmy turned back. He went to a different telephone booth without giving it much thought, but what was in the back of his mind was that he didn't want to talk to Mary on the same telephone that he had just used to call Carl.

He fumbled with the telephone book looking for her family's number. There it was. "Alexander L. Hall." He placed the call and waited, drumming his fingers. He would just say that he happened to be in town and wanted to say hello. That's all.

A woman's voice answered the telephone and Jimmy asked if he could speak with Mary Hall please.

"Who may I say is calling?"

"This is an old friend of hers. Jimmy Harper."

There was a long pause and the sound of footsteps. A moment later the woman's voice returned, "Miss Hall is not receiving calls tonight."

"Oh. But I need to speak with her. I just want to say hello to her…"

There was no sound on the line. Jimmy realized the woman had hung up.

Well, damn it, he thought and hung up. He felt angry and guilty and foolish. Maybe he shouldn't have tried to phone her. Well, at least he'd made an attempt. He wouldn't think about it. Maybe a change of scene would help.

FIUE

Jimmy got into a cab in front of the hotel and showed the driver the back of Felton's card.

"Pluto's Lair," the cabby said with a chuckle and handed the card back, giving him a look that Jimmy couldn't decipher.

Was Pluto's Lair the sort of elegant ballroom that Diggs was envisioning for his musicians? The taxi drove Jimmy to a part of town that had a large Negro population. Coming from Portland, Jimmy had never seen so many dark-skinned people in one place, a prospect that both excited and unsettled him. The taxi drove down a main thoroughfare thick with traffic. For block after block there stretched a string of lighted signs for clubs and cafes. The sidewalks were crowded with people, mostly black, but many whites as well. Some Negro men were decked out in dapper suits, some dressed to the nines in full evening wear, and dark-skinned ladies wore evening gowns and furs. All of these appeared every bit as elegant as the tailcoats and ball gowns that Jimmy had seen the rich white sorority crowd wearing the night before.

But the taxi didn't stop. It drove past the glittering nightlife. Many blocks beyond, it made a couple of turns into a neighborhood of small dilapidated homes and warehouses. Jimmy remembered Freddy's comment about Pluto's Lair. "It's got a flavor all its own." He wondered what that meant. Maybe this wasn't such a good idea.

In front of a dark boarded-up warehouse on a nearly deserted street, the taxi came to a stop. "This is the place," the cabby announced.

There must be some mistake, Jimmy thought, as a flood of apprehension swept over him. Then he noticed on the opposite side of the street a dimly lighted storefront café that occupied the first floor of an old two-story wood frame building. Out front a few cars were parked under a single streetlight.

"You sure this is the right address?" Jimmy asked.

"Pluto's is in the basement below Big Joe's Café."

"Drive up the street a ways," Jimmy said. "I'll get out at the corner."

The cabby drove ahead and pulled up to the curb. Jimmy rolled down the window and looked back down the street.

Just then a group of Caucasian men emerged from a concrete stairwell leading from a basement entrance under the café's foundation. They all wore suits except the last one who was dressed in a white waiter's jacket. They lingered there on the sidewalk, lighting cigarettes and talking. Something in the way the men were standing and relating to each other gave Jimmy a sense that something about them was different. By the light of the streetlamp, he saw the waiter put his arm around the shoulder of one of the other men, and they kissed on the mouth. Was that what Freddy meant by "a flavor all its own"? Jimmy wondered. His apprehension became mixed with erotic anticipation. He paid the cab driver and, gathering up his courage, stepped out of the safety of the vehicle. The taxi drove off leaving him alone on the corner. A fluttery billow of nervousness rose in his gut, like the familiar stage fright he felt before playing music. Well, he said to himself, you came to Chicago for an adventure, so you damn well better have one.

There were no street numbers on the buildings and no sign for Pluto's Lair, but a small board above the storefront read "Big Joe's Cafe."

Jimmy could just make out a jazz band playing inside the building and he could feel that something was going on here—no matter how unlikely the spot. Still, he thought twice before crossing the street toward the group of men standing on the sidewalk.

As he took a few tentative steps toward the club, two cars drove up and stopped under the streetlight. The first was a long black automobile with a liveried chauffeur, who got out and opened the back door. So this is what they mean by slumming, Jimmy thought. He walked a few steps closer.

Three young men stepped out of the limousine. They were all costumed in French-style 18th-century coats with matching breeches and coiffed in powdered wigs. A fourth person emerged in a Marie Antoinette costume of satin and lace, topped off by an outlandishly tall wig. Jimmy was reminded of French paintings from a college art history class that he'd taken with Mary. One of the dandies held the lady's hand as she stepped down from the car, holding up her skirts.

"Oh, Lillian," she addressed one of the young men, "do help me with my train." The deep voice gave away the gender of this feminine vision.

"Not me," the other replied. "I told you, Dorothy, you should have dressed as a charwoman this year."

"Oh, hush, Lillian, dear," said one of the others with a giggle. "I tell ya, you sisters take the cake." He bent down to gather up the back of Dorothy's skirt. "Here, let me help you, sweetie. Now, I hope you girls will try to get along this evening. Come on, Dorothy. I can't *wait* to see if Erica will perform tonight." The group made their way toward the club entrance with much tittering and chatter.

Jimmy felt a visceral disgust. It was a spectacle he had not witnessed except for little Sylvia at the brothel, which now seemed to belong to another world. Out here on a public street, the gender reversal had a sickening effect.

The second car was a taxi. Two figures in hooded capes climbed out and followed the French entourage to the basement entrance.

The group of men smoking on the sidewalk were watching

these arrivals. The waiter laughed and said, "Well, it looks like the girls have arrived. I guess I better get back."

"We'll catch you later, Harvey." One of them gave him a kiss.

"Thanks, Harvey, good night." The others waved good-bye and all but the waiter walked away up the street. Harvey turned and went down the stairs.

Jimmy paused a moment longer then took a deep breath and followed. He hung back at the top of the stairs as Harvey knocked on the heavy door. When it opened Jimmy could hear music and he saw dim blue lights and a doorman.

"Hi, Harvey." The doorman admitted the waiter. Now Jimmy went down and he could feel the music playing inside. Even from this distance he could tell that this was the kind of music he had come to Chicago to hear. His excitement increased, and he stepped up to the door before it closed.

"Good evening," said the doorman. Jimmy held out Danny Felton's card.

"Is this Pluto's Lair? Danny Felton told me he was looking for a piano player. I need to see someone named Eric."

The doorman looked at the card, then raised his eyebrows and studied Jimmy for a moment. "Just follow that fella. Any of the bartenders can tell you where to find Eric."

And with that, Jimmy passed through the door into another world.

Jimmy found himself in a wide industrial hallway. He could hear the music better now and it was hot jazz, like he'd heard on the records that Mary had given him. But this was even better. His heart beat faster.

A motley crowd of people lit by the dim blue lights milled about beneath a mass of pipes and ductwork lining the high ceiling. Harvey made his way through the crowd and disappeared behind maroon curtains down the hall.

A makeshift coat check stand had been set up near the entrance and the couple in hooded capes were talking to the female attendant. Removing these outer garments, the two figures revealed themselves to be tall beautiful Negro women, one costumed as Cleopatra and the other in a flamboyant gown of orange and scarlet beadwork that formed tongues of flame licking upward from the floor-length hem in a bonfire of color. As they handed over their cloaks to the attendant, Jimmy heard Cleopatra say, "They were arguing over some floozy, and let me tell you, she was nothing that was worth fightin' over. So we just left them there and caught a taxi down here by ourselves." They all laughed.

"Anabella!" came a shrill cry as a heavy black woman rushed over and embraced the woman in red and orange, and the three moved on chattering down the hall.

Jimmy approached the coat check stand and handed his

overcoat to the attendant. When she handed him the claim stub and thanked him for his tip, he realized that the coat-check girl was a man. Jimmy tried not to let his surprise and uneasiness register on his face. He turned toward the source of the music and walked on down the hall.

He passed the French entourage he had seen outside. One of the gentlemen dandies gave him the eye, and he immediately looked away.

A few people were dressed in conventional business suits and tuxedos, but most wore costumes or masks. A man in a toga joked with a satyr, naked from the waist up. Next to them, a Roman centurion in a breastplate puffed on a large cigar and laughed. A mulatto man in an Elizabethan gown escorted a young white woman dressed as Charlie Chaplin's little tramp. A heavyset man in a tuxedo with a cigar in one hand was kissing the young woman at his side. Their faces parted from the kiss, as Jimmy passed, and he realized that the two were women.

As he neared the maroon curtains, the band caught Jimmy's ear again. Yes, this was real jazz. The music mixed with the din of voices and laughter.

Jimmy passed through the heavy curtains into a large crowded space, which might have once been a furnace room. From the top of a short, wide flight of stairs that led down into the dance hall he looked out over the crowd. The smell of cigars and cigarettes, alcohol and perfume hung in the thick air. Panels of painted canvas had been placed around the room to hide the furnace equipment. The duct work on the high ceiling was poorly camouflaged by festooned ribbons that caught the different colored lights hung around the room. A bar was set up along one wall, manned by tuxedoed bartenders, and waiters in crisp white jackets moved about the room carrying trays of drinks above their heads.

The decor and the sharply dressed staff told him the place was made to appeal to a higher class of patrons. Still there was no denying that it was a dive, and, indeed, if more had been done to improve the place, the resulting pretension would have destroyed its demimonde charm, driving away the very clientele it seemed to attract. Indeed, along one side of the room a raised platform was cordoned off with an ornate theatrical balustrade of flat pasteboard, and there sat the upper-crust patrons in white tie and ball gowns.

Dancing couples packed the middle of the room and, around the periphery, revelers drank and talked at small tables. On a wide stage at the far end of the room, five Negro musicians were playing up a storm. Jimmy stopped in his tracks, enthralled.

This was the kind of music he had heard before on three-minute phonograph records. But that was a pale shadow compared to this live band in front of an excited crowd. It was gut bucket blues with a tailgate trombone. This was the real thing.

There was some quality to it that Jimmy couldn't put his finger on. It might have been something about the timing and the rhythm. Everything was feeling and intuition and pulsating, rhythmic drive. At the same time, the music had a relaxed quality that opened out into a place that white bands, including his own, couldn't touch. This sound had a looseness that allowed growing and slackening tempos, improvisations, creative surprise and freshness, the very qualities that Diggs Monroe thought made it sound sloppy. With all his anxious energy, Diggs had a compulsion to clean up the music and file off all the rough edges, the very stuff that gave black music much of its character and appeal.

Jimmy was intoxicated by this music. He would have given anything to play like that.

While he stood entranced at the top of the stairs, a couple entered behind him and jostled past, bumping against him. Jimmy stepped aside and turned his attention to the crowd below which was the same odd mix as in the entry hall.

He made his way down the stairs and between the tables over to a line of people queuing up to order at the bar. While he waited, he lit a cigarette and watched the crowd. He had never seen such uninhibited dancing. There was an atmosphere of mad abandon in the room, as if no excess were too extreme. A young woman dancing wildly nearby climbed onto a table and began removing her clothing. A crowd formed around the table clapping and cheering her on. A couple of men accompanying the girl tried to restrain her and help her down. The table overturned and some bystanders were pulled down onto the floor in the commotion.

At another nearby table sat two young black women. One was dressed in a white gown with feathered wings and tinsel halo. The other wore a red dress and horned headpiece and smoked a cigarette from a ruby-crusted cigarette holder. Between them sat a white man in a priest's cassock, drinking red wine from a small glass. As Jimmy watched them joking together, he realized the two Negroes were young men. The fellow in red caught Jimmy staring and smiled at him with a seductive lowering of her eyelashes. Jimmy promptly turned his attention to the bandstand at the far end of the room.

The musicians were tearing into another hot tune. The instruments wove and dodged in among each other, tiptoeing around the melody, all propelled forward by the driving rhythm. Jimmy was in heaven.

The music came to a close and as Jimmy began to applaud, he felt a hand on his shoulder.

"Well, look who's here," said a voice in his ear. "It's Kid Piano from Oregon." Danny Felton was dressed in white tie and tails. "Glad you found your way here, kid. You've arrived on an auspicious occasion. It's our annual costume ball. Let me buy you a drink."

Jimmy hesitated.

"Maybe it's my attire," Felton said. "I just came from the symphony. Am I overdressed?"

A man dressed as Louis XIV squeezed past, holding his glass above the jostling crowd.

"Well, it looks like no one is overdressed here tonight. What will you have?"

Still Jimmy hesitated, speechless.

"Oh, now don't be bashful. We're all friends here at Pluto's Lair." He turned to a handsome young dark-haired man in a business suit who stood beside him and said, "Aren't we, Herman?"

The man smiled and said, "Yes, sir."

Felton turned back to Jimmy. "Your name was Jimmy, right?" and he held out his hand.

Jimmy shook his hand. "Yes, Jimmy Harper."

"This is Herman, my assistant."

They shook hands.

"Tell me what you're drinking, Jimmy Harper. Gin? Or I'll tell you what. How about some authentic single malt Scotch whiskey? Best quality. Twelve years old. You don't see that too often these days."

Still Jimmy had trouble mustering a response.

"Come on. I'm buying."

"Sure," Jimmy said. He was wary of Felton. But at the same time, he was fascinated, and Felton's congeniality was winning him over.

Felton turned to Herman. "Have Roscoe give us some of the special stuff." Then turning back to Jimmy, he said, "Come join me, Jimmy Harper. I've got some music people you'll want to meet." He laid his hand on Jimmy's back and guided him toward the pasteboard balustrade. Without hurrying Felton moved his hand up to the nape of Jimmy's neck, and with each step, Jimmy could feel, through that hand, the slight limp in Felton's gait. Their destination was the raised platform where the well-dressed society set was seated.

Felton's table had a good view of the stage. It was filled with a group of people joking and laughing. A short wiry white man sporting a precise little mustache was engaged in loud conversation with a beautiful dark-haired woman in a Pierrot costume, and a Negro man in horn-rimmed glasses whispered in the ear of a tall blonde woman with a vivacious smile. A big man sat silently at one corner of the table keeping a close eye on the surrounding crowd.

Felton introduced Jimmy around the table, and the big quiet fellow, Sullivan, stood and pulled up an extra chair at Felton's bidding. The wiry little man, named Anderson, owned one of the big dance palaces in town, and the bespectacled Negro man, named Pettit, was introduced as a city alderman and a lover of jazz. The dark-haired Pierrot was a journalist, and the vivacious lady an actress. Jimmy was impressed to be in such distinguished company.

The band began to play again, and they had to lean toward each other to make themselves heard. Felton asked Jimmy if he'd seen much of the city. Jimmy explained that the band was so occupied playing college dances that he hadn't had time to see many of the sights. "Our band is busy trying to line up more work."

Felton leaned in close and put an arm around the back of his chair. "Well, maybe we can help you out, Jimmy boy."

Herman arrived with the drinks and took a chair on the other side of Felton. As Felton sipped his drink, Jimmy caught the glint of a diamond on the onyx ring on his left hand. The band began to play another number and the wiry little Anderson and the female journalist got up to dance.

The Negro politician had turned his chair toward the stage to watch the band, and Jimmy leaned forward, partly to speak to the alderman and partly to put some distance between himself and Felton. "I'm interested in hearing some of the colored bands while I'm in town," Jimmy said.

Pettit leaned back and turned toward Jimmy. "You'll want to go hear the band at the Checker Club. It's one of the best jazz bands in town. But Eric could tell you where to hear the best blues."

Felton leaned in and said he would arrange for Jimmy to meet Eric and the rest of the band at Pluto's. "Eric knows a lot of Negro musicians," Felton said.

Jimmy looked up at the bandstand to pick out the pianist. A shiny concert grand stood on one side of the stage looking incongruous in this setting, but there was no one at the keyboard. To one side of the bandstand on the floor below was an old upright, but no piano player sat there either. Meanwhile the band was going to town. "Where is the piano player?" Jimmy asked.

Felton and Herman smiled at each other. "Getting ready for his act," Felton said.

Jimmy sipped the smoky Scotch whiskey and listened to

the band play. A tall slender man approached the table and after getting a nod from Felton, he whispered something in Felton's ear. Felton nodded again and the man left. Sullivan kept his eye on everything but never said a word. Felton put his hand on Herman's knee, and Herman leaned in as Felton said something in his ear. Herman sat back and chuckled.

The music gathered itself into a closing cadence, and Anderson and the journalist returned to the table. Anderson told a joke about a baseball player and everyone laughed except Sullivan. A cherub-faced waiter came round to take orders for drinks. Jimmy recognized him as the muscular blond boy with Freddy at the brothel. Felton beckoned the waiter with a finger and, when the waiter leaned down, Felton said something in his ear. The waiter nodded. Drinks were ordered. The band launched into another number.

Felton leaned over to Jimmy and asked, "Do you like opera?"

Jimmy nodded.

"Good," Felton said smiling and he settled back in his chair.

When the blond waiter returned with his tray full of drinks, he slipped Felton a small envelope. As the waiter handed Jimmy another Scotch, Felton introduced him. "Jimmy, this is Roscoe. Roscoe, here, works at the opera and he has been kind enough to arrange for some tickets for me."

Roscoe bowed and turned back toward the bar. "I hope you'll allow me to treat you to the opera next Wednesday."

Jimmy didn't know what to say. He hesitated, then replied, "That's a very generous offer. Let me see what my band has lined up."

Felton smiled in a way that made Jimmy uncomfortable. "Keep that evening open. We'll talk later." He leaned back and took out the diamond-studded cigarette case. "Cigarette?"

Jimmy hesitated, then took one in an effort to be polite. It was a foreign brand.

Felton took a cigarette for himself, and Herman offered Felton a light from a gold cigarette lighter, then lit Jimmy's.

Again Felton smiled his discomforting smile and Jimmy turned to watch the band as the music wound to a close.

There was a pause as the band members adjusted their instruments and shifted their chairs. Then there was a long drum roll and the audience quieted down. The cymbal crashed and one of the band members stood up and announced, "Ladies and gentlemen, tonight we are pleased to welcome to our stage a very special attraction. Allow me to present our very own Miss Erica DeChez." There was unrestrained applause, punctuated by whistles and cheers, and as the lights dimmed, the band struck up a slow intro that Jimmy recognized as "St. Louis Blues."

A tall Negro woman appeared in a spotlight beside the stage. She climbed to the platform and walked at a leisurely pace across the bandstand to take up a position next to the curve of the concert grand. She wore a low-cut white-beaded dress and her hair was ornamented with a rhinestone tiara with white ostrich plumes. She moved with immense dignity and a calm grace. A hush fell over the room.

The blues intro glided to a close and the woman's voice opened out into the room, soaring into an entrancing wail.

"I hate to see...that evenin' sun go down
O, I hate to see...that evenin' sun go down
It makes me feel like...I'm on my last go round."

As the song lyrics unfolded from her crimson-painted lips, one hand rose in a simple, eloquent gesture, and a large rhinestone ring flashed on her finger.

"St. Louis woman...wears a diamond ring
She pulls my man around...by her apron string...
If it weren't for powder...and this store-bought hair
That man I love...wouldn't go nowhere.
Nowhere."

She can really sing the blues, Jimmy said to himself. At the same time, he knew the performer was not a woman. The shoulders and arms were too muscular, and the voice was too deep. Yet she performed with such authority, such convincing style and demeanor, that she was unquestionably believable as a female blues singer. The audience was captivated and hung breathlessly on every note.

When the number came to an end, the whole room erupted in thunderous applause with prolonged hoots and whistles. Miss Erica made a gracious bow and smiled and bowed again. She had the most beautiful smile.

"Thank you," she said and waited for the ovation to subside. "Thank you very much."

The band began a more up-tempo number and the clapping subsided. Miss Erica swayed to the rhythm of the introductory vamp, then swung into Mamie Smith's "It's Right Here for Ya."

She directed the wit of the lyrics toward different men in the front row of tables as she slinked across the stage and descended the steps to the level of the audience. The spotlight followed her through the crowd as she made eyes at various patrons, stroking the cheek of a Negro man here, running her fingers through the blond hair of another fellow there, gesturing amorously to a man in drag. In an instrumental break between verses, she turned and moved toward the bandstand, with her back to the audience, exposing a shocking expanse of brown skin above the low cut back of her gown. Miss Erica climbed step by step to the stage, accentuating the sway of her hips as she ascended. At the top of the steps, she turned her head slyly toward the audience and resumed the lyrics over one shoulder. Then, she crossed the stage to the piano where she finished with a flourish. Another ovation followed.

When the applause began to die down, she spoke out, quieting the crowd.

"Thank you. Welcome to Pluto's Lair. Now all you lovely queens out there who got all dressed up just for tonight, be sure to see Lulu at the table in the back to sign up for our Belle of the Ball contest. Lulu, stand up and wave to the crowd so they'll know who you are. Doesn't she look like a million bucks tonight, folks?"

Applause and cheers went up around the hall.

"Our winner will be awarded 35 dollars tonight, so don't miss out on this opportunity to strut your stuff. Remember, 'It's Right There for Ya.'" She placed one hand on her hip and gave a bump to the right as the drummer struck the bass and followed up with a crash of the cymbals.

"Now, I want to do a very special song for all you ladies out there. It's a song my mama taught me when I was just a little girl and I've always followed Mama's advice."

The band broke into the introduction and Erica DeChez walked to the front of the stage.

"Reefus Green from New Orleans
He's the laziest man I ever seen
I was in my backyard washin' hard
And I asked him to get me some lard.

He made me so doggone mad
And I stayed mad all day
He knew I could not fry my meat without lard
And this is what I said:

I need a-plenty grease in my frying pan
Cause I don't want my meat to burn.
You know I asked you once to get me some lard
But it seems that you cannot learn.

You know I use plenty grease every day
But I ain't did no frying while you was away
I need a-plenty grease in my frying pan
'Cause I don't want my meat to burn.

I need a-plenty grease in my frying pan
Cause I don't want my meat to burn.
You know I asked you once to get me some lard
But it seems that you cannot learn.

My fryin' pan was on the stove, gettin' hot
I said "Sweet Papa, put some grease in my pot."
Now I need a-plenty grease in my frying pan
Cause I don't want my meat to burn."

She didn't need to add much to accentuate the lyrics.

Another wild ovation followed. Miss DeChez bowed again and again. Then she strolled over to the concert grand, taking her time as the applause died down, and settled onto the piano bench. As she began to play a slow solo introduction, the audience settled down. Then her voice welled up in an achingly beautiful blues song, captivating the audience again and holding it riveted to the stage.

After a couple more numbers, she left the stage to rapturous applause, which did not die down until she returned for an encore. She left the stage again, and the audience's response brought her back for a second encore. When she left the stage a third time and didn't return, the crowd's long applause began to dwindle. The band took a break, and the audience stirred as conversation rose to fill the room.

Felton leaned into Jimmy and said, "Ain't she something?"

"You bet," Jimmy agreed. "He's—, uh, she's swell."

"Yes, that's some real artistic talent," Felton said. He fastened his attention on Jimmy and asked, "What do you plan to do with your talents, Jimmy Harper?"

"Well, Diggs—he's the band leader—the Diggs Monroe Jazz Orchestra—he wants us to play at those big hotels downtown."

"The Diggs Monroe Jazz Orchestra. That's impressive. From the sound of it, Diggs Monroe seems to have some real ambitions. That's the only way to get ahead. You have to set your mind on where you're headed and keep climbing toward it. Now, if playing the piano is what you really want, I'll be glad to help you out by putting you in contact with Erica DeChez. Maybe we can even arrange to have that band of yours play at Pluto's some night. But mark my words, Jimmy Harper, the only way to make it in this world is to bulldoze ahead. You must keep moving forward. Never look back." Felton leveled his gaze at him and a chill ran through Jimmy's bones.

Herman got Felton's attention and said, "Excuse me, boss, we have an appointment to get to soon."

"Ah, yes," Felton replied, "business before pleasure, eh, Jimmy?" He laid his hand on Jimmy's knee, and again Jimmy caught the glitter of Felton's ring. "You telephone my office in the next few days and make plans to drop round. We can have a nice private little chat. We ought to be able to work something out." Felton paused and eyed Jimmy. "And we'll see what we can do to help out that band of yours—the Diggs Monroe Jazz Orchestra." He stood up. "You'll let me know about the opera, too, won't you? Next Wednesday." He looked at Jimmy for a moment longer, then turned. "Say, Herman, would you be so kind as to take our young friend Jimmy Harper backstage and show him where Erica is?"

Felton said his farewells to Anderson and Pettit, shaking their hands. Then he reached out and shook Jimmy's hand and said, "Let me hear from you." The big silent fellow Sullivan stood up and began to lead the way through the tables. Danny Felton followed and disappeared into the crowd below.

Herman stood up. "Excuse us, everyone. This way, Mr. Harper."

"Nice to meet you all," Jimmy said with a little bow and followed Herman.

The crowd on the floor below was so thick that Herman paused at the stairs, waiting for an opening in the drunken, noisy throng. Jimmy sensed someone following close behind him and he could hear a woman's voice saying, "I painted a portrait of a piano player once." It was Mary. It couldn't be anyone else. The memory of his phone call to her home earlier in the evening was still painfully fresh in his mind. Had she gotten his message? Was she avoiding him?

The crowd jostled Jimmy and he bumped into Herman. Behind him Jimmy heard a bright, clear laugh that he knew was Mary's. But he knew he mustn't turn around and confront her. What had Danny Felton told him? "Keep moving forward—and never look back."

Then Herman moved ahead as a group below made for the bar. Jimmy felt a sudden panic. Carl had urged him to talk to Mary. This might be his last chance to see her. Maybe he still loved her. An image of Elsa at the brothel flashed through his mind. Maybe he could still find Mary sexually attractive. He remembered the muscular blond Roscoe dancing with the lovely society girl. Maybe life could be the way Jimmy had always thought it would be. Maybe it could still work out. He reached forward and grabbed Herman's arm and called, "Herman, wait just a minute."

Jimmy turned back and saw Mary standing behind him. A young woman at her side was speaking into her ear, and Mary was laughing.

She wore a yellow headband around the bobbed hairdo that had surprised him so that summer in Portland, and she was wearing the same yellow dress that Jimmy remembered from the night of their ill-fated engagement.

In that moment he knew Mary Hall was lost to him. He felt no desire for her. It was the same face that he remembered with fondness. But it was the fondness of friendship, the comfortable, upholstered chassis of a platonic love that was not going anywhere. In that moment he understood her feminine desire for the pulsating sexual engine driving toward marriage and children, something he could no longer offer, even though he wished he could.

Mary looked at Jimmy. There was a moment's hesitation, then a flicker of recognition, and the smile faded from her face. A hardness came into her eyes.

"Mary. Hello. It's Jimmy," he said. "Jimmy Harper."

She stared at him, and Jimmy knew that she had already slipped away.

"I know," Mary said. "I can't see you, Jimmy. I'm sorry." She turned abruptly and said to the woman beside her, "Come on, Carol, we have to be going." Then Mary vanished into the crowd.

"Mary," Jimmy called after her, his hand reaching out into the empty space left in the crowd. But she was gone.

Jimmy felt a tug on his arm and heard Herman saying, "Come along, kid." He stepped down from the platform and allowed himself to be guided forward past the bandstand. He knew something had irrevocably disappeared from his life.

SEVEN

Herman led him on through a door into a short hallway. A couple of men from the band were lounging there, one reading a newspaper, the other smoking a cigarette and drinking a glass of beer.

"Good evening, fellas," Herman said in passing and knocked on the first door on the right.

A falsetto voice inside responded, "Who's there?"

"It's Herman," he called through the door. "I have to talk with you."

"Go away."

"Mr. Felton sent me."

"To hell with Mr. Felton."

"Now, Erica, he's been good to you. Didn't he give you a raise in pay and that new grand piano?"

"The old upright was just fine."

"Come on, Erica, open up. I have someone you'll want to meet. We haven't got all night." Herman began to open the door, but a powder puff hit him in the face and fell to the floor as the door banged shut.

"Hey, now don't kill the messenger," Herman said, brushing the face powder off the front of his suit. "Mr. Felton sent me with a new piano player for you to take a look at."

The two musicians in the hallway had been ignoring this exchange, but they now looked up at Herman and Jimmy and traded glances.

"You still want that job Mr. Felton offered you at the Checker Club, don't you?"

There was a pause.

"Okay. Come on in," the voice called.

Herman opened the door into a large empty storage room with a rack of costumes and a makeshift dressing table set up near the doorway. Erica DeChez was sitting before a large mirror surrounded by light bulbs. She had taken off the tiara and plumage but still wore her wig. The white beaded dress was partially covered with an open-front smock and a towel was draped across her lap. She was removing her makeup.

She made a face at Herman, and then Jimmy caught her eye.

"Oo la la! A handsome ofay boy," she exclaimed, watching Jimmy's reflection in the mirror. "Well, come on in. Don't be afraid. I won't hurt you. I'm only a wolf in sheep's clothing." She laughed and winked at Jimmy in the mirror.

"Erica, this is Jimmy Harper. The boss says to give him an audition and buy him a drink. Excuse me now, but we've got an appointment."

"Well don't hurry back," Erica said.

Herman slipped out and closed the door, leaving Jimmy alone with the singer. She regarded him in the mirror for a moment. Then, wiping her hands on a towel, she turned around. Extending her arm with the back of her hand upward, as if to be kissed, she said, "Erica DeChez. Enchanté." There was a coy seductiveness in her expression.

Jimmy hesitated. He noticed the smooth brown skin and the muscles of the extended arm, the pectoral development of the smooth chest above the low neckline of the beaded white gown. Erica's eyes shone with a hint of mischief as she smiled up at him.

Jimmy couldn't help letting out a little laugh as he took her hand and kissed it, noticing the large rhinestone ring and catching a whiff of makeup and face cream.

"Pleased to meet you, Miss DeChez. I'm bewitched by your act. You've got a terrific delivery."

"Well, sugar lamb," she said, "as the saying goes, the cock crows, but the hen delivers."

Jimmy laughed. "So I've heard."

"Do you sing and dance?"

"Yes."

"Do you wear a dress?"

"No, of course not." Jimmy's response came out with more emphasis than he intended.

"Well, it isn't a crime. Not yet, anyway. Do you think God wears a dress?"

"What?"

"Is God male or female?"

"Well, male, I guess."

"Oh?" she said with a giggle and turned back to face the mirror. She lifted a glass of red wine from the dressing table and took a drink. "Excuse me, I'll be done here in a moment." Then glancing at him in the mirror she added, "Tell me all about yourself—and your musical background."

Jimmy began relating a brief history of his music education while Erica removed her wig, revealing a skull-hugging mesh cap. She watched him in the mirror and listened as she placed the wig on a wooden head form on the dressing table. Next she took off the false eyelashes and when Jimmy paused to watch, she said, "Oh, don't stop. I'm all ears." She pulled her smock closed to protect her gown and proceeded to wipe off her powder and paint. She interjected a coquettish "Ooh" or "My, my" in response to Jimmy's history. Then she turned her chair sideways from the mirror and slipped out of her shoes and stockings with a coquettish glance toward Jimmy. He tried to ignore her flirtations and jabbered on.

Standing up, Erica interrupted Jimmy's account. "Now, I must dress for my next act. In the interest of decency, I'll have to ask you to turn around while I change. I've repeatedly asked the management for a dressing screen for this room so I can at least have a little privacy. My fans are so insistent. But no action on the part of the management." She made a little circling motion with her finger, and Jimmy turned around to face into the darkness at the back of the room.

"No peeking, now," Erica said. "Please go on with your story."

Jimmy continued recounting how he'd been introduced to blues and jazz recordings while he was studying music in college. Erica was silent for so long Jimmy began to wonder if maybe she'd taken offense, and he inadvertently glanced back over his shoulder. Erica stood there naked except for the hair cap and a brassiere, bending over with her head down, stepping into a pair of boxer shorts. In the moment before he turned away, Jimmy caught sight of the dark skin of the circumcised cock.

Unaware that Jimmy had turned around, Erica asked, "Which recording artists do you favor?"

Jimmy took a deep breath, gazed up toward the ceiling, and began listing favorite performers, many of them female blues singers, and talking enthusiastically about specific passages on certain tunes. He explained that his friend Mary had given him many of the race records, and that she had bought them from a Negro maid.

"Oh, I see. Why, those are some of my favorite performers, too," Erica exclaimed in falsetto. "Now, who is this Mary? Is she your girlfriend?" she teased.

Jimmy started to explain that Mary was just a friend, but a lump rose in his throat unexpectedly and he choked on the words.

Erica didn't seem to notice, and Jimmy paused to regain his composure.

"I'm finished," Erica interrupted. "You can turn around now."

Jimmy turned to find a tall handsome Negro man in white tie and a crisp tailcoat. "Hello, I'm Eric Halsey," he said in a deep manly voice. Then he smiled. He had the most beautiful smile. It was a smile that Jimmy immediately fell in love with.

Eric extended his hand. Jimmy had not noticed what large, attractive hands Eric had. They laughed and shook hands.

"Look, Jimmy, I have to get back to work, but I'd like to hear you play the piano. Can you stick around till closing time?"

"Sure thing," he said. "Besides, I want to hear your band play some more."

Eric donned a silk top hat, opened the door for Jimmy, and they stepped out of the dressing room.

One of the black musicians remained alone in the hallway. He sat in a chair preparing to inject himself in the arm.

"Monkey, don't do that shit here," Eric said. "Use my dressing room if you have to."

Jimmy looked on in dismay remembering Freddy in that basement room. Monkey grumbled and gathered up his equipment.

"And don't be late for the show. We start in just a few minutes."

Monkey withdrew into the dressing room.

"Damn it," Eric said, "one of the best clarinet players in town."

Then as if nothing had happened, Eric led off down the hall asking how long Jimmy had been in town. Jimmy was glancing back toward the dressing room, churning with curiosity. He recovered his attention and replied adding that he wanted to hear more Negro bands. Eric said that could be arranged and took Jimmy through the doorway into the dance hall.

The room was abuzz with anxious excitement.

"We're getting ready for the Belle of the Ball contest," Eric said. "I'll fetch us a drink and then I have to get back."

As they headed toward the bar, Eric was accosted by the tall Negro woman in the gown of flames.

"Erica, darling. Where have you been keeping yourself? Don't you look handsome in that get-up."

"Hello, Anabella." They kissed cheeks. "How is every little thing?"

"Just fine. Everything is runnin' smoothly. Oh, Eric, I just loved your show tonight. Now, why the good Lord didn't give me any musical talent, I will never understand." Then noticing Jimmy and looking him over, she said, "Sister Erica, have you been sucking on this sweet youngster?"

Eric's hand rose to rest on his hip. "Now, talk nice, Anabella, or I'll scratch your eyes out. He's a musician."

"Ooo. Pretty, and talented, too. Won't you come and have a drink with Anabella, young man? What's your name, sweetheart?"

"Anabella, this is Jimmy. Now you keep your hands off him while I'm working."

"Well, I'll try," Anabella replied, eyeing Jimmy, "but it won't be easy."

Jimmy was embarrassed by these attentions, but he smiled and laughed.

"We've got to move along, Anabella honey. There's a show to put on. But I'll be keeping my eye on you."

"And I'll keep my eye on your young friend."

Eric led Jimmy off through the crowd toward the bar.

"Who's she?" Jimmy asked. "Is she your girlfriend?" He tried to imitate Erica's prying question in the dressing room when she tried to sound him out about his relationship to Mary.

Eric laughed. "No. She's just another drag."

"You're kiddin'. You mean she's a fella?" Jimmy looked back over his shoulder toward Anabella. "Are you sure?"

"What do you want me to say? That I've sucked her cock?"

Jimmy was shocked by the language. He looked back again, partly to hide his embarrassment and partly to study Anabella in this new light. "Boy, she sure had me fooled."

"Yes, she passes. She's had practice," Eric said. "She always wears a dress. But she's not a performer. She's just a street drag. She dresses like that because she prefers women's clothing."

Jimmy was confused. It was a surprise for him to learn that there were gradations within the world of transvestites. "But you were just wearing a dress."

"Well, let's just say that I'm smarter than she is. I do it for money."

"So you're a drag prostitute?" Jimmy joked. Then, fearing that his remark might cause offense, he added, "I mean, you wear a dress for pay."

Eric laughed. "You're quick, Jimmy. I never thought of it like that before, but you're right. I guess that makes you and me music whores, doesn't it?"

They laughed and crossed to the crowded bar. Without waiting for a bartender, Eric slipped behind the counter and brought down a wine bottle. "Do you like Bordeaux?"

Jimmy hesitated, unfamiliar with the name.

"You'll love this. It's divine." Eric poured out two glasses. "Some of the best red wine in France." He handed Jimmy one of the glasses and then raised his to Jimmy and took a drink. Jimmy followed suit.

"I used to work behind the bar before I started playing with the band." Eric took another long drink.

A black waiter with a little mustache slipped behind Eric for glassware. "Hey, good show tonight."

"Thanks, Jasper," Eric replied. "How's things?"

The waiter leaned in close and whispered in his ear.

Eric shook his head and said, "No. We'll talk later."

Emerging from behind the bar, Eric raised his glass to Jimmy and took another swallow. Jimmy took a sip. Eric began to lead him toward the stage.

"Erica, my darlin', where you been all week?" The baritone voice belonged to a tall husky Negro who appeared out of the crowd. He wore a sharp-looking street suit with a diamond stickpin in his carefully knotted tie. "I ain't seen you forever, sugar." He put his arm around Eric's shoulder and leaned in and kissed him on the mouth.

"Say, Reggie, I'm sort of tied up right now," Eric said, coolly working his way free from the advance.

Reggie noticed that Jimmy was with Eric and looked him up and down. The tone of his voice changed from honey to acid. "Oh, I see." An angry hostility came over his face. "I see you savin' a little piece of vanilla cream pie for yo' dessert."

"Look, Reggie, I've got to be movin' along." Eric gave Reggie a sharp look and started to escort Jimmy away toward the bandstand.

"You little hussy," Reggie said, grabbing hold of Eric's arm and casting a threatening eye at him and then at Jimmy.

"Reggie, dear, you'll spill my wine. Now don't make trouble. I'm not your woman." Eric took hold of Reggie's hand and pushed it off his arm. Then he stared Reggie down for a moment, to make sure Reggie got the message.

Reggie stood there without moving, and his expression changed from hostility to sorrow. "Erica," he pleaded.

"I'm sorry, Reggie. I've gotta go." Eric took Jimmy's arm and led him off toward the bandstand.

"You bitch," Reggie called out after them before he disappeared into the crowd.

"Who was that?" Jimmy asked.

"Oh, he's just some rough trade who's gotten the notion in his head that he's my husband."

"Husband?" Jimmy didn't understand.

"Oh, he thinks he's my lover. Very possessive, you know, one of those he-man types." Eric looked at Jimmy. "You're not jealous, are you? Well, don't worry about him. He's not even a music whore." Eric laughed and led the way through the crowd.

As they approached the stage, he said, "I've got to get back to work." He drained his wineglass and set it on a nearby table. "We've got a very special show now. Save a dance for me afterwards." That beautiful smile unfolded across Eric's face and shone its blinding light on him. Feeling bashful, Jimmy nodded and smiled back, and Eric headed off, tipping his top hat to greetings from the crowd as he passed.

Jimmy found a place at the side of the room and sat tasting the Bordeaux as he watched Eric return to the bandstand. The musicians, including Monkey, reassembled onstage, and Eric took his place at the piano bench, looking resplendent in his white tie and top hat. They launched into a fast tune and the dance floor filled up. Jimmy realized that he felt a comfortable familiarity with Eric, as if he had known him for a long, long time.

The music washed over Jimmy and he looked around the room. The pasteboard balustrade of the wealthy set platform caught his attention and he felt a stab of heartache remembering Mary. He thought back on their friendship, the music and the art that they shared an interest in. But it was an idealized romance, not a love affair. He had thought he wanted a heterosexual relationship, to be able to conform to that "normal" majority that ruled the world of weddings and baptisms that seemed to come so easily to other people. For him that was a false dream.

What was left was his desire for the bohemian part of Mary's world, the unconventional world of music and art and sensibility. Now what he saw in Mary was an upper middle-class girl who represented the respectable world that was not his. She must have been out slumming with her girlfriend or maybe they were there on a lark with some gentlemen friends. He knew that tomorrow she would be back in her conventional life with her middle-class family.

Now Jimmy found himself in an exciting new world of talented black musicians and intriguing characters, a world that challenged all his notions about life. Jimmy began to feel right at home.

He watched the band and paid special attention to Monkey, who was making music with his clarinet that Jimmy had never heard from Howard's playing. Eric was on the mark. Halfway through the tune, Anabella and Cleopatra approached Jimmy's table and asked if they could join him. He nodded and gestured toward the empty chairs. They watched the band and exchanged pleasantries, and Anabella was cordial and well-behaved.

After a couple of numbers, the band paused. There was another drum roll and Eric came down center stage. Again the spotlight held him in its beam, his white shirt and tie gleaming. The audience applauded as he smiled and tipped his top hat, then they became quiet.

"Ladies and gentlemen," he began, "it is time for the event you have all been waiting for, the Parade of Beauties." The band burst into a fanfare and then was silent.

"Oh, we must get ourselves ready," Anabella said and she and Cleopatra left Jimmy's table and headed for the back of the room.

"All of you lovely contestants who have signed up for a chance to become the Belle of the Ball, the time has come to strut your stuff. Now, I will read off the names of the contestants and each of you come forward over here to the left of the bandstand by Miss Gloria—wave your hand, Gloria honey—and walk across the stage this way..." He swished across the stage to indicate the direction of movement, while the audience hooted and whistled. "...to show yourselves off to our audience and our judges down there. Then continue on around the room in that direction." Eric nodded to the drummer. Another long drum roll ended in a crash of cymbals. Eric began reading off the names of the contestants as the band played a muted "Pomp and Circumstance." With each name, another lovely creature rose from the crowd and made her way down to the bandstand, mounted the stairs, and crossed the stage at a slow pace, illuminated by the spotlight. Although there were a number of more conventional flappers, many of the gowns were as fashionable as anything Jimmy had seen at the Redfield dance. Others were more flamboyant like costumes he had seen at vaudeville shows and theater productions.

As each contestant made her appearance, cheers and applause erupted from different parts of the crowd where her particular coterie of supporters and fans were gathered. "Dorothy Gish," was announced, "playing the role of Marie Antoinette," and the beauty Jimmy had first seen getting out of the limousine appeared out of the crowd. She was escorted across the stage by her entourage of fancy gents. The gender reversal that had sickened Jimmy on the street earlier, now amused him. Nancy and Nadja were announced as "The Priest's Dilemma," and Jimmy watched the colored angel and devil fall under the spotlight as the priest in his cassock escorted them across. A Negro named Rhody was called. She wore a tight-fitting floor length skirt spangled with shimmering blue and green beads, but she was bare from the waist up except for large scallop shells covering her breasts. The whole ensemble was topped off with an elaborate coif decorated with sea shells, strands of pearls, and colorful tropical fish. She was announced as portraying the "Daughter of Neptune."

An explosion of raucous applause arose from several quarters as Anabella was called up in her fiery gown. Her ensemble was now topped off with a curious hat, which burned with real flames blazing forth like a crown of fire as she paraded across the stage.

"Tonight, Anabella appears as the Great Chicago Fire," Eric announced and wild applause followed.

The Parade of Beauties continued to wind their way around the room in a line of colors that rivaled the rainbow. Some made strange-looking women, but many were indistinguishable from the "real" women in the audience and some were more beautiful. After the last contestant had crossed the stage and made the circuit, the band played a couple of dance numbers while the judges deliberated.

At last came the moment of truth, and there was another fanfare as Eric came to the center of the stage. A long drum roll ensued and then he proclaimed, "The Belle of the Ball...the most lovely creature at our festivities this evening...is the elegant...the exquisite...the incomparable...Miss Anabella."

There was a chorus of shrieks and cheers as the whole house burst into thunderous applause and the band broke into a regal march. Anabella strode to the stage, radiant and triumphant, her headdress in full blaze. Eric presented her with a huge bouquet of roses, and she paraded back and forth several times, graciously curtsying and waving to the cheering crowd. Eric took center stage again and holding up his hands to quiet the crowd, announced that he would lead off the first dance with the Belle of the Ball. Anabella handed the bouquet of roses to an attendant, as another helped her remove and extinguish her flaming headdress. Then Eric led Anabella to the dance floor, and as the band played a waltz, the two of them whirled gracefully about the room. At the end of the dance, they returned to the stage, and Eric thanked the crowd and invited everyone to continue dancing. Anabella took a seat in a decorated chair that had been hoisted onto one corner of the stage. The spotlight encircled her as a crowd of fans surrounded the foot of her throne.

It wasn't long before Eric found Jimmy at his table near the side of the stage.

"Come dance with me," Eric said.

"But we can't. I mean, you're not wearing a dress."

"Oh, Jimmy. Of course we can. Look at all these men dancing together—even those college boys over there. Come on."

Jimmy let himself be persuaded, and they made their way to the dance floor. "Go ahead, you lead," Eric said. "I know how to follow."

They took a few turns around the floor amid the lavish costumes, which were now in motion with the dancing crowd.

As they passed the front of the bandstand, Reggie appeared out of nowhere and accosted them. He slapped his hand on Jimmy's shoulder and whirled him around.

"It's time for me to dance with my girl."

Eric stood back and said, "Reggie, you're too drunk to dance."

"Erica, you will dance with me."

"No. I think it's time you headed home to sober up."

"I am gonna dance with you."

"Am I going to have to ask Mr. Jefferson over at the bar to take you outside for a lesson in etiquette?"

"Can't you see he doesn't want to dance with you?" Jimmy said in Eric's defense.

"Shut up, you little fairy," Reggie said and gave Jimmy a shove. "Erica, I ain't gonna argue with you."

"And I'm not going to dance with you."

"Well, you're not going to dance with this little ofay faggot," Reggie said as he drew a pistol from inside his suit coat and aimed it at Jimmy's face. Jimmy froze.

"Reggie!" Eric shouted, holding out his hands. Someone in the crowd screamed. The music stopped playing and a silence fell over the circle surrounding Reggie as he held the gun. Jimmy felt like a pawn in a chess game about to be sacrificed for the queen. He was petrified. He'd never had a gun pointed at him like this.

Then, cool as could be, Anabella arose from her throne and

called out Reggie's name. Crossing the stage and descending the steps toward him, she positioned herself between Jimmy and the barrel of the pistol. After a pause, she held out her hand and in a calm voice said, "Give me the gun."

There was a long silence. A shiver went through Reggie's body. He slowly lowered his arm and laid the pistol in Anabella's palm.

A couple of men in the crowd grabbed Reggie from behind, and a number of club bouncers and waiters rushed over to take control of the situation. But it was all over. Reggie became docile, bowing his head, and allowed himself to be lead him away. Anabella handed the gun to one of the bouncers and said, "I don't have any use for this, honey."

Eric turned to the bandstand and motioned for the musicians to resume playing. The music started up again, and in a moment it was as if nothing had happened.

Jimmy stood stunned and silent.

"Thank you, Anabella," Eric said.

"Oh, don't mention it, Erica darlin'. I don't think you'll have any more trouble from Reggie. Not tonight anyway. He's basically harmless. He just gets a little ornery when he's had too much booze. Now I think I deserve a dance with your friend, don't you?"

"What do you say, Jimmy?" Eric asked, putting an arm around Jimmy's shoulder.

"Why…sure," he said. He still felt dazed. He wasn't certain what had just happened. "Of course."

He held out his arms to Anabella, and they danced off into the crowd.

While they danced Jimmy thanked Anabella for interceding.

"It was nothing," she said. "I'm not trying to excuse what Reggie did back there, but you should know that he saw his daddy killed by a gang of Irish boys back in the 1919 riots and a man just doesn't forget about such things any too easy. So it ain't personal. Don't take it on yourself. He just doesn't like white boys. You'll excuse him if he doesn't like you messing with Erica. Even though Erica isn't his girl or anything like that. But then it's a funny thing, 'cause you know Erica's granddaddy was white."

"What?" Jimmy was astonished.

"Yeah, his grandmama was a house servant to a wealthy white man down South and he took a shine to her and set her up as his mistress with a real nice place of her own and everything. He must have loved her a lot. Of course, it was all done on the sly. No one was supposed to know. But everybody did."

Marie Antoinette danced past with one of her gentlemen, and her train brushed Jimmy's leg.

"And when Eric's mother, Heleena, was born, that southern gentleman supported her like she was his own, which she was. Sent her away to give her a good education and all. Maybe that's when it started, with Heleena being separated from her mama. That nice white man got to keep seeing her mama, while Heleena went away to fancy schools up North. So, I understand. Heleena took a dislike to the both of them."

A white waiter carrying drinks dodged by them as they whirled along the edge of the dance floor.

"And before that southern fella died, he left Eric's grandmama a whole mess of money so she would be provided for. I guess that's why Eric's mama is so straight-laced and brought Eric and his sister up so prim and proper. She must have felt that her mother was some kind of whore. I think she always carried that thing against her mama, when really all that her mama was trying to do was get on in the world."

Through the crowd Jimmy caught sight of Eric in his white tie and tails, and tried to imagine his white grandfather.

"And she did a good job of it too—a woman who was born into slavery—providing a good home for herself and her child and making sure Heleena had everything she could want. And, Lordy, Heleena did get an education, you know, and all the advantages. Got to be a school teacher and got herself a proper marriage. Turned out to marry a good black man who takes care of her. Why, she ought to be grateful to that old woman, not spiteful."

"Boy, you sure know a lot about everybody," Jimmy said.

"Oh, I make it my business." Anabella said. "I spend time sitting with the women folk sometimes, the mothers and the sisters, in their kitchens, and I hear the talk. I sit quiet and I listen and I hear the talk."

As the bar closed and the last of the revelers straggled out, the bartenders and waiters scurried about clearing away empty glasses and wiping down the tables. A grey-headed Negro janitor began lifting the chairs up onto the tabletops and sweeping up the sequins and beads and stray feathers strewn across the floor along with the cigarette butts and broken glassware. Eric, still in his white tie and tails, stood by the grand piano, speaking in a low voice to Monkey who kept gesturing with his clarinet. The other band members had taken off. Jimmy came forward past the upright piano on the floor beside the stage. They noticed him and fell silent. Eric greeted Jimmy with a smile and introduced the other musician. Jimmy was surprised to see how alert Monkey was after his earlier drug incident, but he already knew after hearing the band that Monkey was one hell of a musician. Eric invited Jimmy to come on up and take a seat at the grand piano.

"Play something for us," Eric said.

Jimmy played a couple of tunes that Diggs' band used to do. When he finished, Eric and Monkey applauded, but the clapping was swallowed up by the echoing silence that had settled over the expanse of the empty bar room.

"Nice playing," Eric said. "You're very proficient."

Eric sat down on the piano bench next to him and played one of the tunes over again to show how he would handle the piece. Monkey came in on the clarinet, improvising around Eric's lead. Jimmy liked the difference in sound and paid close attention while he watched Eric's playing. When Eric and Monkey finished, Jimmy played a few selected phrases to ask Eric how he had achieved that sound. Eric repeated the passages slowly.

"I can't tell you exactly why I play it that way," Eric said. "Sometimes, you know, it just seems as if these musical notes were preordained by God." He laughed.

Jimmy tried certain passages again. Then a smile broke over his face and he said, "I see what you're doing."

"Yeah, now you're on the trolley," Eric said as Jimmy played. He was loosening up now and he started to catch on.

"Do you know 'Gladstone Blues'?" Eric asked. Jimmy shook his head. "Here, I'll teach it to you." Eric played the tune through, and then Jimmy accompanied Eric in a duet. Jimmy thought it was a superb jazz melody. Monkey came in with his clarinet. When the number came to a close, they all laughed, and Monkey complimented Jimmy's playing.

"Thanks," Jimmy said. "That's a great tune."

Jimmy and Eric both sat at the piano bench trading musical passages and stories. Eric mentioned Scott Joplin's Red Book and played a piece. Then Jimmy played a different piece from the same collection and told Eric about discovering it when he was studying music in college.

Jimmy was surprised to find out that Eric first learned classical piano music from his mother. Eric played part of a short Bach keyboard piece. Then Jimmy played a passage from Mozart.

"Hey, I like that melody," Eric said. "Let's see what we can do with that." Eric jumped up from the concert grand and scrambled down the steps from the stage. Standing next to the old upright, he took off his top hat in a salute to Jimmy. "Thank you Jimmy, thank you Wolfgang," Eric said, playing the master of ceremonies again and making an elaborate theatrical bow. Then he set his hat on the upright and settled on the wooden swivel stool in front of the keyboard.

"Play that one more time," Eric said.

Once again Jimmy's fingers moved over the keys of the grand piano and Mozart's melody filled the air. Eric repeated the melody and then began improvising it into a jazz tempo. After a bit, Monkey joined in on the clarinet. Jimmy came in, adding a countermelody.

The waiter named Jasper came over carrying a nightcap and sat down to listen near the bandstand. As the musicians cranked up the heat, the janitor paused to listen, swaying to the music as he leaned on his broom. Despite the size of the empty hall, it began to take on the cozy privileged intimacy of a club after closing time.

They had played a few varied tunes, when one of the bartenders came over and told them it was time to lock up.

Monkey began packing up his clarinet. From the upright piano, Eric smiled his broad smile at Jimmy who was getting up from the concert grand.

"Jimmy, I think you'll work out just fine, playing here at Pluto's."

Eric turned to the bartender and called out, "Hey, Geno, I have to change my duds. I'll be out in a minute. Will you call for a taxicab? There's a rent party at Jewell's flat in my building. You should all come along."

Jimmy had never heard of a rent party and Eric explained that one of his neighbors was raising money to pay the rent by charging admission to a party at her flat. The barkeep said he had to be getting home, but Monkey and Jimmy agreed to join Eric.

Eric came back shortly in a suit and tie. Before leaving, he stopped behind the bar and grabbed a bottle with a blue label and tucked it inside his coat.

"A contribution to the rent party," he explained with a smile toward Geno. The bartender waved and said good night.

NINE

The rent party was in full swing when the three men arrived. Eric's building might have been a large fashionable brick-front home a few decades earlier, but it had since been divided into apartments. Jimmy could hear a band playing inside as they climbed the stairs to the front stoop, and Monkey opened the front door for them. The party was in a flat on the main floor. A Negro man was collecting admission outside the apartment door, and he hesitated when he saw that Jimmy was white. "It's okay. He's with me," Eric explained. The three musicians paid up and the man pushed open the door to admit them.

Jimmy hesitated outside the doorway. He had never been in a situation where he was the only white man and he didn't know what to make of it. Monkey slipped inside, and Eric put an arm around Jimmy's shoulder and led him into the packed apartment.

"You can leave your overcoat here by the door." Eric had to raise his voice to make himself heard over the music and talking and laughter. "Let's get something to drink."

As they made their way through the crush of bodies and the smoky air, Jimmy caught a glimpse of the musicians playing jazz in the living room. Only a few people were actually dancing—it was too crowded to dance—yet all the bodies in the apartment seemed to pulsate with the beat of the music. Laughter and animated conversation filled the air, but the talk was so full of slang that Jimmy couldn't make out half of what was being said. There was a kind of energy in the place that he had never experienced before.

Eric and Jimmy squeezed through to a small kitchen where a bar had been set up. Eric greeted a slender, fashionably dressed young woman who was serving up drinks. He handed her the liquor from inside his coat and said, "A contribution from Pluto's."

She smiled and gave Eric a little hug across the table, as he said, "Looks like you got your rent paid." The woman eyed Jimmy with a suspicious coolness.

Eric made the introductions. "This is my friend Jimmy Harper. He's going to be playing piano at Pluto's. Jimmy, Jewell Carothers. Give us a couple of glasses of gin."

Jimmy could tell that Jewell did not like him. Was it only the color of his skin she didn't like? Is this how colored people feel in a crowd of whites? When Eric started to pay for the drinks, Jimmy protested, "You already got me a drink at Pluto's. Let me get these." Jimmy hoped this gesture might soften what seemed to be Jewell's disapproval, but she took the money without returning Jimmy's smile. During this transaction, an unfamiliar smell caught Jimmy's attention. It was a pungent, green odor, wafting in from a kitchen window that opened onto a wooden porch at the back of the building where a group of people stood smoking and laughing.

Drinks in hand, Eric led Jimmy back through the noisy crowd to where the music was coming from, greeting people along the way, occasionally introducing Jimmy.

The music was intoxicating, and Jimmy couldn't get enough of it. While a heavy woman with very dark skin engaged Eric in talk, Jimmy drifted off toward one corner of the living room, drawn by the music. Monkey was blowing his clarinet along with a trombone player, a saxophone player, and a pianist. Jimmy found a spot near the upright piano where he could see the woman at the keyboard as her long slender fingers moved over the keys. He sipped his drink and watched and listened, mesmerized. The music was so spontaneous it struck him as completely different from any arrangement he had ever played with Diggs and company. Even if Diggs could be persuaded to go along with it, Jimmy wondered how his band could achieve such a sound. He kept trying to figure out how these musicians were making it happen. The instruments wove in and out of each other like birds playing tag, and the music filled Jimmy with an itch to play like that.

A man at Jimmy's elbow spoke, "Didn't you come in with Eric Halsey?"

Jimmy looked at him. "Yes," he said, aware of a sense of pride.

With a knowing smile, the man said, "He sure seems to favor you white boys." Without a hint of malice or irony, he shook his head and laughed good-naturedly.

Jimmy blushed and turned back to watch the piano player. He tried not to think about the man's remark and trained his eyes instead on the keyboard. The woman's left hand was churning out a rolling bass, the likes of which Jimmy had never heard. His study of her technique was interrupted by a commotion at the front door, but Jimmy could only make out incoherent hollering and laughing.

"Hey, Grandy," someone cried out. Others called out greetings. A wiry older man with graying hair came into the crowded living room, weaving as he walked. He was escorted by a heavyset fellow carrying a guitar case. The crowd parted to make room for them. From the look of the wiry fellow's disfigured eyes, Jimmy guessed that he was blind. He was unstable on his feet, and he answered the barrage of greetings with slurred responses. Someone offered Grandy a straight-backed chair in the middle of the living room and he sat down.

A woman standing near Jimmy leaned in toward the man beside her and said, "Hey, isn't he Grandy Roberts, that blues singer from Louisiana?"

The jazz musicians finished off their piece and Grandy applauded.

"Come on, Grandy. Now you play us a song," one of the jazzmen said.

"Yeah, sing us some o' dem blues, Grandy." There was a murmur of encouragement, as the crowd encircled him.

The heavyset escort opened the instrument case and handed a battered guitar to Grandy. He fumbled lifting it into his lap, and he draped his arms around its body, adjusting himself in the chair. The crowd in the living room quieted down. The escort took off his felt hat and placed it on the floor in front of the chair. The attention in the room focused on Grandy.

Jimmy felt the anticipation as the guitarist began to pluck the strings. A series of notes built into chords that grew into the throbbing beat of a blues introduction. The room fell silent and the quiet gradually spread out to the noisy crowd in the next room, like the widening ripple from a stone tossed in a pond.

An unearthly moan materialized from the man with the guitar and little by little rose in volume and intensity. The earlier remark locating Grandy in Louisiana caused Jimmy to imagine a mist rising out of a swamp. Words, then verses formed out of the moan, propelled forward by the unrelenting rhythm of the rising and falling guitar notes.

Between Grandy's drunkenness and his rural southern accent, Jimmy could only understand a word here and there, but the lyrics that Jimmy could make out had to do with train stations and ramblin' and jail houses, with crying over the gal who would not do him right and with beating up on the woman who did him wrong.

This music conjured up the feelings Jimmy experienced when he proposed to Mary and it seemed that all hell had broken loose—a petrifying terror, a desolate loneliness. And the sorrow he felt earlier in the evening when he knew Mary was lost to him.

The voice that carried all this emotion had a raw sound. Yet with all his rough-hewn style, with all the gravel and whiskey in his voice, Grandy's tenor fell on Jimmy's ear with a melodious rightness, and his facility with the guitar, slurring the notes to match the human voice, all fit together.

In his blindness, Grandy played with a complete self-absorption, and as he continued, he seemed to lose all self-control. Something else took over. The people listening became gathered into the music.

Jimmy felt a combination of horror and fascination. This was no vaudeville show Mamie Smith blues like Jimmy was used to from records, nor the "Blues" music of sweet refinements played by his own band. It was obvious that the blues meant something entirely different to Grandy than to Diggs. This was a different continent. Jimmy heard something dark and painful in this swamp music that made the hair stand up on the back of his neck and it scared the hell out of him. If this was music, Jimmy began to have doubts about what he had gotten himself into.

After Grandy had sung for a time, he seemed to return to the present of the apartment and he paused in silence. Gradually, applause broke out, along with cries and whistles, and it rose to a thunder, accompanied by a shower of coins aimed at the hat on the floor. Jimmy noticed Eric standing across the room clapping and looking at him through the crowd. Eric nodded his head and gave him a knowing smile. Jimmy smiled back and shook his head in disbelief.

Grandy called out for "that bottle." When the escort told him they had drunk it all, he became belligerent. Jewel came forward with one. Jimmy recognized the blue-labeled bottle that Eric had brought from Pluto's Lair. As Grandy took it, he held onto Jewell's hand and said, "Is that the hand of some sweet young thing? I do believe I smell an oven full of sweet jelly roll."

Jewell laughed and said, "I think you're shopping in the wrong store, Papa."

He put the bottle between his legs and held onto Jewell's hand. "From the sound of that pretty little voice, I bet you're a fine-lookin' woman. Now tell me, baby, I bet you can shake that thing." He kissed her hand while his other hand felt for her leg and began wandering up under her skirt. "Give me a taste of your goods, pretty mama."

Jewell freed her hand from Grandy's grasp and slapped his arm away from her dress with a hard audible smack as she took a step back. "No deal, Grandy. The bank's closed."

"Aw, now, honey, have mercy on a poor old blind man."

Jewell laughed and said, "I love your music, Grandy, but you're barking up the wrong tree."

"Oh, now baby, just give me a little chance. Why, honey, my jones is a rolling machine. I can really ring that bell for ya."

"Why don't you put those hands on your guitar and play us another song," Jewell suggested.

"Oh, you one of these high-class Chicago gals. Ol' Grandy ain't good enough for ya." He turned his attention to the gin bottle and unscrewed the cap. "I see I can't win with that gal," he said with a sly smile toward his audience, and he took a long swig from the bottle. A few people in the crowd laughed.

Monkey called out, "Take it easy, Grandy. That's no lady to mess with."

"Well, if there's ladies present, they better clear out before I start playin' again, cause they ain't gonna like what I got to sing about."

The old man took another sip and placed the bottle on the floor between his feet. Then the guitar sounded and the singer began again. His song was full of sexual innuendoes and metaphors so explicit that it made Jimmy blush. When Grandy finished, there was general laughter and more hoots and applause. More coins pelted the felt hat.

Then Grandy raised his head and turned his face as if he were surveying the room with his blind eyes. "Is they some ofay boy here among us?" The room fell silent and all eyes turned on Jimmy. His discomfort was unbearable.

"Mercy, mercy." Grandy shook his head. "He in for a heap o' troubles."

Jimmy felt like a deer caught in the headlights, his mind confused. What did Grandy mean? And how could Jimmy possibly respond to such a pronouncement?

Grandy paused, put the bottle to his lips and holding it inverted above his head, he swallowed again and again. The silence in the room became restless. Someone called out, "Leave that bottle be and play us another song." When he tore into his next piece, it was with a renewed ferocity, and the song was darker and more frightening than anything that came before. Jimmy imagined that with that last swig, Grandy must have sucked out of the bottle some malevolent spirit.

In the midst of this song, a woman's angry shouts reverberated from the hall outside the apartment. The door opened and the voice burst into the room as a struggle broke out at the entrance.

"Where is that no good, two-timin', yellow-bellied dog? I know he's in there. I hear him singin'. Why, that….I got a straight razor with Grandy Roberts' name on it. Let me at 'im."

It was obvious that alcohol was doing the talking, yet there was a visceral tone in the woman's voice. The place it came from was as primitive and animal as Grandy's blues, but this was no musical performance. The sound of her voice sent a chill deep into Jimmy's bones.

Several men managed to bar the woman's entry and force the door closed. Her cries could still be heard from outside as another woman's voice shouted back at her. Grandy paused in the middle of his song. His escort called out that they had to get out of there and began gathering up the hatful of coins. Grandy tried to stand, and the escort took the guitar, while two others pulled Grandy up. They supported him under each arm and walked him toward the kitchen.

"See if you can get him out the window and down the back porch," Jewell called out. "I don't want that man's blood all over my carpets."

Grandy balked and turned back, calling out, "Gimme that bottle. I ain't leavin' without mah hooch." The escort finished picking up the last of the coins and snatched up the bottle.

"I got the bottle, Grandy," he said. "Let's make tracks." The men rushed Grandy off toward the back of the apartment.

The woman's shouting from the hallway receded out the front door, down into the street, and subsided into the night. Laughter broke out here and there around the room. The chatter of conversation returned.

Soon a voice called out, "Hey, Eric, you play something."

"Okay," Eric said, sitting down at the piano. "Monkey, you and Joe help me out." He nodded to Monkey and a tall man holding a cornet. Jimmy watched Eric's fingers strike a chord and begin to wander around the keyboard. He loved watching Eric's large square hands moving over the piano keys. The other two musicians joined in and Eric's voice crooned the lyrics. The room changed shape again. The upbeat jazz was balm to Jimmy's soul following the frightening darkness of Grandy's blues.

The crowd began to thin out. Jimmy could see a hint of daylight coming in through an open window. The gin he'd drunk earlier had him feeling right at home, but he was beginning to lose steam.

Eric played a couple of numbers. More people said good night and left, until only a few remained listening to the music in the living room. Jewell wandered in from the kitchen. The sky out the window became gray.

Eric finished playing and paused. Then he turned to Jimmy and asked him to play something. Jimmy held up his hands, refusing. Monkey and Joe urged him on, and he hung back until Eric stood up and gestured to the piano stool, and Jimmy let himself be persuaded. The alcohol and his own desire to play moved him forward and he settled in at the piano. As his hands touched the familiar keyboard, he relaxed. Remembering the Mozart melody that he and Eric played earlier, Jimmy began to play a variation of it. He tried to twist it into something bluesy but he couldn't make it sound right. A wave of doubt and panic came over him, and Jimmy could feel his cheeks redden. He stopped playing. There was a dead silence in the room. Jimmy froze at the piano. The other musicians were quiet.

Then Monkey, holding up his clarinet, said, "Hey, that's the tune Eric played earlier at the club, ain't it, Jimmy? Say, let's try something more familiar. Like that Gladstone Blues. You remember that one. It goes like this." The clarinet played the melody and Joe joined in.

The sound of the music calmed him and Jimmy let his fingers

pick out the chords of the tune. He followed as best he could, trying to add a flourish here and there, but he knew he wasn't playing his best. His confidence was shaken and he felt stiff and lifeless.

After what felt like an eternity, the other players brought the tune to a close. There was a smattering of polite applause and Monkey said, "You played that real nice." Jimmy didn't want to turn around from the piano but he couldn't stay at the keyboard. He stood up and half-turned, making a shrug and a gesture with his hands. His eyes darted around the room, but he didn't see Eric. Jimmy averted his eyes from the people in the room and headed toward the kitchen. As Joe and Monkey started up again, he heard a voice behind him saying, "That white boy plays like he's got a board up his ass."

Jimmy went into the kitchen hoping to find Eric. There he found Jewel pouring Eric a drink and laughing. As Jimmy approached them, they exchanged glances.

"Well?" Jewel said.

Eric turned toward Jimmy and smiled. "Have a drink," he said holding out the glass that Jewell had just poured.

"I've gotta get going, "Jimmy said.

He saw that Eric sensed his distress.

"Have this," Eric said, pressing the full glass into Jimmy's hand. Then he filled another for himself and glanced at Jewell. "Jimmy and I ought to be shoving off."

She stood there without smiling and made no response.

Eric put an arm around Jimmy's shoulder and led him to the front door.

Jimmy found his overcoat and they went out into the hall. As he slipped on his coat, Eric guided him to the stairs, and they climbed three flights. At the top Eric opened a door that led out onto a small flat area of the roof.

Toward the eastern horizon, the clear sky was just beginning to turn pink. Overhead, some stars still twinkled. The air was cold and crisp, and Jimmy felt reinvigorated. Across the rooftops, a few lighted windows showed in the dark buildings. Jimmy breathed deep. He was relieved to be away from the party.

"I saw what happened," Eric said. "Don't worry about it. I've been playing with those fellas for years. You've never played with them before in your life."

"Oh, it wasn't their fault." Jimmy looked off at the dawn and sighed. "I just feel like such an amateur."

Eric touched his glass to Jimmy's and said, "Well, here's to initiation by fire." They both took a drink. A shiver ran through Jimmy.

"That blues singer—his name is Grandy?" Jimmy asked.

"That's right."

"What did he mean…when he said I was in for some trouble?"

"Oh, who knows? Don't think twice about that. He was drunk. Besides that, he's crazy in the head."

Jimmy looked toward the pink glow and took another deep breath, then let it out in a long slow sigh.

"It's cold out here," Eric said and put his arm around Jimmy's shoulder, pulling him against his long tall body. "Let's go back in. I've got a surprise for you."

TEN

They descended a flight of stairs to the second floor and walked down the hall to a door at the back of the building. Eric handed his drink to Jimmy, took out a key ring, and unlocked a padlock on the door with one key, then the door lock with another. Jimmy followed him inside as Eric turned on a fringed lamp on the bedside table by the door.

It was a small crowded room with a double bed, an upright piano, and a table by a window. The lamp's rosy glow revealed a rich chaos of images. In an attempt to hide the ancient water-stained wallpaper, pictures and postcards had been tacked up all around the walls. Prints of African mask paintings by Picasso reminded Jimmy of pictures that Mary had shown him to explain her cubist portrait. Lithographs of Tahitian women by Gauguin hung next to postcards of Egyptian mummy cases and Islamic calligraphy. Pictures of erotic couplings from Hindu temple sculptures hung next to mechanical drawings by Leonardo da Vinci. It was like a review of the art history class that Mary had persuaded Jimmy to take in college.

Curtains of deep maroon velvet covered the single tall window. In front of it, on a table draped with a paisley shawl, sat a cracked blue ceramic vase full of fading burgundy roses next to a white plaster statuette of Michelangelo's David and a wooden African sculpture with an enormous phallus.

Books and magazines and sheet music were scattered about in disarray on every surface including the tumbled covers of the bed. An open closet looked as if an explosion from within had expelled brightly colored clothing, leaving it draped over the top of the door and hanging from the doorknob. The wrought-iron foot rail of the bedstead was festooned with a blue shirt, a green kimono, a red dress. Above the piano hung a botanical illustration in a crooked gilt frame beside a postcard of the Taj Mahal, and crowning the room, a shimmering gold fabric with an intricate emerald-colored border had been tacked in swags across the ceiling. As Jimmy raised his eyes to examine the fabric, Eric said, "Beautiful, isn't it? It's a sari."

"A sorry?" Jimmy said.

"You know, an East Indian woman's garment. It was a gift from an admirer."

Eric closed the door behind them, and after removing a stack of sheet music from an ornately carved straight back chair, he offered Jimmy a seat. Jimmy squeezed between the piano and the bed, crossing over the floral pattern of the Persian carpet, and sat down. The chair creaked and wobbled as he sat and leaned over to place the two glasses of gin on the table. Eric undid his necktie as he went over to a steam radiator and opened the valve. The pipes began to hiss and thud, and Eric said, "It will warm up in no time. You can take off your overcoat. Before long I'll have to open the window. Just wait and see." He laughed and slipped sideways between Jimmy's knees and the bed. Opening a Victrola cabinet, he cranked up the drive mechanism. A gleam sparkled in Eric's eye as he turned to Jimmy and poised the needle over the black record spinning on the turntable.

"This is the world's greatest blues singer."

"Better than Grandy?" Jimmy asked.

"Ha," Eric laughed. "Well, that Grandy's somethin' else again. Listen to this."

He set the needle down and it scratched into the groove. After the simple piano introduction, an extraordinary female voice billowed out of the Victrola and filled the room. It was a big voice, as wide and as deep as the oceans separating America from a dark and distant continent. The voice had some of the lonesome train whistle of Grandy's music, and it carried all of Grandy's authority and sureness. Yet it was simple and direct, and had a great beauty and rich polish that Grandy's drunken, country roughness lacked. Grandy's voice was all broken glass and jagged edges, where this female voice was all rounded and smooth. Grandy's music was like the cry of a wounded animal, an involuntary response to a harsh and hostile world. The fear and terror in Grandy's music had summoned up a defensive fortress around Jimmy's heart. But the melodious sweetness of this woman's voice slipped softly into the back door of Jimmy's heart, as if it had discovered the kitchen door to his soul. Perhaps it was some feminine key to the male ear, some deep-seated memory of the lullabies of mothers, but this billowing song got to Jimmy in a way that Grandy's could not. With a voice like that, Jimmy thought, she could sing anything and I would fall in love with her music.

When the record was over, Eric looked at Jimmy and said, "That's Bessie Smith, Queen of the Blues."

Jimmy shook his head in awe. "Please, play some more."

Eric played another Bessie Smith before there came a banging on the ceiling of the room below. Eric laughed and closed up the Victrola. "I guess we'd best keep it quiet."

"Where did you get those records?" Jimmy asked, his voice quiet. Eric sat down on the piano bench near Jimmy, their knees almost touching.

"My father works as a Pullman porter and he buys up the newest race recordings and sells them to colored vendors in towns along his way. So he gets all the latest music and I get my pick. These records just came out this summer."

"Are there stores where I can buy some?"

"Why, sure. I can take you to a few places. And there are some bands in town you ought to hear."

"You must know the city pretty well. Have you always lived in Chicago?"

"No. I was born and raised in St. Louis. East St. Louis. Then my father got an opportunity for a better position and we moved to Chicago—when I was 10."

"How long have you been playing the piano?"

"Like I mentioned at the club, my mother taught me. She's a piano teacher, see. So I started early. Then later on I went to Fisk University in Nashville and graduated with a degree in Music."

"Say, that's swell," Jimmy said. "I hear they have a great music program there."

"You've heard of it?" Eric sounded surprised.

"Yeah," Jimmy said and after a brief pause, he added, "this girl I used to know, she saw the Fisk gospel choir perform once." His mind drifted off to another place for a moment, and then he added, "Here. In Chicago. That's where she saw them perform."

"No kiddin'? I sang in that choir for a while," Eric said. There was a moment of awkward silence. They each picked up a glass and drank the gin.

"Well, tell me this," Jimmy said, "Did the other boys make fun of you for playing piano when you were growing up—back in St. Louis?"

"Oh, maybe a little, but mostly they respected me for it. The other kids loved music."

"Hell, the white boys out West sure didn't think that way. They thought music was effeminate, and they considered anyone who played it a sissy. I took a bit of teasing when I was a kid."

"Well, now, I think the place to be—for a musician—is Paris, France. I hear they have high respect for musicians there. And they love jazz. Someday I'm going to go to Paris."

A sudden yawn came over Jimmy before he could stifle it. He finished off the last of his gin.

"Let me pour you another," Eric said. "I've got another bottle around here somewhere."

"I don't know. Maybe I'd better think about getting back. Say, can I use the bathroom?"

Eric showed Jimmy to a bath down the hall. When Jimmy

returned, Eric was partially undressed and sat on the bed in his undershirt. In his lap was a small metal box and Eric was rolling a cigarette. The lamplight gleamed on the dark, smooth skin of his shoulders.

"Muggle?" Eric said.

Jimmy didn't understand.

"Marijuana. Tea. You've never tried it?"

Jimmy shook his head and shrugged.

Eric indicated the corner of the bed. "Sit down and make yourself comfortable. I'll give you a taste. Take off your coat and relax." Jimmy hung his overcoat on the bedpost and his tuxedo jacket on the chair back. His fingers trembled as he undid his black bow tie and tucked it into the tuxedo pocket. Then he unfastened his shirt collar and sat down on the edge of the bed.

Eric finished rolling a fat cigarette and lit it. "Initiation by fire," he said with a smile as he moved in close to Jimmy on the bed. Jimmy recognized the thick green odor that he'd smelled earlier in Jewell's kitchen.

"Now, inhale through your nose," Eric said and turned the cigarette so the lighted end pointed toward his own face. Eric opened his mouth and put his lips around the middle of the cigarette with the burning coal in the hollow of his mouth. Leaning forward, he blew out a thin stream of white smoke from the end of the cylinder. Jimmy leaned in and inhaled the white stream of smoke into his nostrils. "Hold it in a bit," Eric said after removing the cigarette from his mouth.

Jimmy felt a slight dizziness as a warm glow spread through him. At last he exhaled. Eric took a puff and handed Jimmy the thick cigarette. Jimmy took a long puff and held the smoke in. Then a cough erupted and he expelled all the smoke at once. He began to feel lightheaded and he laughed. Eric took the cigarette and smiled, watching Jimmy. There was a twinkle of mischief in his eye that Jimmy recognized from his introduction to Erica DeChez in the dressing room. Jimmy smiled back at Eric, then collapsed on the bed in laughter. A warm sensuousness filled Jimmy's whole body. He looked over at Eric and again he saw Erica DeChez sitting on the bed looking back at him. The sound of the Bessie Smith records and Erica's performance earlier filled Jimmy's mind and colored his perception of this unusual creature.

"I keep hearing Bessie Smith in my head," Jimmy said and hummed to himself for a moment. "Didn't I hear you do one of these Bessie Smith songs tonight? Her style has influenced you, hasn't it?"

"Yeah. I did one of her songs tonight. She gives me a lot of inspiration. I've seen her perform here in Chicago."

"Her music is so different from Grandy's blues."

Eric laughed. "That Grandy. What did you think of him?"

"He scared the hell out of me."

Eric laughed again. "Yeah. Well, there's no surprise there. The story goes that Grandy sold his soul to the Devil to get back his eyesight. But the Devil double-crossed him. Instead of giving him the ability to see, the Devil gave him the ability to sing the blues." He puffed on the cigarette.

Jimmy shuddered. "Well, we sure don't hear that kind of music out West, at least not where I come from. Why, they don't even let you sing some Mamie Smith songs at certain places back in Oregon. I was singing that song you did tonight, 'It's Right Here For Ya,' at a country dance back home, and the Ku Klux Klan stopped me from singing."

A cloud passed over Eric's face, then an opaqueness drained all the expression away, and Jimmy could no longer tell what Eric was thinking. "Sounds like a pretty rough crowd to me," Eric said. "I'm glad I missed that performance."

"Hell," Jimmy said, "I was so mad I could have killed one of them."

"Anger never does any good," Eric said. "I understand what you're saying, but anger is no way to deal with people. You have to learn to be smarter than they are." Eric paused, then continued, "I remember one night—Erica DeChez was playing piano and a fight broke out."

To hear Eric talk about his alter ego as a different person both fascinated and confused Jimmy.

"One fella pulled out a straight razor. It was like that nitwit Reggie tonight. Well, I'd been having one of those nights when everything clicks, you know?"

Jimmy nodded.

"So Erica walked up to the front of the stage and just said, 'Put the blade away, honey.' And as simple as that, the fella put the razor away. But I wasn't about to walk right up to the fella like Anabella did tonight. That sister was really taking a risk. Reggie could have blown her head off. Man, she's got more balls than I do. I don't know why it is, but a man wearing a dress has a special power if he knows how to use it."

"I wonder what would have happened if Anabella had been there the night those Klan bastards stopped us from playing."

"She would have been lynched," Eric said.

Jimmy realized that he had forgotten about their difference in skin color and he became embarrassed. He realized that he had never been in danger of being lynched—not for playing Negro music, not for simply walking down the street. Not the kind of danger Eric would have found himself in.

"Say, Eric, Anabella told me…she said that your grandfather was a white man."

"That girl has the goods on everyone. Yeah, it's true. A quarter of the blood in these veins is white. Probably more. Who can say for sure what a colored man's ancestry really is after more than 300 years of slavery? Isn't it funny how if a person has a single drop of African blood he's considered colored? Why isn't it the other way around? If I have a drop of Caucasian blood, why is it I'm not considered white?"

"Anabella said Reggie's father was killed by some white fellas," Jimmy said, "and now he hates whites."

"Yeah, I know all about that. The whole race issue weighs real heavy on Reggie's heart. That's why I say anger is no way to deal with people."

They were quiet for a moment.

"I have this idea," Jimmy said, "that music should be able to stop people like those Klansmen at that country dance in Oregon. I've always imagined that in a proper world, an orchestra should be able to stop a bullet, instead of the other way around. You know what I mean? I want to learn to play that well. A magician—uh—excuse me, I mean, a musician—ought to be able to stop a gun."

Eric laughed. "You had it right the first time," he said. "Musicians are magicians."

"Yes," Jimmy agreed. "But then how can a musical performance be so powerful and yet so fragile at the same time?"

"Music only exists in that instant of the present moment, on that razor's edge between the past and the future. But it passes so quickly. In less time than even the flowers of May. That fragility, as you put it, is the exact source of music's power."

They were both quiet for a time. Then Eric reached out and took the cigarette from Jimmy.

"Exhale," Eric said, and took another long drag on the cigarette. He brought his face down close to Jimmy's where he lay on the bed as Jimmy let out his breath. Then Eric put his mouth over Jimmy's mouth and forced his smoky breath into Jimmy's lungs.

The gesture took Jimmy by surprise and he felt amazed at what was happening to him. The air that had been inside of Eric now filled Jimmy's lungs. The sensation of Eric's lips on his own inflamed Jimmy's imagination.

Eric pulled back and dropped the cigarette into an ashtray beside the bed. For a moment he looked into Jimmy's eyes. "I like ofay boys like you."

The exotic sound of the phrase further bewitched him. Eric leaned in and gently kissed him, long and slow. Jimmy gave in to the warmth of the smoky drug and the kiss and the smell of Eric's body. He raised his hand and ran it over Eric's short nappy hair and down his neck to the smooth dark skin of his back.

Eric pulled back and regarded Jimmy for a moment with

that mischievous smile. "Would you like to sleep with a man or a woman tonight?"

Jimmy wasn't sure what Eric meant, but memories of Mary Hall and Elsa flashed through his mind and without giving it any more thought, he said, "A man, I guess."

"Hmm." Eric smiled and seemed to be contemplating all the possibilities. Then he began unfastening Jimmy's pants and said, "Let's see if the two of us can churn some cream together."

As he allowed Eric to remove his clothes, Jimmy wondered what he was letting himself in for. He had known Carl for some time before he and Carl had sex, but Jimmy had only just met Eric. Yet he felt that he had known Eric for a long time. Maybe it was the muggle, maybe it was because it had been such a long, strange night. Jimmy felt a connection with Eric, this strange being who was part male and part female, part black and part white. Could it be true that, being both male and female, Eric was privy to esoteric knowledge? Could Eric teach him some secret wisdom? Jimmy wondered if he could learn to love Erica DeChez, and through her, maybe he could learn to desire women. Maybe he could learn to desire Mary Hall.

As Eric removed the cufflinks and studs from Jimmy's tuxedo shirt, Jimmy noticed the pink on the palms of Eric's hands. He admired the smooth dark skin of Eric's biceps and shoulders, and he reached out and stroked Eric's arms. He closed his eyes and there was no way of knowing the color of Eric's skin, this dark skin he was touching. Jimmy wondered what it was like to live inside skin the color of Eric's. But color is only skin deep, isn't it, like beauty? How could something which seemed like such an insignificant difference cause such a vast gulf between two whole races? I guess I'll never know, Jimmy thought. There is a whole, wide history here inside this dark body beside me, a whole lifetime of experience that I will never know, never understand—all attached to the color of this skin.

When Jimmy was naked, Eric jumped up and stripped off the rest of his clothes. Then he crawled onto the bed like a stalking panther and began moving his pink palms slowly over Jimmy's body and kissing his skin.

As they began to make love, Jimmy found that Eric's skin smelled of spices and coffee and something dark and musky.

Jimmy became aroused and Eric reached down and caressed Jimmy's genitals.

"I like your member," Eric remarked.

Jimmy looked down and noticed the different colorations of Eric's circumcised penis. I guess I'll never know, he thought again.

"We're both circumcised," Jimmy observed. He reached out and fondled Eric's cock, which was also growing erect.

"Yes," Eric replied, "some societies seem to favor that religious mutilation." He bent down and ran the tip of his tongue around the circumference of Jimmy's cock, directly below the head where the foreskin would have been. "Imagine all the sensations they deprived you of when they cut off that pound of flesh." Eric looked up at Jimmy and said, "I like your taste." Then he moved up and gave Jimmy a long passionate kiss as they continued touching each other.

After a time Eric sat up and said, "Why don't you roll over and let's see about churning some butter."

"I…" Jimmy said, and hesitated.

"You…?" Eric asked. Jimmy didn't say anything, struggling to formulate his thoughts.

"We," Eric said and he gave Jimmy a long sensual kiss. Then he rolled Jimmy over onto his stomach and reached into a bedside drawer and took out a jar of Vaseline. He began massaging Jimmy's buttocks, working toward the center.

Finally, Jimmy found his voice. "I've never done this before."

"A virgin." Jimmy heard Erica DeChez's voice exclaim with surprise. Eric stretched his long dark body alongside of Jimmy's and nuzzled his ear and stroked him tenderly with his hand. "Well, you sweet lamb, let me initiate you," Erica DeChez said. He inserted the tip of his tongue in Jimmy's ear. "Don't worry. I'll be gentle."

Eric applied a liberal amount of the lubricant and continued to massage Jimmy's back side, working his way in toward the anus with a gentle, massaging motion, and easing a finger inside. After a time, Eric positioned himself and started to rub his erect cock against the crack between Jimmy's buttocks. Then Eric raised his hips and at last he began to press against Jimmy's sphincter.

After one long moment of agonizing pressure, Eric's member began slowly penetrating the orifice.

This can't really be happening to me, Jimmy thought. I can't do this. Thoughts of all the effeminate men in costume at Pluto's that night flooded Jimmy's mind. I'll turn into one of those.

Jimmy's anus contracted and he felt an intense pain. He experienced a doubt whether he could endure it, and he turned his head to look back at Eric.

"Please, Eric. No," he said. "I can't..." Tears stung his eyes.

Eric stopped. There was a silence. Eric pulled back and rolled onto his side next to Jimmy.

He reached out his hand and stroked Jimmy's back. "What is it, honey lamb? Tell me what's the matter." It was Erica DeChez's voice again.

"I don't know," Jimmy said as a tear rolled down his cheek.

"What are you afraid of, sugar?" Erica asked.

"I...I don't know." A sob shook Jimmy and he buried his face in the bedcovers.

"There, there, sugar lamb," Erica said, stroking Jimmy's head. "There ain't nothin' wrong, honey. Everything's gonna be all right." They were both quiet for a time and Eric placed his arm across Jimmy's back and hugged him close. Jimmy's tears subsided.

After a silence, Jimmy sniffled and turned to Erica and said, "Won't this turn me into a woman?"

"Oh, Jimmy, you sweet innocent boy," Erica said, as she rolled away from Jimmy onto her side and propped herself up on one elbow. "You're acting like trade."

"What do you mean?" Jimmy said.

"Oh, you know, some men think that you should never be on

the receiving end of another man's cock or you lose your manhood. Like Reggie. Trade is what we call he-men like that. Supposedly normal fellas who will let another man be their woman, but who won't reciprocate. You know what I mean? Real men. But then, what girl doesn't like to have a real man. Erica DeChez certainly does." She looked up toward the heavens, raised her arm, and ran her hand over her hair in a theatrical gesture. Then she turned her gaze back on Jimmy. "But I say that you can't fully understand your manhood until you've experienced the female role. A man can be trade and a fairy and a faggot—all at the same time. Look at me. Sometimes I'm a woman and sometimes I'm a man. Just because I let some other man brown me doesn't mean I'm not a man. Just because I wear a dress or pluck my eyebrows doesn't mean I'm a woman. Sex is not a black and white matter. Don't be afraid to open yourself up to new experiences. Relax, Jimmy, it's okay to let your hair down. You don't have to be ashamed of sensual adventures."

"But isn't that what turned you into a woman?" Jimmy insisted. "Isn't that what turned all those fellows at Pluto's into fairies?"

"Oh, Jimmy, Jimmy," Erica said with a sigh.

Jimmy buried his face again. Erica let him think for a while as she stroked his back.

At last Eric said, "I think I understand what's bothering you."

Jimmy wiped his eyes with his hands and turned his face toward Eric.

"You're afraid of what's already inside you, Jimmy."

"How do you mean?"

"Life is always moving—through all of us. Open yourself up to it. You need to find a way to let it go. That's the trouble with your music."

Jimmy looked at Eric with surprise and anger. "My music?"

"You see, Jimmy, your problem is that you want to control everything. You play from your head and not from your heart. Your music comes from your brain. Sometimes you just have to let it happen. Be spontaneous. You've got to learn to loosen up and just let the music move through you. Let the piano play you. You're afraid to let go and let the music take over."

Jimmy felt a surge of resentment overcome him. He shot Eric an angry glance and turned away.

"Now, don't you be mad at Erica, honey. She's just trying to help you out." Eric waited a moment for Jimmy to understand.

"Let me tell you a story." Eric said and paused for a moment to be sure he had Jimmy's attention. "Once upon a time, there was a young god who created and created and created. It seemed that there was no end to what he could do. Then one day he had a doubt. And because of that one small, little doubt, he found that he could no longer create." Eric didn't say any more.

Jimmy was quiet for a long time. Then he said, "Is that the end of the story?"

"Yes," Eric said. After a moment he continued, "Don't be afraid to open yourself up. Life is just flowing through you. Trying to control it won't make it better or last longer. You don't use it up. You create more of it by giving in to it. Play with wild abandon."

Jimmy turned back to Eric. "But what about order and form and discipline?"

"That's why you practice and practice and practice," Eric said. "Yes, we have to strike a balance between technical discipline and musical passion. Between Apollo and Dionysus. But you have to get to know Dionysus too. I know you've mastered the disciplined end of the piano. You need to get in touch with the passionate end of it. Let the emotion flow through your playing."

Jimmy moved over and hid his face in Eric's shoulder as he clung to his body. He was a stranger in a strange land. In Chicago with the gin and the muggle, the brothel and Pluto's Lair, all of his points of reference were gone. The boys in the Diggs Monroe Orchestra would never understand what Jimmy was doing in Eric's bed in the early morning. Carl Holman and Oregon and all the things Jimmy knew were far, far away. Eric was the only sympathetic soul Jimmy knew and he clung to him like a life raft.

He didn't want to lose him and he decided he would do anything to retain his favor.

"That's the end of Miss DeChez's pedagogy for today." Erica put her arms around Jimmy, cradling him in her arms and rocking him back and forth. "Now, what do you say we go back to practicing your lessons?"

Jimmy looked Eric in the face and gave him a long kiss. Then he reached down and began fondling Eric's member, and their kisses continued to increase in passion.

When he became aroused, Eric rolled Jimmy onto his back and, cupping his hands behind Jimmy's knees, raised Jimmy's legs in the air. First, he used his tongue to open Jimmy up. Then, after a time, he repositioned himself so that the two of them were face to face and Eric eased his member into place and ever so slowly leaned forward. They looked into each other's eyes, and a little smile glowed on Eric's lips. Jimmy made an effort to relax, let go of all effort, and then the pain was not so great. Without hurrying, Eric entered. After that Jimmy felt a great comfort settle over him. Like taking Eric's smoky breath inside his lungs, he took Eric's cock inside his body. Crossing their bodily boundaries, they became joined.

Eric was still for a time, letting Jimmy relax into the sensation. Then, after a bit, Eric began to rock gently and the stroking filled Jimmy up with a pleasure he had never imagined.

Jimmy heard a deep moaning sound that he could not place. At first he thought it was Eric vocalizing with each stroke. And then he realized that it was his own voice, his own body responding to Eric, as each thrust filled him. Waves of sensation washed over him, surging and receding.

Jimmy felt at last open and receptive. He had unfurled himself wide, given himself over to Eric completely, and there was nothing left for him to hide or withhold. Here I am, he thought. This is life. Take me, world.

After Eric's climax, his movements subsided. Jimmy floated for a long time in a state of complete and utter relaxation. The world would continue and life would go on, and whatever happened, Jimmy was ready to receive it. He began to wonder why he had ever been so reticent in the first place.

At last, they uncoupled and lay in each other's arms for a time, gradually returning to the world of gravity and dimension.

"Tell me now. Is God male or female?"

Jimmy's mind stopped. He could not answer. After a long silence he said, "I don't know."

"Um hm," Eric said and held him affectionately.

After a while Eric said, "Erica desires you."

It took Jimmy a moment to understand Eric's meaning. "I've lost my erection," Jimmy said. He was unabashed.

"Let me see what we can do about that," Erica said and she took Jimmy's member in her mouth.

When Jimmy became erect, Eric said, "Erica wants you to be her Shez Bo."

"What?" Jimmy said.

"Be my Chaise Beau."

"Okay, I'll be your Jazz Boy."

Eric rolled back and laughed. "No, no. It's French. Chaise Beau. He's the strutter who takes the cake at the cakewalk, the good boy who sits on the throne, the one who deserves the favor of the chair of honor."

"I'm not sure I understand."

"Here, let me show you how Erica likes it. Sit on this chair." He draped a towel over the seat of the straight-backed chair and Jimmy sat down. Erica handed the jar of Vaseline to Jimmy, saying, "Here, use this." Jimmy used a bit of it to grease himself.

"Oh, don't you be stingy with that stuff," she said. Then she leaned in and sang softly in his ear.

"I need a-plenty grease in my frying pan, 'cause I don't want my meat to burn."

Jimmy laughed. Erica took a generous amount of the petroleum jelly and lubricated Jimmy's cock with her hand. In order to whet his appetite, Erica bent down and helped herself to a taste of his nipples. She licked and nibbled. It was something Carl had never done and the novelty of these newly discovered sensations excited Jimmy's blood.

Once Jimmy was well-oiled, Erica greased herself, and then she straddled Jimmy's lap and gently settled herself down. The chair creaked and groaned as they moved.

They passed hungry kisses back and forth and their tongues tasted each other. Now their bodies were connected at both ends, Jimmy realized with pleasure, creating a curious wheel of involvement.

Erica was in ecstasy. A moan sounded deep in her throat.

"Oh, yeah, jazz me, baby," she whispered. Her words excited him.

But this all seemed very inconvenient to Jimmy, as Erica held him by the shoulders and rode him up and down. He couldn't find the glide that sparked him. He wanted more leverage, more freedom of movement.

This may be Erica's favorite position, Jimmy thought to himself, but I guess it isn't mine. He remembered Carl saying that people dream up all different ways to have sex. Jimmy wanted to satisfy Erica's tastes, whatever form they took.

It took some work on Jimmy's part, bucking and thrusting, but eventually he achieved orgasm. And Jimmy was happy to please Erica who was clearly enjoying their shared pleasure.

They sat for a time with their arms wrapped around each other as they luxuriated in the subsiding heat. Erica dismounted with a smile and said, "See, Jimmy, you're still a man." Then she leaned in and kissed him.

Erica put on the green kimono and handed Jimmy a bathrobe and a clean towel. She slipped out into the hallway to see if the bathroom was vacant and shortly returned and beckoned to Jimmy. They both used the bathroom down the hall, taking turns at the toilet. Eric cursed the landlord when he couldn't get any hot water, and they had to wash up using the cold. Sharing the bathroom together seemed, to Jimmy, almost as intimate as sharing sex.

When they returned to his room, Eric peeked out through the curtains and announced, "The sun is shining, jazz boy. It's time to go to sleep."

ELEVEN

When Jimmy woke up, it was past noon by the bedside clock. He was hungover and disoriented, and it took him a minute to remember where he was. Eric was asleep beside him. Without the magic of gin and muggle, the lavishly decorated room looked a bit tawdry with the light of day sifting in around the drapes. The room was quiet except for Eric's soft breathing, but Jimmy could hear people moving around in other parts of the building and noises came up from the alley behind. Lying there next to Eric's sleeping body, Jimmy remembered all that had happened the night before and he didn't know what to make of it.

He felt he had done something ultimate, tasted forbidden fruit. He was the same person, but he was changed somehow. He had taken an irrevocable step across some invisible line, crossed over into another world that intrigued and amused him. There was no turning back.

At the same time he felt anxious to get back to the familiar world of the Diggs Monroe Orchestra, which was not as exciting, but comfortable from long wear. What was the band up to? When were they supposed to play next? Oh, my God, we have that private party this afternoon. Didn't Diggs say we were leaving the hotel at 2? He was in a panic to get back to his hotel. He had to get dressed.

Jimmy didn't want to awaken Eric, so he slipped out of bed and searched around for his clothes, which he found scattered about on the floor among Eric's finery and sheet music and decorative clutter.

As he pulled on his clothes, Jimmy wondered if the fellows in the band would see that he had changed. Would they notice some outward difference? Well, he couldn't worry about that now. He had to find his way back.

He was tying his shoes and wondering where his cuff links and shirt studs had ended up, when Jimmy heard the bed covers rustle and then the bedstead creaked as Eric shifted his body. Looking up he met Eric's sleepy gaze. Eric blinked and started to raise his head, then groaned and fell back on the pillow. He rubbed his face with his large brown and pink hands. "Oh, boy," he said. When he uncovered his face, he grinned at Jimmy and said, "Hey, jazz boy."

Jimmy felt uncomfortable and unsure of himself. "Hi," he replied with a quick smile, and bent down to finish tying his other shoe.

"How are you this morning, sugar?" Eric propped himself up on his elbow.

"I'm okay," Jimmy said. "Only I don't think it's morning. And I'm pretty hungover. Look, I gotta get back to my hotel. I forgot that I have to play for a fancy party this afternoon. With the band, you know."

"Sure," Eric said, rolling back onto his pillow. He stretched and sat up. "Say, honey, hand me those black pants on the foot of the bed there, and come give mama a big good-morning kiss." Jimmy pushed down his anxiety and brought the trousers to Eric. Eric kissed him and peered into Jimmy's face, searching out his mood. "You sure you're all right?"

Jimmy nodded and tried to avoid Eric's gaze. "I'm just scared I'll be late getting back. I have to be there at 2."

Eric smiled and patted Jimmy's cheek. "Don't worry. You've got time." Then he moved to the other side of the bed and, with his back turned slipped into the pants. He fished the blue shirt off the foot rail of the bed and slipped into it.

"I can't find my cuff links," Jimmy said.

Eric pointed to Jimmy's overcoat on the bedpost. "I stashed all that in your coat pocket. I've got to run to the privy." He ruffled Jimmy's hair with his hand as he rounded the foot of the bed toward the door. "Be right back. Don't you run off."

When Eric returned, Jimmy had finished dressing and was combing his hair at the dresser mirror. Eric said, "Give me a minute to pull myself together, here, sweetheart, and I'll help you find a taxi."

As Eric dressed, Jimmy fidgeted with his clothing and then looked over the Bessie Smith records. He remembered the rent party and Grandy and all that music. "Hey, thanks. Thanks for playing these records for me." Jimmy turned. "Thanks for everything."

Eric finished adjusting his clothes and walked over to Jimmy. He placed a hand on each side of Jimmy's head and looked into Jimmy's eyes. "It was my pleasure." He studied Jimmy's face and then kissed his lips. Jimmy folded Eric in his arms and Eric returned the embrace.

"Look, I've got to run now," Jimmy said moving away from him. "But I want to see you again."

"I'll be at Pluto's Lair every night this week," Eric said. "Come back and see me. I'll take you to some after-hours clubs."

Then Eric went to open the door for Jimmy and said, "Come on, I'll show you the way."

Jimmy attracted numerous stares from the colored faces on the street as he and Eric walked together looking for a cab. The sun was shining and there was something raw and invasive about the clarity of day. Jimmy wished it were still night, with its secretive, enveloping comfort.

By daylight, Jimmy saw that this was not a pretty part of town. The buildings were old and in disrepair, with windows in need of glass, yards in need of care, streets in need of paving. Some of the lots were vacant and filled with trash. In an occasional glimpse between the buildings, Jimmy could see laundry hanging out in the backyards, a chicken coop here, a vegetable garden there.

As they passed along the sidewalk, approaching a more commercial area, Jimmy heard singing. Eric put his hand on Jimmy's shoulder and said, "Hey, come in here a minute, Jimmy. You've gotta hear this."

Jimmy hesitated.

"It won't take long," Eric said and he ushered Jimmy into a storefront church.

The front room of the establishment was empty except for an old Negro woman. She sat swaying to the music and humming to herself next to a collection box. The singing spilled out from an open doorway into the congregation hall. The old woman wore a white dress and an unusual white headpiece, which was plainly the uniform of her sect. As Eric and Jimmy approached, a sun-filled smile spread across her face and she nodded to them.

"Welcome to the house of the Lord," she said. Her expression betrayed no surprise or even a hint of acknowledgement that Jimmy was white. She radiated an unconditional love and her face glowed. Jimmy was so enthralled by an essence that radiated from her that he was overcome with a gratitude that insisted on showing itself. He dug in his pocket and produced a dollar bill, which he deposited in the collection box.

"Bless you, chil'," she said, the warmth of her smile still illuminating her face. "Jesus loves you." Jimmy couldn't help believing her.

They passed through the doorway into the back of the large hall.

The sound of the singing hit Jimmy full in the face. He hadn't stopped to think that it was Sunday until the gospel song filled his ears and his eyes saw the small congregation swaying and clapping their hands, women in their white church dresses and distinctive head pieces, and men in their Sunday suits, some wearing high-topped country shoes. Jimmy remembered Mary Hall's fondness for Negro spirituals and her descriptions of hearing the Fisk College choir. But nothing could have prepared him for this.

The passion in the room almost knocked him over. A feeling of overwhelming joy and love swept through him. It was as if the doorway to his soul had been thrust wide open by the enormous force of the emotion in the room and he was left defenseless and vulnerable to the fiery winds of the Pentecost. Jimmy could feel the power of the Lord moving through the congregation, Love made manifest.

From their vantage point at the side of the room, Eric and Jimmy could see the small choir in front dressed in their long white robes. Near them stood a preacher beside a lectern, raising his voice with the rest of the congregation.

"Are you washed
In the blood
In the soul-cleansing blood of the Lamb?
Are your garments spotless?
Are they white as snow?
Are you washed in the blood of the Lamb?"

The standing congregation moved and surged with song, nearly submerging the sound of the old upright next to the choir. An occasional shout of "Amen!" went up from the crowd, above the rhythmic singing. "Hallelujah!" came a cry from across the room as a large man raised his hands in the air. Others raised their arms to the heavens in supplication. The wildness of the scene, the complete abandon, was nothing like the quiet reserve of the Protestant religious services Jimmy was used to when he played the organ at the Episcopal Church back home.

A few rows in front of them, a small woman—probably in her late teens—raised her arms and let out an involuntary cry. She made her way out into the aisle and began moving toward the front, tears streaming down her cheeks, her hands swaying over her head. A slow wail arose from her throat. Then a violent jolt shook her body. Her white headpiece fell half-off and hung beside her face, still pinned to her hair.

"I have sinned," she screamed. "I have sinned. Forgive me, blessed Father." Another jolt went through her. She fell to the floor convulsing. Words that were not words flew out of her mouth.

A woman who had been sitting with her came out into the aisle and knelt beside the girl. She clasped her hand and cried, "Lord, have mercy. Lord, have mercy on her soul." A large woman seated nearby came to the girl's side and cradled her head in her lap.

Moans and sobs and cries racked the girl. Her arms and legs jerked. A small spot of blood appeared on the front of her dress, between her legs. The red stain spread out from the center as her pelvis thrust with the convulsions. Someone handed a white shawl down the row out to the aisle and the large woman used it to cover the girl's midsection.

Jimmy's face went clammy as a cold sweat broke out, and he began to feel light-headed. A dizziness and nausea overcame him. He wasn't sure if he was about to pass out or vomit, and before he knew what he was doing, he turned and ran out onto the sidewalk. He was halfway down the block before he stopped and leaned against a building. He doubled over and held his head, bracing his elbows against his knees and gasping for breath, hoping that he would not be sick. Then Eric was beside him with his hand on Jimmy's back.

"Keep your head down and breathe deep," Eric said. "You'll be all right in a minute. Everything's going to be fine."

Jimmy glanced up and saw a passerby pause to stare at him and then carried on, glancing back. Before long, he felt better and he slowly stood up.

"How are you doing?" Eric asked.

Jimmy said he was okay.

"Let's walk a bit," Eric said. "Do you feel well enough to walk?"

Jimmy nodded.

They walked half a block and found a stoop to sit on. Jimmy took out a handkerchief and wiped his face.

"I don't know what happened back there," Jimmy said.

"It can overpower you to be in the presence of God if you aren't prepared for it," Eric said.

Jimmy took a deep breath and put his handkerchief away. "What happened to that girl on the floor?" Jimmy asked.

"Oh, it's hard to say. Maybe she was feeling guilty and the mercy of the Lord was more than she could bear. Maybe she caught a glimpse of the world the way God sees it, and it was too much for her."

Jimmy pondered this for a time. After a while he felt he had sufficiently recovered his equilibrium, and he said he had to get going. He was shaken and he wanted to get back to familiar surroundings where he could feel his feet on the ground.

They walked a couple of blocks to a busy commercial street where Eric hailed a taxi. Jimmy thanked Eric again and shook his hand before getting into the cab.

"I'll look for you at Pluto's," Eric said and closed the car door.

Jimmy waved and as the taxicab moved on, he turned back to watch Eric standing on the curb until the cab rounded a corner.

Jimmy rolled down the window and let the cool air flow over him. His head began to clear and he tried not to think of anything.

As the cab drove north, there were fewer and fewer colored faces and more and more white ones. Jimmy began to feel that he was back in more customary surroundings.

But why must there be this animosity between the races? Jimmy wondered. He was feeling such a kinship with Eric, such closeness and affection, that skin color seemed such an arbitrary and artificial difference. Black and white didn't seem to make much difference at Pluto's Lair. But then neither did male and female.

Jimmy wasn't sure what it was about Eric that he found attractive. Was it his physique, or the smoothness of his complexion? His smile played a part, and his quick wit, and his musical talent. Maybe even his peculiar ability to become male or female by turns made him attractive. But Jimmy didn't think the color of his skin had anything to do with it.

Still, as the taxicab moved into the white part of town, he felt he was passing into a different world, and his link with Eric and that milieu began to lose its spell over him. He felt more at ease, and he was surprised at his sense of relief to be among Caucasian faces again.

And although he was only vaguely aware of it, Jimmy also knew that he was returning from a world where he didn't know if the person before him was male or female—back to the world where there was no question that men were men and women were women and they all knew their places.

Like Oregon and Portland, familiar territory. And Jimmy thought of Carl and their conversations about marriage and sex. About his own reluctance to perform certain acts and how that reticence no longer made any sense. He wanted to talk to Carl and tell him everything that had happened and explain to him—

But Jimmy couldn't think about Carl right now. He was about to face Diggs and the band. He realized that he had glimpsed another world, and he wasn't sure how he could ever fit back into the world as the Diggs Monroe Jazz Orchestra dreamed it. Well, there is no turning back the clock, he thought. All I can do is plow ahead and face the music.

As the taxi approached the Firestone, Jimmy became anxious all over again. Would the fellows in the band see a change in him after what had happened with Eric? He knew he was changed, utterly, but did it show on the outside?

TWELVE

It was after 2 when Jimmy climbed out of the taxi and paid his fare. He had never been late to an appointment with the band before and he hoped that would stand him in good stead this once. Still, he was anxious about how Diggs would react since there had been so much uneasiness between them lately.

As he entered the hotel lobby, Jimmy saw Diggs and Bill and Larry waiting together. It was worse than he had feared. Diggs was pacing back and forth, pulling back the sleeve of his tux to check his watch, and when they saw Jimmy approach, a coldness came over their faces.

"You're late," Diggs said.

"I'm sorry, fellas."

"I told you we had to leave here at 2 sharp," Diggs began. "I swear, Jimmy…"

Jimmy held up his hands and cut Diggs off. "Now, it's only ten after."

"It's a quarter past 2, and we have to be set up to play by 3," Diggs shot back.

"Look, Diggs, I'm all set to go. I just have to run upstairs and grab my music."

"Well, for God's sake, hurry up," Diggs said. "Howard and Chuck are bringing his car around front. You can ride with them. I'll tell them you'll meet them out front here."

Jimmy ran up the stairs two at a time. In the room he

scrambled to gather up his sheet music and headed back. As he raced down the hall, he saw a colored maid filling a linen cart and he took notice of her with an interest that was new to him. He found himself wondering where she lived and what her life was like. He slowed his pace a bit to smile and say "Good afternoon," as he passed, and she looked up and returned his greeting.

Larry was waiting alone in the lobby when Jimmy returned. A cool smirk crossed Larry's face.

"Hey, lover boy," Larry said.

For the first time, Jimmy hated him, but somehow he didn't care now what Larry must be thinking.

"Diggs went to get his car. Chuck and Howard are waiting for you out front. Let's move."

Jimmy didn't say a word, just hurried toward the door. Larry, who was so sure he knew the score, was ignorant of the vibrant world Jimmy had just left.

Out at the curb, Jimmy was relieved to see Howard at the steering wheel with Chuck beside him. Jimmy greeted them and climbed into the back. Diggs came driving around the corner with Bill and called out the driver's window to Howard. "Follow me." Larry jumped into Diggs' car and they were off.

On the drive out, Chuck and Howard talked about the bands they'd heard the night before. Jimmy was bursting to tell them about the great Negro band that played hot jazz at Pluto's Lair, about Grandy's cold blues at the rent party, even about Eric's blues singing and the Bessie Smith records, and... But he knew he couldn't tell them all this. Instead, he said he'd heard the hottest jazz in the world at a couple of dives, but that it was nothing Diggs would approve of.

"So how come you showed up dragging in at 2 o'clock in the afternoon?" Chuck asked, turning to face Jimmy in the back. Images of Eric flashed through Jimmy's mind and he allowed a coy smile to come over his face. "Well, I sort of met this woman and one thing led to another..."

Chuck turned to elbow Howard and said, "What did I tell you?"

The private party was like nothing the band had played before. The home was a palatial estate looking out on the vast lake. Howard followed Diggs' car as it pulled off the street into a wide circular drive. The band was directed to park behind a large garage that housed several limousines. A number of house servants were dispatched to help them carry their instruments through a back entrance up to a second-floor ballroom with windows opening onto a terrace that overlooked a large lawn and garden stretching off toward the water.

Diggs was bustling around making sure everyone and everything was in its place by 3. But once they started to play, Diggs began to calm down, and the jitters with which he had infected the other band members evaporated.

This was strictly a society affair and they played society music. With all the South Side rhythms and other musical licks that still filled his head, Jimmy had to struggle to stick to the arrangements they had rehearsed. By 5, when the party was in full swing, the swanky environment began to feel more comfortable. The band was sounding more relaxed, and Jimmy was feeling loosened up. He tried some variations in one of the piano parts. He couldn't help himself, after all the tough, jumping jazz and lowdown, gut bucket blues that steamed through his brain from the night before. Diggs shot him a look that let Jimmy know that his inventions were not appreciated.

At his first opportunity, Diggs made his way over to the piano and said, "Don't push it."

Jimmy didn't say anything. He sat tight and looked back at Diggs.

"You know what I'm talking about. Don't do it," Diggs repeated, then with a brusque turn he walked away.

The party broke up around 6. While the other fellows were packing up their instruments, Diggs cornered Jimmy alone.

"Just what do you think you are doing? This is the most

important engagement we've had since we got here and you try to ruin it by sneaking in some of that nigger music. This is high society. That kind of sound just doesn't go here. They want to have civilized music that stays in the background."

Jimmy wasn't going to fight about it. With the thought of playing piano at Pluto's in the back of his mind, he didn't have to. Besides, he knew he couldn't win, not with Diggs. He would do what he could to keep the peace. "I'm sorry," he said. "It just sort of slipped out. Don't worry. It won't happen again."

After they got back to the hotel, the band went to their now customary diner. Diggs asked for the titles of popular new songs that they had heard the night before. He was compiling a list to take to the music store the next morning. The song that stuck in Jimmy's mind was "Gladstone Blues," so, in an effort to make some contribution, he mentioned that title. He wanted to show the others that he was carrying his weight and hadn't been wasting his time the night before. But once he got started, he couldn't contain himself and he went on to tell them about hearing Bessie Smith's records from "this girl" he'd met. "Bessie Smith is the hottest Negro blues singer in the country," Jimmy said. "'The Queen of the Blues' they're calling her. She's the berries."

Diggs dismissed Jimmy's enthusiasm. "I don't think Negro blues is going to get us the kind of work we want in this town. Now listen. Our money is running low. This party today paid real well for three hours work, but if I can't find us more work fast, we're in trouble. Everything is more expensive here than I planned on. We have to economize. Let's think about moving into less expensive quarters. Howard, can you and Chuck look into finding someplace cheaper?"

"Cheaper than this fleabag?" Larry laughed and so did the others.

"I've been working my frat connections and I was able

to arrange for free rehearsal space with a piano at the college tomorrow afternoon from 1 to 5. We'll meet in the hotel lobby at noon. We should be able to use that rehearsal space all this week. We've got that frat dance on Tuesday evening. I'm still trying to set something up for next weekend too. I think I'll have that nailed down by Wednesday. Okay, now, there's also the music union angle. I'm working on it, but it's turning out to be trickier than I thought. It may cost us a bundle. I'll let you know what happens with that."

Bill and Larry said they wanted to go out after dinner to take in another white band at a nearby club. "You fellas come along," Larry said. "Afterwards we plan to check out one of those places downtown that has taxi dancers."

Diggs said he had to make some phone calls back at the hotel, and Howard said he had a date with a girl he'd met. Jimmy said he wasn't interested, and Chuck said he wanted to go back to the room to get some sleep.

After dinner, they all walked back to the hotel. Jimmy said he needed some air and walked off down the sidewalk. Behind him he heard Bill say, "What's eating him?" Then he heard Larry's derisive laugh, and the reply, "I can just guess." Jimmy kept walking and turned the corner.

He grabbed the first cab he could find and went to Pluto's. He couldn't stop thinking about Eric and he was desperate to talk to someone. Eric was the one person he knew in Chicago that he felt he could trust.

THIRTEEN

At Pluto's Lair, the scene was significantly different from the night before. As Jimmy passed through the maroon-curtained entrance the sparse crowd displayed none of the dazzle of Saturday night. On the stage at the far end of the room, Eric was playing the piano by himself. Eric's presence reassured him and Jimmy felt a sense of relief. At the same time, seeing Eric sent a rush of sensual excitement through him.

There was no sign of the band. Just a handful of couples in street clothes moved around the dance floor. The platform where the slumming rich had clustered during the costume ball was empty. Jimmy felt out of place in his tux. Well, Eric is in his tux, Jimmy thought, and so is the bartender. Will people think I work here?

As he walked toward the bar, he recognized the bartender Roscoe. The only people at the bar were two young men engaged in an ardent conversation. Jimmy watched as Roscoe served their drinks and wiped down the surface of the bar. He remembered the scene in the basement of the brothel, and he remembered seeing Roscoe leave with Danny Felton that night. Once again, Jimmy noticed Roscoe's pretty-boy face with its angelic, child-like features. What was Roscoe's relationship with Felton, and what was that deal with the opera tickets? And how did this same fellow end up at that sorority dance with an heiress on his arm?

Roscoe approached and Jimmy ordered a gin.

"Say, let me ask you something," Jimmy said as Roscoe got down a glass. "Danny Felton introduced you to me last night, remember?"

"I meet a lot of people here," Roscoe replied.

"I thought I saw you at that sorority ball at the Redfield Ballroom Friday night."

Roscoe gave Jimmy a sharp look. "You trying to make trouble, buddy?"

Jimmy was shocked at his vehemence.

"Wait a minute. You've got the wrong idea. I was playing in the band at that dance. I just thought maybe I saw you there."

"So what's it to you if you did? You must have me confused with somebody else." Roscoe poured the gin.

"Sorry," Jimmy said. "I was just trying to be friendly. Look, I'm new in town—from Oregon. Jimmy's the name. Jimmy Harper. I'm a friend of Eric's." Jimmy extended his hand to shake. "I'm hoping to take the job playing piano here."

Instead of shaking hands, Roscoe handed Jimmy his drink. He studied Jimmy for a moment. "Yeah, everyone knows Eric likes white boys." Roscoe's tone was not friendly, and again, Jimmy was surprised at his animosity. Roscoe continued to study Jimmy for a moment, and then he turned and put the gin bottle back behind the bar.

Jimmy paid for the drink and added a generous tip, hoping Roscoe would warm up to him, then tried again. "Danny Felton said you work at the opera."

"Yeah." Roscoe scooped up the money and continued to eye Jimmy with suspicion.

"What kind of work do you do there? Are you a singer?"

Roscoe laughed. "You're a regular joker. Do you think I'd be working here if I was an opera singer? No, I'm an usher. But I've got my eye on a manager position there."

"Mr. Felton said you arranged some opera tickets for him. Is he on the level?"

"Oh, you bet he is. He's a real opera fan. He's got a private box there and all that." Roscoe warmed a bit as he talked about the opera. "I always usher Mr. Felton and his wife to their box. They sometimes take important personages as guests. He goes every chance he gets."

Jimmy was surprised to hear that Felton had a wife.

"You must like the opera, too," Jimmy said.

"And how, it's the cat's meow, let me tell you. I've seen some of the world's greatest singers since I've worked there."

"Yeah? Who've you seen?" Jimmy asked.

Roscoe named the famous Mary Garden and then some other singers that Jimmy didn't recognize. "When I was a kid, my pop took me to see Caruso sing there. I told myself, I'm gonna work here someday. It's a nifty job."

Jimmy nodded, then said, "Mr. Felton says he can help my jazz band find work. Is he really all that well connected?"

"Listen, Mac, if there is one thing that you can count on in this town, it's that Mr. Felton is well connected. He got me my job at the opera."

"Well, let me ask you this. What, uh,…how is it he got you a job at the opera?"

Again, Roscoe shot Jimmy a suspicious look. "Because I asked him. I just told you, I've always wanted to work there. Since I was a kid. Boy, you ask a lot of questions." He picked up a bar towel and began polishing the glasses.

"What I mean is…is he just a nice fellow? What does he get out of it?"

"Yeah. He's a nice fellow," Roscoe said with emphasis and gave Jimmy a look. "If you're nice to him, he's nice to you. Okay?"

"Okay," Jimmy said. "Thanks for the drink."

Jimmy found an empty table near the stage. Eric broke into a smile and nodded at him as Jimmy sat down. He loved that smile. And he loved listening to Eric's solo piano. The music soothed him and made him itch to try out some new ideas in his own playing. And it made him question Diggs Monroe's musical judgment.

At the next break, Eric joined him. "Hey, jazz boy. I didn't expect you back here so soon, but I'm sure glad to see your face." The words lifted Jimmy's spirits.

"Boy, it's sure quiet tonight. Nothing like last night."

"The place closes early on Sunday and Monday nights. Besides, last night was something special."

"So that explains it," Jimmy said. "I'm glad I got here early."

"Let me take you to a black and tan club later on. There's a band you ought to hear."

Jimmy had never heard of a black and tan club, so Eric explained it was a joint that had a colored band and welcomed both black and white clientele.

"You mean like Pluto's Lair?" Jimmy said.

"Well, Pluto's is kind of a special place. Come along with me later and I'll take you to the Checker Club. Felton wants me to move over there pretty soon. More pay. You'll find it a lot classier."

"So is that why Felton has a piano job opening here?" Jimmy felt daunted by the prospect of trying to replace Eric.

"I'll be there three nights each week, but I'll still be performing here part of the time."

Jimmy felt reassured. "I keep hearing about the band at the Checker Club," Jimmy said. "I'm curious to catch their act."

He listened to Eric play until around midnight when the place closed. When Eric joined him, Jimmy asked what new popular tunes the Diggs Monroe outfit ought to learn. Eric said that the music he knew probably wasn't appropriate for the crowd Diggs was playing for.

Jimmy asked him about certain passages that Eric had played earlier in the evening. "Like this," Jimmy said, and went over to the upright next to the stage. He played a few phrases. Then Eric pulled up a chair from one of the nearby tables and sat down beside Jimmy and played the passage again.

"It's these blue notes," Eric said, and he demonstrated. Jimmy repeated the passage. Then Eric corrected Jimmy and played another phrase. Jimmy repeated the new passage. After a while Eric moved to the grand piano on the stage and again he played a bit and then Jimmy repeated it. Before long they were engaged in a full-blown improvisation in a call-and-response conversation, each one commenting on the previous passage of the other. For Jimmy, it was a relief to be playing what he was feeling, freed from the straightjacket of Diggs' control. Playing music with Eric opened him up to new possibilities and pushed him to take chances and try out new inventions. They played for half an hour until Roscoe told them it was time to lock up.

On the way to the Checker Club in the back of a taxi, Jimmy asked Eric about the job at Pluto's.

"What's with your band?" Eric asked.

"Things aren't working out so well."

"Boy, you fellas have come a long way together. What's the problem?"

"Oh, God, Eric," Jimmy sighed. "It's a lot of stuff. I guess the biggest thing is that Diggs wants to play this corn-fed society music and I like the music I hear down here when I'm with you."

"This is a tough racket, this music business. I know a lot of musicians that are happy to be making a buck playing any kind of music. If your band has work, stick with them. You may have to make the music you love after hours. Like we did tonight."

"But what about the job at Pluto's? There I could play the kind of music I like."

"You've got it if you want it. But think about this deal with your outfit. It sounds to me like Diggs is a go-getter with some high-toned connections."

Jimmy admitted that was true. And that was the problem. Still he agreed to think it over.

The taxi took them to the street where Jimmy had seen all the brightly lit clubs on his way to Pluto's Lair the night before.

"Paris may be the City of Light," Eric said, "but this part of Chicago does its best to turn night into day." The sidewalks were crowded with colored people as before, with many white faces in the crowd as well. And other faces could have been colored or white. Jimmy wasn't sure.

The cab let them off near a busy corner. The whole street was alive with people, all moving with rhythms that Jimmy was unused to seeing. Eric caught Jimmy's bedazzled look.

"Welcome to the Stroll," he said with a smile and led Jimmy off through the foot traffic. They passed a boisterous crowd of men clustered around a dice game on the concrete doorstep of a closed shop. A group of women dressed to the nines moved along with the crowd, soliciting aggressive greetings from young men along the walkway. Jimmy felt intimidated by this world, but Eric seemed to embrace it all, revel in it. He was open to everything.

A group of people at the curb had gathered around a young man in a snappy suit seated at a soapbox. He shuffled and fanned and laid out playing cards. He spied Jimmy and called him to come over. His dexterity with the cards and his line of patter was so captivating that Jimmy stopped before he knew what was happening.

"Take it easy, Mooncalf," Eric said laying his arm around Jimmy's shoulder. "This white man is flat broke."

The card shark greeted Eric by name and said, "He don't look like he's flat in that sharp tuxedo."

They laughed and Eric directed Jimmy on down the walkway.

"What was that?" Jimmy asked.

"Just a skin game. Don't pay him any attention. He'll suck you in and have your wallet before you know what hit you."

They came to the corner and paused as a car turned in front of them. A gorgeous woman in a green brocade gown and a fur coat was crossing the street away from them. An approaching group of men accosted her with flirtations. "Hey, pretty mama."

"Don't look now but that's our friend Anabella," Eric said

in Jimmy's ear. She reached the far side of the street, and as a limousine passed by, she turned to watch it. Eric waved and caught her eye. Anabella smiled and blew them a kiss, then turned and proceeded on down the street. Jimmy watched in amazement. She looked for all the world to be a woman, and there she was, out brazenly sauntering down a public street.

Eric maneuvered Jimmy through the auto traffic to the opposite corner and pointed out a music store. "You said you were interested in buying some music. You ought to be able to find anything you want here." Then he pointed off down the side street. "And there is the L train station one block over that way. So you can drop in any time you like."

Jimmy peered into the darkened windows of the music shop and then looked around to memorize the street signs.

"The Checker Club is right down the street," Eric said. "Follow me."

They heard the sound of blues as they passed a knot of spectators surrounding a drunken singer with a guitar leaning against a doorway.

"Hey, look, Eric," Jimmy said, stopping to watch. "It's Grandy."

They paused and watched through the gathering crowd listening to the music. Grandy was singing.

"All you see that glitters
Does not turn out to be gold.
I say, all you see that glitters
Does not turn out to be gold.
Death took away my baby
And now I find I done growed old…"

The heavyset fellow who had been escorting Grandy at the rent party stood beside him now holding out the felt hat, which clinked with coins as the small audience tossed in their offerings. Jimmy dug out a quarter and pitched it into the hat.

Eric nudged Jimmy on, and down the block he stopped at a door under the sign advertising "The Checker Club." They walked through a tiled vestibule to an inner door attended by a large colored doorman in a tuxedo. As they approached, the doorman appraised Jimmy, then saw that he was with Eric.

"Evening, Mr. Halsey," he said. Then turning to Jimmy with a broad smile, he added, "You must be here for your music lesson tonight. Come right on in."

"Maybe he's here to teach us a thing or two," Eric said.

"He that good?" the doorman asked.

"Time will tell," Eric replied as they passed inside.

The place was very posh compared to Pluto's, just as Eric had suggested. Potted palms and ferns and other exotic plants gave the room a feeling of lush tropical forests. A polished teakwood bar with a shiny brass foot rail stretched before a huge beveled glass mirror in a mahogany frame. Flanking the mirror above each end of the bar stood two large African-style statues, one female and the other male, carved from ebony wood in an angular geometric style. These figures looked down through a jungle of hanging plants onto the black bartenders who were doing a brisk business below. Colored waiters in white serving coats bustled about the room.

A Negro band dressed in tuxedoes was playing hot jazz like nobody's business beyond a large black-and white-checkerboard dance floor crowded with well-dressed couples. Surrounding the main floor was a second-story gallery, festooned with leafy vines, twining and draping their tendrils down from above. Tables covered with white linen lined the upper gallery where patrons sat eating and drinking as they gazed down over an ornate wrought-iron railing onto the spectacle below.

The clientele was largely colored, but Eric seemed to know a number of people both black and white. They greeted him with a wave or shook his hand as he and Jimmy made their way to the bar. A distinguished-looking white gentleman greeted Eric and called to one of the bartenders to get Eric anything he wanted. The man seemed a bit drunk. Eric addressed the man as Mr. Horton and introduced Jimmy, and the man told the bartender to pour one for Jimmy, too.

They stood at the bar a while, listening to the music and drinking. Horton asked Eric if he was going to sing "one of those indigo ditties tonight." Eric said, "Maybe later." A blonde came up and told Horton that she wanted to dance, and the two of them drifted off toward the dance floor.

A lively young black woman with a sparkling smile approached Eric and gave him a hug. Eric introduced her to Jimmy. He recognized her as the piano player at Jewell's rent party. Her name was Alice and she seemed to know a lot about music. A tall blond man came up and asked how soon Eric would start playing piano there. Eric told him two weeks.

During a pause between numbers, Eric, Alice, and Jimmy made their way to a table that had been vacated near the bandstand. As they took their seats, the trombone player in the band greeted Eric from the stage. Jimmy recognized the musician as another one of those at the rent party, he felt a twinge of shame.

The band began to play again. Jimmy liked this band even better than the one at Pluto's Lair, but he couldn't quite say why. The music was more relaxed and open than the music at Pluto's. It had a refined stateliness that took its sweet time getting where it was going, taking surprising side trips along the way. Jimmy was impressed by the cornet player. There was a long, thrusting line through his solo breaks that powered them forward while rising naturally out of the composition. Meanwhile, the entire group of musicians played with an ensemble teamwork that held the music in a balanced fullness. Jimmy loved the sound of it.

From time to time Eric leaned over and, speaking in Jimmy's ear, remarked on the different solo breaks or pointed out elements of technique. Alice commented on the performance of one musician or another. Jimmy was carried away by the playing.

One of the waiters came up and said something to Eric, who

excused himself, saying he would be back and left with the waiter toward a gaming room in the back.

Jimmy gave Alice a puzzled look and she leaned in to his ear. "Maybe it's about the gang wars with the Micks." Jimmy didn't understand but noted the remark. They sat for a time, listening to the music and making an occasional comment. Alice asked if Jimmy cared to dance and she led him to the dance floor and showed him some new steps. When they got back to the table, Eric had returned. The waiter came by again and Eric insisted on buying more drinks, explaining that he was celebrating, but he became coy when Jimmy asked about the cause for celebration.

"A bit of good luck" is all that Eric would say.

The band took a break and one of the members came up and asked Eric to play with them during the next set. Eric agreed. A girlfriend of Alice's joined them for awhile, and then the two of them left to go to the powder room.

A stage manager announced the "Tiger Lilies" as the next act, and there was a round of applause as a different piano player took the stage and struck up a tune. A chorus line of five light-skinned Negro girls clad in skimpy orange costumes took the stage. After a dance number, they were joined by a man who sang some amusing novelty songs.

Soon after that, the band reassembled and Eric joined them at the keyboard. During the set, Jimmy's gaze wandered along the upper gallery as he listened to the music. All at once he recognized Danny Felton dressed in white tie and tails sitting at a table by the railing. Next to him sat a beautiful, young dark-haired woman. Herman and the big silent fellow Sullivan were seated with them, along with another couple. Before he could look away, Jimmy realized that Felton was staring right down at him. Felton smiled and nodded. Felton's presence made him feel uneasy as he remembered Felton's hands on him at Pluto's. Jimmy hastily turned away to watch the band.

As he sat there drinking and listening to Eric and the other musicians, Jimmy thought of Felton's offer to help find work for the band. Diggs' rebukes to Jimmy for trying to make the music more interesting flashed across his mind. Jimmy wasn't sure he wanted to help find work for the band, but then again, maybe Felton could help them get engagements at clubs that preferred hot jazz. Would Diggs go for that? Jimmy wondered as he took another sip from his drink. The glass was nearly empty, and he was considering ordering another when Herman appeared at his table.

"Hello, Mr. Harper," Herman said. "Mr. Felton would be pleased if you would come and say hello."

Jimmy glanced up at Felton, who nodded at him.

Jimmy couldn't think up a plausible excuse, and besides he felt that declining was not an option, so he followed Herman through the crowd to the upper level. As they approached Felton's table, Jimmy saw that they were in the middle of a meal. Felton stared over at Jimmy. That sly, discomforting smile crept over his face. Jimmy looked away and glanced around the table, admiring the group's evening wear.

"Well, we meet again, kid piano," Felton said, rising to his feet and extending his hand.

Jimmy said hello and shook his hand, forcing a smile.

"Jimmy, I'd like you to meet my wife. Darling, this is Jimmy Harper, the piano player I was telling you about."

The dark-haired woman seated next to Felton put down a forkful of what looked like smoked salmon and, without rising, reached out to take Jimmy's hand.

"I'm so pleased to make your acquaintance," she said. "My husband has told me what a fine musician you are. I hope he will be a help to you." Up close she was even more beautiful than from across the room.

"Thank you," Jimmy said.

"Will we get to hear you play this evening?" she asked. "Surely, that can be arranged." She turned to her husband.

"Why, of course. You'll play for us, won't you." It was a command, not a question. "I'll make it worth your while. Herman, talk to the stage manager and have this young fellow play during the next break. What do you say, Jimmy Harper?"

Jimmy was so struck by Felton's wife that he turned to her and said, "It would be an honor to play for you."

"Good," Felton said. "Herman, show our young friend here down to the stage manager and make sure he plays next."

"Pleased to meet you," Jimmy said and made a little bow in the direction of the wife.

As Herman escorted Jimmy away from the table, Felton followed close behind. He placed his arm around Jimmy's shoulder and spoke in his ear. "Come see me before you leave tonight."

Jimmy nodded, though he felt hesitant, and Felton said, "Good boy," and slapped his back. "We'll talk later."

Herman led Jimmy downstairs to the stage manager. He said something in the manager's ear, and the stage manager nodded and looked Jimmy over. Then Herman returned to the upper level.

"Stay up here by the bandstand," the stage manager said leaning in to be heard. "What's your name again? Jimmy Harper?"

Jimmy nodded.

"I'll announce your name and you can come right up on stage by these stairs here."

Waiting to play, Jimmy decided that maybe this was an auspicious coincidence running into Danny Felton. Maybe this was a sign that Jimmy could make it on his own without the band. Again he thought about the friction with Diggs and weighed the merits of continuing with him, let alone helping the band find work.

The set was over then and the stage manager was introducing "a talented new piano player, Mr. Jimmy Harper."

During a round of polite applause, Jimmy went straight to the piano. It was all so sudden that he didn't have time to think or prepare. He just started to play. He was not thinking about anything in particular, but he remembered his sense of freedom playing with Eric earlier that evening at Pluto's. In the back of his mind he kept remembering what Eric had told him about letting go and allowing the piano to play him. His fingers took over. Or maybe the piano keys took over his fingers. Jimmy wasn't sure what happened. He found his mind wandering back over all that had come to pass to bring him there, Mary Hall and Elsa and Erica, the friction between him and Diggs and the fellows in the band, and his longing to see Carl.

Before he knew it, he had come to the end of his musical train of thought. There was a brief silence and then an avalanche of applause. He hadn't noticed how quiet the room became while he played, but the thunderous applause, laced with cheers and whistles, was gratifying, and Jimmy's attention returned to the present. He stood up and took a couple of short bows, then left the stage. The applause continued.

Eric came up to Jimmy and smiled and put an arm around his shoulder. "Great playing," he said.

Jimmy returned the smile, and Eric led him back to their table.

As the ovation was dying down, Jimmy glanced to the upper tier through the haze of cigarette smoke. There Mrs. Felton stood, still applauding, and at her side, also clapping, was Danny Felton, staring down at him with that unsettling smile. Jimmy looked away.

As the Tiger Lilies started another dance number, Jimmy said, "I could use another drink."

"Let me get one for you" Eric said. "You sit tight and I'll be right back."

Jimmy was feeling a bit dazed. Some of the members of the band had taken seats at their table. They all had words of praise for his performance. Alice had rejoined them and was sitting in the lap of one of the musicians. She leaned over toward Jimmy and said, "You play like an angel, sweetheart." Jimmy was humbled and flattered.

Eric returned with drinks for them both. Before long the band began to play again with their regular pianist. The next time Jimmy glanced up to the upper gallery, Danny Felton and his party were gone.

Sitting there with Eric, Jimmy began to relax and unwind from his performance. He sipped his drink and listened to the band play. They were really laying it down.

After a while, Herman approached their table. He nodded a greeting to Eric and turned to Jimmy.

"The boss wants to see you before he leaves," Herman said. "Come with me."

Jimmy glanced at Eric and then got up from the table.

Herman led Jimmy to the front of the club and down a side hall. An old Negro janitor came toward them wheeling a mop bucket, and he and Jimmy nodded to each other in passing. They approached the door to the men's room, and Jimmy was surprised to recognize Sullivan standing in front of the doorway.

"Sorry, the washroom is occupied," Sullivan said, stepping forward to bar Jimmy's way.

"He's okay," Herman said. "Let him in. He's that musician the boss likes." Sullivan gave Jimmy a quick pat down and waved him on. Herman held open the lavatory door and gestured for Jimmy to enter. He was confused but stepped inside and the door closed behind him.

Jimmy glanced around. A piney smell of cleansing soap hung in the air. The restroom seemed to be empty. A row of vertical porcelain urinals stretching down to the tile floor, which was damp and clean as if freshly mopped. Beyond the urinals, mahogany panels enclosed the toilet stalls.

Maybe Herman had gone to round up Felton, Jimmy thought, but this struck him as a peculiar venue for a meeting. He felt awkward standing there alone, waiting in the men's washroom, so he took advantage of the opportunity to relieve himself. Stepping up to the far urinal, Jimmy undid his fly.

His stream had just started to run down the porcelain when he heard the sound of urine beginning to tinkle in the toilet stall next to him. The sound echoed off the tile.

Jimmy's urine flow stopped. Just visible under the dark wooden partition at his side, Jimmy caught the highlight off a black patent-leather shoe. Someone was standing facing the toilet urinating. Was it Felton? Try as he might, Jimmy could not get started again. The person in the stall finished up and there was the sound of the fixture flushing. As he fumbled to fasten his fly, Jimmy heard behind him the sounds of footsteps coming out of the stall and walking across to the sink. Then there was the sound of running water.

When Jimmy finished with his fly and turned around, he found himself facing the back of Felton's tail coat, as Felton stood vigorously washing his hands at one of the sinks. Felton was watching Jimmy in the mirror.

"Well, hello, Jimmy boy," he said with that peculiar smile. The white of his teeth was as bright as his tie. "Say, that was one hell of a performance you gave." He took a white cloth towel from the stack next to the basin and turned off the faucet using the towel, then began drying his hands. "My wife was very impressed. She said if there is anything we can do to help you out, all you have to do is ask."

Jimmy stood dumbstruck.

"Don't neglect to wash up," Felton directed him.

Jimmy stepped up to one of the sinks and began washing his hands. Felton finished drying and came over to stand next to him.

"You know, I haven't heard from you about the opera. It's not polite to ignore a special invitation for a private box at the opera."

Jimmy's mind was racing. "Oh, yes, the opera," he said, averting his eyes and drying his hands. "It's just that I don't know yet what the band has lined up..."

"Well, that's okay, Jimmy boy," Felton said. "As it turns out, I've had some important business come up and I have to go to Milwaukee. I won't be back until Friday." Felton leveled his gaze at Jimmy. "So why don't you plan to take some friend of yours to the opera? It's on me. Maybe you know some nice young lady who you'd like to make an impression on. The seats are excellent. As I said, it's my private box. Roscoe will escort you to your seats."

He studied Jimmy for a moment.

Jimmy fumbled for words. "I…uh…"

"They're doing Gluck's *Orphée et Eurydice*." Felton paused. "You haven't forgotten, have you? It's Wednesday evening. It'll be a big night."

"Uh…no, of course not. It's just that with the band and all… and being new in town, you know."

"That's right. What's it called? The Diggs Monroe Jazz Orchestra? Well, now, I might have a proposition for your band. I'll tell you what. Come by my office around noon on Tuesday. I won't be leaving town until Tuesday evening. I'll take you to lunch and we'll discuss your career."

Jimmy hesitated.

"You have my address, don't you?" Felton asked.

"Why, sure. Of course. It's on your card. Uh, noon, Tuesday. Let me see. I'll try to make it. The band has been rehearsing in the afternoons. Can I give you a call and let you know?"

Felton had caught him off guard, but Jimmy felt that declining the invitation was not among the choices Felton was offering him.

"Do that, Jimmy Harper. Give me a call. But remember, I will be out of town until Friday. So let's have lunch Tuesday before I leave." Felton put his hand on Jimmy's shoulder and leaned in closer. "We can become better acquainted." Felton paused, looking at Jimmy. Then he slapped Jimmy on the back and walked toward the exit. There he turned back to look Jimmy in the eye once again. "Call me." With that, he walked out the door.

Jimmy was left standing in the middle of the clean, white tile floor, wondering.

Eric and Jimmy stayed until the Checker Club closed. Alice left with one of the band members. The other musicians stayed on and invited Eric and Jimmy to take turns playing a few numbers with them. Soon Eric said it was time for him to leave. A couple of the musicians were headed to another club for an after-hours session, but Eric declined.

As they left the Checker Club, Jimmy was anticipating that Eric would invite him back to his place again. When they hailed a cab, Eric opened the door for Jimmy but did not get in with him.

"You're not getting in?" Jimmy asked, trying not to sound disappointed.

Holding the car door, Eric leaned into the cab and said, "No. I've got some things to attend to." His tone was confidential.

Jimmy felt a flurry of mixed feelings—panic, desire, anxiety, anger, affection.

"Is there someone else?" Jimmy asked.

Eric leaned in and whispered in his ear, "No. You are my desire. If I were free tonight, I would take you straight home and tear your clothes off, jazz boy." Eric pulled back. "It's just that I've got some urgent business I have to take care of this evening. You understand."

"I keep thinking about that butter churn in your kitchen."

They smiled at each other and Eric said, "You're a sweet kid, Jimmy." He looked off to the side and thought a moment. "Come by Pluto's tomorrow night."

"Okay. Count on it," Jimmy said and reached out for Eric's lapel. Before he thought about it, he pulled Eric toward him and kissed him on the lips.

Eric returned the kiss, then laughed as he pulled away. "See you then, baby." That irresistible smile spread across his face and he closed the door.

ҒOUᴙTΣΣN

Mid-morning the next day Jimmy woke up early while the other band members slept. It had been another late night, but he couldn't sleep.

His mind was in turmoil. Diggs' needling him every time he tried to get creative was becoming intolerable, and colliding with that was the feeling of freedom and exhilaration Jimmy had making music around Eric and that world. But he remembered Eric saying that Jimmy and the band had come a long way together. "If your band has work, stick with them," Eric had said. But Diggs didn't sound so sure that the band could find work, and getting into the music union sounded doubtful. At the same time, the job playing piano at Pluto's seemed pretty secure. But for that to happen, Jimmy would have to deal with Danny Felton and that prospect gave him the creeps.

Unable to sort out his feelings, Jimmy struggled out of bed. He showered and dressed while mulling over his options.

He kept remembering the music store that Eric had pointed out. He wanted to explore the place. And Diggs had asked for the names of popular tunes in order to get sheet music. Maybe Eric was right that he should stick it out with the band. Even though he had misgivings about Diggs, Jimmy still felt a sense of duty to the rest of them. Maybe he could offer them some music that would make them popular and put him back in Diggs' good graces. He decided to give it a try.

Even though he rode the L train, it still took some time for
Jimmy to locate the music shop. But being back in the South Side
neighborhood invigorated him. Black folks were going about their
morning business and newsboys were calling out headlines about
the gangland murders.

As he entered the store, a man at the counter welcomed him.
Jimmy found that the store was well stocked with sheet music
and records. He was thrilled to find all of his favorite music there
and more that he wanted to investigate. But he knew he could
only afford a few pieces of sheet music, and carrying records
around with him was out of the question. He lost himself looking
through the music. After browsing for a long time, he decided on
"Gladstone Blues" and another number he had gotten to know
from the band at the Checker Club. He believed those would be
suitable for Diggs. For himself he found one of the Bessie Smith
songs that he especially liked.

After he paid, he saw that he was going to be late getting back
to the hotel again. But the thought did not cause him to panic like
the day before, and he resolved to take it in stride.

When he walked into the hotel lobby, it was after 1. The
band members were all gathered there waiting. Their conversation
stopped as Jimmy approached, and he could feel all their eyes on
him.

"You're late again," Diggs called out.

"I'm sorry," Jimmy said. "I ran into some trouble."

"Well, you're in trouble with me," Diggs said. "I don't want to
see anyone showing up late for rehearsal with this band."

"Give me a break, Diggs," Jimmy said. "I said I'm sorry."

"You said that yesterday."

Jimmy shrugged and spread his hands. He decided there was
nothing more he could say.

Diggs turned to the rest of the band. "Okay, time's a-wasting,"
he said. "Let's go. Howard, follow my car."

When they reassembled in the rehearsal space at the college, Diggs handed out the photographs from the studio. Everyone was excited to see how the pictures turned out. Each band member got two photo postcards. Diggs told them he wished he could have had more made for each of them, but he was concerned about economizing. He was going to leave a picture and a telephone contact at the each of the venues where he hoped to find them work.

As the others were getting out their instruments, Jimmy approached Diggs with the sheet music he'd bought. He apologized again and explained that he was only late because he had been hunting down some hard-to-find tunes.

Diggs glanced at the music and said he'd look it over later. "Today we need to concentrate on the other new arrangements."

Jimmy nodded and made his way to the piano.

"Let's start with 'Yes, We Have No Bananas,' okay? I know. I know. It's a silly song," Diggs glanced at Jimmy, "but you know we're gonna get requests for it since it's so popular. Let's try it from the beginning."

The tune nearly drove Jimmy crazy, but he kept his mouth shut and he stuck to the notes on the sheet music. He kept thinking of the inventiveness of the music of the colored players at the Checker Club the night before and he wished that he was back there or at Pluto's Lair or with Eric. Any place but here with Diggs.

They played for about an hour and Jimmy was warming up and starting to feel a little better about this band. They were playing one of the few pieces that Jimmy liked and one he thought had potential. At a certain point he couldn't stop himself and strayed off into a variation that the music seemed to call out for.

"Hold it. Hold it," Diggs stopped the band. There was a silence. Jimmy didn't turn around from the piano but he could feel the whole band's attention on him.

"Jimmy, I don't want to tell you again," Diggs said. "Just play the arrangement the way it is written."

Jimmy turned to face the band. "But Diggs, I just want to spice it up a little. Give it a little heat."

"Sophisticated people like to listen to sophisticated music," Diggs said. "We want to make music that is as cool and smooth as satin."

Jimmy felt himself starting to get hot under the collar. "The music in the South Side clubs is more sophisticated than anything you'll ever hear in those big fancy hotels in the Loop." He heard a nervous giggle from Larry.

"And how much money do you think those Negro bands make on the South Side?" Diggs asked.

"The money has nothing to do with it, Diggs," Jimmy said. "The music is better."

"The money has everything to do with it. If you don't eat, you are not going to be playing music for too long."

"But, Diggs, you used to like hot jazz. When I first met you, you were a maniac for it, just like me."

"You've got to play the kind of music that people want to hear."

"The kind of music most people want to hear stinks. This prissy 'sweet music' is dead. At least the colored music has some life to it."

"I'll tell you what your problem is." Anger began to creep into Diggs' voice. "I think you're starting to like those Negro girls as much as you like that Negro music. What's the idea of being gone all night and dragging in late every day and carrying on about some nigger woman blues singer?"

Jimmy opened his mouth to defend himself, but before he could say a word, Larry jumped in.

"I think he's turned punk on us, Diggs, that's what I think. Bet he's tasted some of that black cock and now that's the only thing he wants."

Jimmy couldn't believe what he was hearing. He turned to look Larry in the eye and said, "What the hell?"

"Oh, you're not the only one who goes to the South Side. Bill and I went to the Checker Club last night to hear some of that jungle music. We saw you with that pretty-boy nigger."

"Shut up, Larry," Diggs cut him off and turned to Jimmy. "Look, Jimmy, this is not a Negro band and it's never going to be a Negro band. We aren't going to play that whorehouse kind of music. The sooner you figure that out, the better."

Jimmy felt the blocks of his foundation crack. He stood up from the piano in a daze and started to leave the room. He didn't speak and silence hung thick in the air. He went out the door.

As he walked down the hall, he could hear loud voices behind him in the rehearsal hall. Outside it was a cold, sunny day. A moment later he heard Diggs coming after him, calling, "Jimmy, wait. Listen to me."

Jimmy kept walking. He knew he was too angry to talk, and he needed time to cool down.

"We've got to talk," Diggs called, running after him. "Look, I'm sorry for what I said back there. I shouldn't have said it."

He could hear Diggs' voice growing closer behind him. "Larry was completely out of line. I promise I'll can him if he ever talks like that again. I'll give him a talking to he won't forget. Hey, wait up, Jimmy. We've all been under a lot of pressure lately, but I know we can smooth things over. Look, we've got to stick together. I've already given out photos of the band to promoters." Diggs was now right behind him.

Jimmy felt a sudden surge of anger. Were the publicity photos more important to Diggs than their music? Jimmy remembered Diggs' remarks about Negro girls and whorehouse music, which was now tangled up in his mind with Larry's comments about Eric. The whole band had congealed into one dark and distasteful substance. He stopped and turned back on Diggs. "Listen, you bastard, I've had it with this band and your sweet music and your nasty innuendoes."

"Now, cool down. We can work this out."

"No. I don't want to work this out." He looked Diggs in the eye and unleashed all his anger. "I've had it with all of you bastards.

As far as I'm concerned, you can all go to hell."

Diggs was taken aback and stood there in silence. Jimmy turned and walked away.

"But we've already taken the photographs," Diggs called. He didn't say anything more and didn't follow after him.

Jimmy didn't look back.

FIFTEEN

Jimmy caught a taxicab back to the hotel. He packed his things and counted up his money. Without taking it off to look, he included the $200 in his money belt in his mental calculation. He was in a hurry to clear out. His funds were running low, but he figured that if he was careful, he could get by until he started playing piano at Pluto's. He grabbed his bag and left the hotel.

To conserve his cash, Jimmy decided not to hire a taxi until he had to. He walked around town carrying his suitcase, checking out several different hotels. The suitcase became heavier. It took a while before he found lodging he felt he could afford. The place was run down, but at least he wasn't out on the street. Jimmy decided to pay one night at a time in case his plans changed. It was late afternoon by the time he lay down to rest in his new room.

He had been glad to let the search for lodging occupy his mind. But when Jimmy found himself alone in the shabby room, he began turning over in his mind the scene at the rehearsal. How could they…? He was hurt and angry, and he felt justified in what he'd done. And it was too late to change any of that. He didn't want to think about it anymore.

Now he had to think about what he would do next.

Jimmy felt a gnawing desire to be with Carl. He felt comfortable with Carl. He knew he could trust Carl. For a moment he thought about phoning Carl, then considered using his money for a train ticket back to Portland. But rather than cheering him up, thinking about Carl made him feel sad and lonely. His dark mood conjured up the sound of one of Grandy's mournful train whistles and gave rise to a fleeting fantasy about forgetting everything and hopping a freight train to faraway places and taking up the life of a hobo.

Instead of a phone call, Jimmy decided to drop Carl a note on the back of one of the photo postcards of the band. He searched through his things until he found the cards. Glancing at the photograph Jimmy stopped. For a moment he was transported back to Oregon—memories of venues around Portland where the band had played during happier times. He remembered the country dance when Carl had come to hear them play. Jimmy longed to be with Carl, to talk to him, to seek his advice. He always felt safe when he was with Carl. Right now he didn't feel safe. He didn't know if he could trust Danny Felton. He didn't want to trust Diggs. He wasn't even sure if he should trust Eric. But Jimmy knew that he could always trust Carl.

Yet Carl Holman was far away. Somehow, he felt the photograph belonged with Carl and with those memories. In some way sending Carl the photograph would bring them together. At the same time, sending the postcard away would sever his connection with the Diggs Monroe Jazz Orchestra.

Jimmy found his fountain pen. He made an effort to sound hopeful in a quick note on the back of the photo. He addressed the card and went down to the lobby where he bought a postage stamp from the old man at the front desk.

"Can I leave this with you?" Jimmy asked.

"How's that?" the old fellow asked.

Jimmy raised his voice. "I said, can I leave this with you—to mail?"

The old man pointed to the street and said there was a post box on the corner. Jimmy went out and dropped the card in the box.

With all these memories of Portland and Carl and those early days with the band, Jimmy began feeling sorry for himself. He decided to find some alcohol—never mind his slender finances.

He located a speakeasy a few blocks away, and after a couple of drinks, he felt better. He bought a bottle to take back to the hotel with him.

When he got to his room, he was still unsure about what to do. The river of jazz that had propelled Jimmy forward for so long seemed to have reached a chaotic ocean. He felt lonely and confused. He was without bearings or compass.

Again he thought of packing it all in and taking up the hobo life. Or maybe he would stow away on a tramp steamer and cross the ocean to Paris. He lay down for a while, but his mind was a turbulent sea and he got up and paced the room.

Voices from the hallway came in through the transom, and Jimmy heard people enter the room next door. His room felt too warm, and he closed the valve on the steam radiator. He raised the window sash and looked out at the lighted windows of the building across the way. In an open window on the floor below, he could see a couple dancing with their arms around each other. He heard the hissing of a phonograph needle mingled with the strains of a Bessie Smith song that Eric had played for him. Yes, Eric, Jimmy thought. Eric was his best and only hope.

He began to formulate a plan. He would meet with Felton and talk to him about nailing down the piano job at Pluto's. That would keep him in contact with Eric and the South Side jazz world, and it would give him some income to count on. Hadn't Felton and his wife both said to let them know if there was anything they could do to help out? If Felton was as well-connected as people said and he had taken a liking to Jimmy, then there ought to be some way to make things work out. Maybe he could make some deal with Felton in order to scrape together enough money to take Eric to Paris.

To firm his resolve, Jimmy took a couple of swallows of gin. Then he headed out to find a phone. Avoiding the elderly man at the counter, he found a phone booth in the back of the lobby and called the number on Felton's card. A man answered. It sounded like Herman.

"I need to speak with Mr. Felton, please," Jimmy said.

"I'm sorry, Mr. Felton is not available right now," the voice said. "Can I take a message?"

"Yes, this is Jimmy Harper—the piano player. Please tell Mr. Felton that I am interested in taking the position at Pluto's Lair and I would like to meet with him to discuss it."

"I'm sorry, but Mr. Felton will be unavailable for a few days."

"He suggested earlier that I should meet with him at noon Tuesday before he leaves town. I will be available then, as it turns out. I was thinking that I had a rehearsal planned for then, but I was mistaken."

"Oh, yes... Mr. Harper, the piano player..." The voice seemed to be directed to someone else in Felton's office.

"Yes, tell Mr. Felton that I can come round to his office Tuesday at noon," Jimmy said, "like he suggested."

"Tuesday noon?... Yes, very good. He is expecting you. Yes, I'm sure Mr. Felton is looking forward to getting together with you."

"Thank you," Jimmy said and hung up. He felt a sudden wave of apprehension and he wondered what he signed on for.

He went back to his room and lay down. He was emotionally worn out, and now that he had set a course for himself, he was able to relax a bit. He soon drifted off to sleep.

When Jimmy woke up, it was dark. He didn't know where he was. It took several moments to remember what had brought him there. Diggs and the whole mess. He became angry all over again. He thought again about calling Carl, but he didn't know how much he wanted to tell him. There was no good news, and he wanted to be able to tell Carl something hopeful when he did talk to him. Besides, he had already sent the postcard. What time was it, anyway?

He checked his watch and saw that it was a little past 9. He panicked. How late did Eric say Pluto's was open? Didn't he say they closed at midnight on Sunday and Monday? He still had time to get there.

Jimmy hurriedly washed his face and dressed. He took out the gin bottle and had one last healthy swig. Then he rushed out. He found a cab and told the driver to take him to Pluto's Lair as fast as he could.

SIXTEEN

When Jimmy got to Pluto's, he was relieved to find the place still open, and the crowd was somewhat larger than the night before. The band had the night off and Eric was alone at the keyboard again. When Jimmy heard Eric playing, his nerves were further eased.

He approached the bartender, whom he didn't recognize, and said, "You better fix me a double." He drummed his fingers on the bar and looked around for Roscoe. He was nowhere to be seen, and Jimmy didn't know anyone else in the place except Eric. When the barkeep brought his drink, he took a quick swallow. He watched Eric play until he saw Eric notice him. Jimmy thought he saw a hint of anxiety in Eric's expression—or was it his own uncertain situation he perceived?—before that broad smile broke across Eric's face, and he gave Jimmy a subtle nod. Jimmy raised his glass to Eric in return and finished off his drink. Then he ordered a second and took it over to a table near the bandstand.

Eric was in fine form, and the music was a balm to Jimmy's troubled soul. Soon Eric took a break, and Jimmy approached the stage. Eric smiled and reached down to shake his hand.

"I'm sure glad to see you, jazz boy," Eric said amidst the rising buzz of conversation that followed the music. "I'll come down and join you." Eric motioned to one of the waiters and hopped down from the bandstand. They sat down across from each other, and the colored waiter with the little mustache came over.

"Hey, Jasper. Bring me a gin," Eric said.

"Coming right up," Jasper said and turned to Jimmy.

He raised his nearly-full glass and said, "I'm okay, thanks."

"I was beginning to think you wouldn't show tonight," Eric said. "Hey, you look worried. What's up?"

Jimmy looked down at the tabletop. "It's my goddamned band. We had an argument and Diggs gave me the boot…well, I quit. I moved to a different hotel and…" He broke off.

Eric whistled with surprise. "That's rough," he said. "You boys have been together for a while." He studied Jimmy's face. "No wonder you look like you've got yourself a touch of the blues."

"Aw, it's probably all for the best," Jimmy said. "I couldn't have kept that up much longer, the way Diggs was getting and that music he had us playing."

Jasper brought Eric's drink.

"You going to be okay?" Eric asked.

"Oh, yeah, I guess so," Jimmy said. "I'm just feeling kind of lost—like I've fallen off a ship in the middle of an ocean storm."

"You'll find your way. There are ocean currents."

"Well, I telephoned Felton's office this afternoon and told him I wanted to take the piano job here when you start at the Checker Club. I made an appointment to meet him for lunch tomorrow. He's going to Milwaukee tomorrow night and won't be back until Friday."

"You're kidding," Eric said. He sounded surprised and concerned. He glanced to the side as if he were making a mental calculation. "You're sure about that?"

"That's what Felton told me."

"That's very interesting."

"How do you mean?" Jimmy asked. "He said it was just a business trip."

"Oh, it's nothing. I thought all his business was here in Chicago, that's all." Eric leaned forward. "This will be a very good move for you, Jimmy. You'll do well for yourself here at Pluto's. I think this place is going to become a very successful venture."

Jimmy began to feel encouraged. "I hope so," he said, looking up from his drink. "Maybe there is an ocean current that flows toward Paris. I've been thinking things over, and I want to take you to Paris."

Eric laughed and his eyes sparkled. "Maybe I'll take you to Paris. Hey, maybe we can go to the Paris Opera together."

"And the Eiffel Tower," Jimmy said.

"And the Champs Élysées," Eric said.

They mused about Paris for a while until Eric said he had to get back to the piano. Before returning to the bandstand, he leaned toward Jimmy and said, "You can stick around till closing time, can't you? I've got something back at my place for you."

Jimmy smiled. "You bet. After this afternoon, there's nowhere I'd rather be."

"Good. Stay put. Right now, I've got a song for you. Listen to this next number."

Eric returned to the stage and settled in at the keyboard. He launched into an introduction, and then began to sing.

"I went to see the doctor today
To see what he had to say.
Something must be wrong,
I'm worried all day long.
He said I had a love attack.
I must get my baby back.
He said to do it right away.
This is what he had to say:

You need some lovin' when you feel sad.
You need some lovin' to make you real glad.

You need some lovin' when you feel blue.
You need someone to talk some baby talk to you.

Some sweet caressing every night and day,
Someone to love you in that old-fashioned way.

Kiss you with all of their power,
Repeat it sixty times every hour.

You need some lovin',
Must have it all of the time,
To ease your mind."

Eric kept looking over at Jimmy as he sang, and Jimmy could hear Erica DeChez giving a seductive turn to the lyrics. At first the song made Jimmy laugh. Then Eric's delivery caused a thrill of desire. And, behind all of that, in a secret drawer in Jimmy's heart, he felt a longing to be back in Oregon so he could see his own doctor.

The audience, too, liked the song and paid Eric back with vigorous applause. Eric began to play another song and a number of couples took to the dance floor. Jasper came around again after a while and Jimmy ordered another drink. He listened to Eric play until closing time.

Around half-past twelve Eric and Jimmy headed for the exit and stopped at the coat check to collect their wraps. The attendant told Eric someone was asking for him and gestured to a couch along the wall. There sat Monkey, his face drenched in sweat and his whole body racked with shaking and twitching. When he saw Eric he got up with difficulty and came forward. Jimmy didn't understand, but he felt for the fellow, so obviously in misery.

"You gotta help me," Monkey said. His face was the picture of torment.

"I see you're in a bad way," Eric said. "But I told you before, I can't do anything for you."

"Can't you loan me some cash? I'll pay you back tomorrow..."

"No, we've been all through this—"

Just then one of the barkeeps came toward the exit. He sized up the situation in an instant. Eric exchanged looks with him.

"C'mon, Monkey boy," the barkeep said. "I'll give you a lift in the old Model A—where will it be? Shirley's place?"

"By God, you're a life saver," Monkey said reaching out a trembling hand.

He put an arm around Monkey's shoulder and guided him toward the door. Monkey wasn't too stable. "Get ahold of yourself, now. You know Shirley ain't gonna like this. Can't you make a switch…" They went out the door.

Eric looked on with exasperation. He glanced at the coat check attendant and shook his head. "I don't know about that boy."

"Here, take your coats."

As they were climbing up the basement stairwell toward the street, Jimmy said, "So what's with Monkey?"

"Heroin," Eric answered. "He can't get his hands on another fix and now he's got the sickness." Jimmy was at a loss for words.

At the top of the stairs Eric paused and said he wanted to stop in for a minute at Big Joe's Cafe. He led Jimmy across the front of the building and into the cafe. It was the first time Jimmy had seen the inside of the place. Warm food smells hung in the air, mingling with the clatter of silverware and dishes and the babble of talking and laughing. A lively crowd filled the scattered tables and the row of stools in front of a counter that stretched along one side of the room.

"Wait here," Eric said, just inside the front door, and he walked back to the far end of the counter. Jimmy looked on as Eric approached an enormously round colored man wearing a dirty apron and standing next to an ornate brass cash register. Jasper was sitting next to the cash register talking to the large man. Eric leaned in and spoke to them. All three walked to the back of the room and disappeared behind a curtained doorway. Jimmy sat down on a stool at the end of the counter. Looking around the room, he recognized a number of faces from Pluto's. Soon Eric returned and said he had called for a taxi. They went out on the sidewalk and lit cigarettes and talked while they waited for the cab. Jimmy wondered why Eric hadn't called for the cab from Pluto's.

SEVENTEEN

When they got back to Eric's room, they made themselves comfortable. Eric brought out a box of muggles and lit one, passed it to Jimmy, then went to the Victrola and put on a record. Again Bessie Smith's rich voice filled the room, but this was a song Jimmy hadn't heard. They listened in rapt silence as they passed the marijuana cigarette between them, and Eric got out a bottle of gin and poured them each a glass.

When the phonograph needle began to scrape in the last groove, Eric took the record off the turntable and handed it to Jimmy. "Here, it's for you," Eric said. "It's her latest. I just got it from my father today."

Jimmy took the record and examined the label, then looked back up at Eric. "Say, that's the nuts, Eric. Thank you. This is really special." He looked back at the record and turned it over to read the label on the reverse side.

Eric sat down beside Jimmy on the bed and said, "I think you're really special." He leaned in and kissed Jimmy on the lips, then lay back on the bed.

Jimmy reached over and laid the record on the table next to his glass of gin. He turned back to Eric. "You've been so good to me. How can I ever repay you?"

"Go with me to Paris, jazz boy," Eric said and handed the muggle to Jimmy.

"Boy, right now I'd like to go somewhere far away. But I don't think I could afford to take you that far away just yet. How about New York City? I bet I could afford to take you to New York. Right now. Let's do it. We could leave tonight."

Eric glanced away and after a moment replied, "Yeah, I hear Harlem is a jumpin' place. But, you see, I believe Chicago is the center of the world right now. Do you know about the Mogul Empire—in India?"

Jimmy shook his head.

"The Moguls were the ones who built the Taj Mahal. After they established their empire in the North, they went on to conquer all of India. They became fabulously wealthy. They began enticing all the greatest poets and musicians away from Persia, which had been the cultural capital of the Muslim world. Well, right now Chicago's underworld bosses are hiring all the greatest jazz musicians away from New Orleans. Chicago has the biggest concentration of jazz players in the world. For now I plan to sit tight."

The radiator began making a hissing sound.

"Here," Eric said, exhaling, "let me recite a piece of Mogul poetry for you. They were famous for their rhymed couplets."

Eric leaned back on one elbow, closed his eyes and recited:

"Is thy collar held closed by a ruby stud,
Or is thy silken shirt graced with a drop of my blood?"

He opened his eyes and looked up at Jimmy.

"That's beautiful," Jimmy said.

"Ain't it, though?"

"Let me hear it again."

Eric repeated the verse.

"How'd you learn so much about India?"

"I used to have a butter and egg man who went over there and he told me all about their history. He has a mansion full of Indian carpets and all kinds of oriental art he brought here. He's the one who gave me that Indian sari up there."

"What happened to him?"

"He went to Paris to live."

"Do you speak French?" Jimmy asked.

Eric laughed. "No, but Erica DeChez is working at it. With a name like that! You want to hear my big dream? Someday I'm going to go to an opera at the Paris Opera House. That has to be one of the most elegant experiences in this world."

"Did you learn that from your butter and egg man?" Jimmy asked as he remembered Danny Felton's promise of tickets to the opera.

Eric gave an impish smile and nodded.

"How about going to the opera with me here in Chicago?" Jimmy asked.

"And watch from nigger heaven? Forget that."

"What? From where?"

"The top balcony. As far as I know that's the only place they would let a colored person be seated at an opera in America. When I go to the opera, I want to see and be seen. Gordy, the drummer at Pluto's, has an uncle who was in Paris with an army band during the War. He said, 'I don't care if you got to swim there, get yourself to Paris, France. That's one place on God's green earth where a colored person can live with dignity and respect. And if you are a colored musician who can play jazz, you can live like a king.'"

The radiator pipes began making a clicking sound.

"Well, musicians aren't living like kings here in Chicago, are they?" Jimmy asked. "How much do musicians make here? They aren't living like Mogul emperors. Even those sweet-music, society dance orchestras aren't getting rich, are they? Like Diggs seems to think?"

"The gangsters that run most of the Chicago nightclubs are paying pretty well. And with the tips they throw around, the take home isn't bad."

"But there aren't any musicians getting rich, are there? I mean, really rich."

"Only a handful of headliners, if any. Mainly the ones who go to Hollywood."

"So a fella might just as well stick with playing the music he loves, don't you think?"

"Yeah, I guess. Music, like virtue, is its own reward," Eric said.

Jimmy lay back on the bed and sighed. "I don't know about Diggs. And I don't know about America's taste in music."

"Imagine this," Eric said. "If America was planning to send an expedition to start a colony on a deserted island, do you think they would plan to send a musician? No. No one would think to send a lazy, no-good musician. They would send doctors and farmers and carpenters. But think how much musicians contribute to society. We couldn't live without them. Yet most folks in this country wouldn't think to send a musician to start a new settlement. Now, in Paris, France, I'll bet you one of the first things they'd think of is to send a musician. I promise you, someday my ship is gonna come in and I'm going to Paris. The City of Light."

"Maybe," Jimmy said, "we can figure out how to get enough money out of these Chicago Mogul emperors to get ourselves over to Paris."

"How do you figure on doing that?"

"What if you had the goods on one of them? You could use blackmail."

Eric laughed. "What could you hold over the head of a man who has committed cold-blooded murder? That sounds like a good way to end up at the bottom of Lake Michigan."

Jimmy considered for a time and then asked, "What about your butter and egg man? Maybe you could get some money from him."

"Naw," Eric said. "I've gotta get over to Paris on my own. My sugar daddy fell for some wealthy Indian fella in Bombay. The son of one of those Rajas or something. They're living the high life in Paris now. He doesn't want me complicating things for him."

"Is that how you came by that picture of the Taj Mahal there, above your piano?" Jimmy pointed.

"Yeah. Sugar daddy sent me that. You know that story? About the Taj? The Mogul emperor, Shah Jahan, had the Taj Mahal built as a tomb for his dead wife. And then when it was completed and he saw how perfect it was, he had the architect's hands cut off so the architect would never be able to create anything to rival it. How would you like to have your hands cut off after playing a perfect piano solo?"

"Maybe one perfect creation is enough," Jimmy said.

"Yes. Maybe. Well, at some point society dismembers all of us, doesn't it? All of us who are different from the rest. Those of us who are not deemed good enough to be members of the human race." Eric disappeared in thought for a moment. Then he gave a little laugh and reached over and placed his hand on Jimmy's crotch. "What if, after the one perfect orgasm, they cut off your member?"

"Jesus, Eric. That's gruesome. And I was just starting to feel safe, again."

"Oh, honey, I'm sorry. Everything's all right, baby," Erica DeChez said, moving closer.

"It's okay. It's just that I'm feeling kind of shaky right now. On account of the band and all. I feel like I've been set adrift and I'm not sure if I will sink or swim." Jimmy turned and looked at Eric. "You're my only safe harbor right now."

"Oh, my little sailor, don't you worry about a thing. Erica will be your home port."

Eric turned to Jimmy and reached out to touch his face. Jimmy turned his head and kissed the palm of Eric's hand.

Eric slid nearer on the bed and began kissing Jimmy's face. Their mouths converged and their tongues communicated like mating sea creatures. A tropical current rose in their blood, and Eric said, "Here, I'll teach you how to swim." They began taking off each other's clothes.

When they were naked, Eric said, "Let's try the Pisces position."

"What?"

"You know, the Zodiac sign. The two fish swimming in a circle, chasing each other's tails. I'll show you."

Eric took Jimmy's member in his hand and with the tip of his tongue he stroked the underside. When Jimmy began to grow erect, Eric's lips caressed the head of his cock and sucked it into his mouth. After a time Eric took the full length of Jimmy's penis deep into his throat. No one had ever done that to him before, not even Carl. Jimmy had never even imagined that such a thing was possible.

They repositioned themselves and Jimmy gave it a try. At first, Jimmy kept choking like a man drowning. He paused and came up for air.

"Relax and take your time," Eric said. "You don't have to swallow the whole thing."

Jimmy tried again and soon he began to get the hang of it. Then he paused and said he had trouble concentrating on giving and receiving at the same time. Eric laughed.

"You can play piano and listen to the band at the same time, can't you?" Eric said. "All you need is practice."

Jimmy tried again and this time he began to relax. He realized that their bodies were once again connected at both ends, involved in a curious circle, and the thought pleased him. He gave in to the sensations and let the sea of pleasure engulf him. Soon the surging reached its climax and the rising tide of their passion washed up pearls of sea foam.

They both lay panting like shipwrecked sailors prostrate on an exotic shore.

Later they bathed and settled into bed. Jimmy reminded Eric that he had to hook up with Danny Felton at noon, and Eric set his alarm. Then they cuddled together under the waves of bedcovers and drifted with the current into an ocean of dreams. The last thing Jimmy remembered before descending into the depths of sleep was a vision of the City of Light.

When he awoke in the morning, Jimmy felt like he was on vacation. He was free from the band and he liked the independence. A whole new world opened up for him. He could act alone now, as his own boss. There was no one he had to answer to or consult. And at the moment, there was nowhere he had to be until his noon appointment. He glanced at the alarm clock. It read a quarter past 7.

As Eric slept, Jimmy languished in bed and looked about the room. A pile of books lay on the bedside table. He read the titles on the colored spines. There was a volume of Mogul poetry, two books of French poetry, The Rubaiyat of Omar Khayyam, Tales of the Arabian Nights, a novel by Balzac, and a French grammar. Eric was serious about going to Paris. Jimmy wondered what kind of ship was coming in that Eric had all his hopes pinned on. The dream vision of the City of Light floated like a faint perfume through his consciousness. He remembered architectural stereopticon photographs he had seen of Paris—the Eiffel Tower, the Pont Neuf, the Paris Opera House. He imagined watching *La Traviata* in that opulent marble setting with Eric in white tie and tails sitting by his side. He imagined them walking the streets of Paris together.

Then he remembered Danny Felton's opera invitation. Was Felton going to come through with tickets? He resolved to take Eric to the opera if Felton lived up to his promise. That way Eric would not have to watch from nigger heaven. And what about Felton? Jimmy didn't want to think about that right now. He wondered what Diggs and the others were doing. What would they do about a piano player and singer for that fraternity dance Diggs had lined up? And what if Felton did have a proposition for the band? Jimmy wasn't sure if he wanted to help them out. He might, however, want Diggs Monroe in his debt. An act of largesse like helping the band find a job or helping them get into the music union might smooth over their antagonisms and give Jimmy an advantage. Even if he did not join back up with them, they might prove useful later on. The music business was a small world.

Jimmy lay in bed for a long time considering his present situation. He liked some of the fellows in the band and wanted to remain friends with them. He thought about Howard in college, and Chuck, and he remembered better times playing with the band in Portland. When they first got together, everyone was excited about starting out and giddy about getting paid to make music. Jimmy began to miss Portland and again he had an urge to phone Carl.

At last, he began to feel weary thinking of all that had come to pass. He rolled over and reached an arm around Eric. He snuggled up close and inhaled the sleepy perfume of Eric's body under the covers, and soon he drifted off to sleep again.

EIGHTEEN

The ringing of the alarm clock woke Jimmy and Eric.
"Ten o'clock," Eric exclaimed once he was awake enough to read the clock. "Lordy, but you're an early riser."

After they dressed, Eric insisted on taking Jimmy out to a nearby place for breakfast. As they walked in, Jimmy felt a moment of tension as he looked around the small cafe at all the dark-skinned faces. He was the one white person there. He wasn't sure if the tension was his own apprehension or suspicion on the part of the black patrons. A large woman behind the counter greeted Eric with an easy friendliness that showed they were old friends.

"Hello, Florence," Eric replied. He introduced her to Jimmy and she treated him with a warm smile. The tension seemed to melt away as fast as it had arisen.

They took a table by themselves in the back of the room and Florence came over. Eric ordered biscuits and gravy with link sausage, but Jimmy mentioned his lunch date with Felton and ordered nothing but a biscuit and coffee.

Eric seemed troubled and distracted. Jimmy sensed that something was preying on his mind and he tried to think of something to cheer him up. After Florence brought their food, Jimmy leaned forward and spoke so as not to be overheard. "Eric, remember what I said last night about taking you to the opera here in Chicago? I was serious. Would you go to the opera with me on Wednesday night?"

Eric's face was blank for a moment. Then a faint smile flickered before it was replaced by a frown and then a laugh.

"You're kidding me, aren't you?" Eric said.

"No, no. Danny Felton offered me tickets to his private box for Wednesday evening. He said he wouldn't be able to use them himself. That's when he told me he would be out of town until Friday. He is supposed to give me the tickets when I see him today. He told me to bring some young lady that I was trying to make a good impression on. Well, I'd like to make a good impression on you."

Eric looked at Jimmy for a minute. "No one is going to let a colored man sit in a private box at the opera."

Jimmy was dumbfounded. He couldn't make it all fit together in his mind. Why not? Why couldn't Eric go to the opera? This wasn't just some poor, uneducated country nigger. This was Eric. Eric, who dressed in white tie on the stage and played Bach on the piano. Why shouldn't he be allowed to sit in a box seat at the opera? Then Jimmy realized this was a question that Eric asked himself every day of his life. No wonder he longed to go to Paris.

Jimmy felt embarrassed and naïve. "Well, I am a country bumpkin, ain't I?" he said, trying to summon a laugh. "I'm sorry. I didn't...I didn't think...." He buttered his biscuit, and considered. He wasn't ready to throw out his idea and Eric's dream of going to the opera. "I wonder if there isn't some way to...what about Roscoe? He works at the opera. Maybe there is some way he could get you in to Felton's box seats. Felton said he would escort me and my young lady to his box."

"I think you're dreaming. Danny Felton may like our nigger music but he doesn't want any niggers sitting in his private box at the opera." Eric sounded resigned. He took a sip of coffee. Then he seemed to pick up the idea and turn it over in his mind. "You must have remembered what I said about my dream to go to the Paris Opera."

"Yes, I remembered." Jimmy looked at Eric and a feeling of

love welled up in his heart. "Maybe we're both dreaming. But what's wrong with having dreams?"

Eric seemed to be turning the idea over to view it from yet another angle. "Well, we may not be able to sit in Felton's box seats… But I'm sure we would be allowed to sit in the upper balcony. Even that might be worthwhile."

"You're sure you wouldn't mind watching from up high?" Jimmy asked. "Say, look, is Roscoe working at Pluto's tonight? Let's ask him. Why couldn't we use Felton's tickets to get us in the door? And then maybe Roscoe could seat us in some other part of the theater."

"I don't know," Eric said. "Still…I would be very interested in attending this opera." He was turning something over in his mind.

Jimmy let the subject drop. If Eric didn't feel comfortable going to the opera, then it would be no compensation for Eric's kindness, and Jimmy simply wanted to do Eric a favor. He decided to turn the conversation in a different direction. "What did you mean last night about your ship coming in?"

He felt Eric stiffen as his fork remained suspended over his plate. He looked off to the side and said, "Oh, there's a deal I've been working on. I can't talk about it now." He took a bite of food and then glanced at Jimmy, who felt he'd made a mistake by asking.

Florence came by and filled their coffee cups. Eric seemed deep in deliberation, trying to work out some puzzle in his mind.

By the time they had finished, Eric had settled something in his deliberations. "Okay, Jimmy," he said. "Let's plan to go to the opera together. You go ahead and talk to Roscoe about it at Pluto's tonight. He should be tending bar this evening. I can guarantee that you'll have more luck talking to him than I would. But make it sound like Felton said it was okay for you to bring me with you, you understand? I bet if you do, he'll be more likely to help us."

Jimmy agreed. He knew that Eric understood the situation much better than he did.

"Meanwhile, I'll arrange for someone to play piano at Pluto's Wednesday night so that I'll be free. Oh, and don't say anything to Felton today about taking me to the opera with you. Let him think you're taking some white girl. He mustn't know anything about me going." Eric paused, then added, "It's just that I know he would object because of the race problem. Anyway, he'll find out soon enough once it's all done with."

Again Jimmy agreed.

Florence came around to clear their plates. "Say, Florence, I need to talk to you," Eric said. "Excuse me a minute, Jimmy." He got up and followed her past the counter and into the kitchen. In a few minutes Eric returned to the table.

"Come on, jazz boy," Eric said. As they were making their way out, Florence emerged from the kitchen door and she and Eric exchanged goodbyes.

"Pleased to meet you," Jimmy said in parting.

Florence said, "The pleasure is mine. Now, you come back again real soon."

When they were out on the street, Jimmy looked at his watch.

"Heck, I'd better get going if I'm going to be at Felton's by noon."

Eric said he had some business to attend to as well.

"Remember," Eric said, "don't let on that you plan to take me to the opera with you."

Jimmy reassured him, and they agreed to meet again that night at Pluto's. Eric hailed a cab for Jimmy. He seemed to know the driver and, handing him some money, told him to take Jimmy anywhere he wanted to go.

ПIПЄTЄЄП

As the cab wound through traffic, Jimmy was still unsure how to approach Felton. He had to talk to him about nailing down the piano job at Pluto's. That he knew for sure. And he had to get the opera tickets, though what all was behind the intrigues with Eric and Felton concerning the opera Jimmy didn't understand. Maybe he was better off not knowing.

Jimmy also wanted to find out about Felton's proposition for Diggs and the band, if he had one. Whether he would present Felton's deal to the band as a kind of peace offering, he wasn't sure yet. And maybe he could cook up some deal with Felton and make enough money to take Eric to Paris. He didn't understand Felton well enough to plan ahead. Everything seemed up in the air at this point, and Jimmy knew he would have to improvise.

Danny Felton's office was on the second floor of a new office building. In the granite-walled entryway, his name was on a directory between the elevators and an ornate staircase. Jimmy felt increasingly uncomfortable about this whole encounter and he thought it would calm his nerves if he walked up to the second floor.

At the top of the stairs, he followed a sign directing him toward Felton's office. Down the hall, two men seated outside the door watched him as he approached. That familiar nervousness arose in his stomach as he walked toward them, but now the sensation was tinged with a kind of terror.

Jimmy steeled himself and nodded to the two door guards, but before he reached for the knob of the door where Danny Felton's name and the words "Property Management" were painted in gold on the frosted glass, he hesitated. Well, he told himself, I have to at least find out what he can offer me at Pluto's. He opened the door.

Herman sat at a large desk talking on the telephone. Sullivan sat in a corner by the door reading a newspaper. Another frosted glass door stood ajar into an inner office.

Herman acknowledged Jimmy's entrance and said into the phone, "Just a minute." He placed his palm over the receiver, nodded to a chair, and said, "I'll tell the boss you're here as soon as I'm done." Herman ended his call and hung up. Then he disappeared into the other room.

Jimmy took a chair and tried to remain calm. Sullivan glanced up from his newspaper without changing his expression and looked Jimmy over. He laid the newspaper aside and stood up. "Let me check you out, kid," he said. "Stand up and raise your arms."

Jimmy froze.

"Don't get nervous. I just wanna make sure you're not packin' a gun."

The big gent patted him down, then, satisfied, went back to the newspaper.

Before Jimmy could collect his wits and sit down, Danny Felton entered the room. He wore a well-tailored suit and a diamond stickpin in his tie. Herman followed, carrying a briefcase. Felton greeted Jimmy. "Good to see you, young fellow. Glad you could make it. Glad you could make it. I've made reservations for us at the Grove Hotel. I think you'll like it. It's one of Chicago's best. Sullivan, keep your eye on things here. Shall we go?"

Herman opened the door to the hallway. Felton placed a hand on Jimmy's shoulder and said, "Now, I want to learn all about you, Jimmy Harper." The two men seated outside the door nodded to Felton as he and Herman escorted Jimmy out.

A car and driver waited out front and delivered them several blocks away to a small, well-appointed hotel. All this time Felton kept Jimmy talking, questioning him about his past. Even though Jimmy distrusted him, Felton's interest and attention won him over and calmed his anxiety. He told Felton about growing up in Oregon and about his musical background in college.

"Did you hear that, Herman? A college man," Felton said.

Once the maître d' had settled them at a linen-covered table in the bustling dining room, Herman gestured with a nod toward one corner of the room and told Felton that their friend the mayor was seated across the way. Felton caught the mayor's eye and they nodded to each other.

"Well, now, Jimmy boy, here are those opera tickets I mentioned," Felton said, fishing a small envelope out of his breast pocket. "As I told you, I'll be out of town on business until Friday so I won't be able to attend. I told you, didn't I, that it's Gluck's *Orpheus*? It's traditional for a woman to sing the part of Orpheus, since the part was written for castrato. But it's hard to come by one of those these days—even though there are lots of men around who don't have any balls. Isn't that so, Herman?" Felton looked at Herman and they both chuckled. "You'll like the opera. It has a happy ending. The two women go off together and live happily ever after. But you would know all that, being a college man."

Jimmy told Felton that he had studied a little about opera while in college but had never seen one performed.

"Oh, then this will be a special treat for you." He held out the envelope, and the black onyx ring gleamed on his finger.

"Gosh," Jimmy said. He took the envelope and looked at the tickets. "Well, yes, as it turns out, I am not playing with the band Wednesday night so I'll be able to use these tickets. I know a young lady who will enjoy going. She'll be very impressed. Thank you." He tucked the envelope in his breast pocket.

A waiter came by. Herman asked for the special and Jimmy the luncheon salad. Felton ordered the *fettuccine al funghi* with truffle sauce. When the waiter was gone, Felton asked about Portland, and Jimmy described some of his favorite places. The more he talked, the more homesick he became. Before he knew it, he found himself telling Danny Felton about Carl.

Felton showed particular interest when Jimmy mentioned his good friend was a doctor.

"It's always good to know someone in the medical profession," Felton said glancing at Herman. "What's his name again?"

"Carl Holman," Jimmy said. "He works in a small clinic in downtown Portland with a couple of other doctors."

"Tell me about the business and industry out there in Portland," Felton said.

Jimmy gave his impressions from his limited knowledge on the subject. When he mentioned that Diggs Monroe's father was in the warehouse business, Felton wanted to know his name and some of the particulars.

They finished their meals and a waiter came round to clear their plates.

"Seymour, tell the chef that this truffle sauce is ambrosia," Danny Felton said.

"Yes sir, I'll pass that along. Are you gentlemen interested in dessert?"

Felton and Herman declined dessert and ordered coffee, but Felton encouraged Jimmy to try the chocolate-covered banana. "It's a specialty of the house," he said.

Jimmy said coffee would be plenty, but when Felton insisted on treating him to dessert, Jimmy didn't argue.

When the waiter had moved away, Felton pulled out his gold cigarette case and lighter. He offered Jimmy a cigarette and lit it for him, then lit one for himself.

"Say, I've got a story for you, kid piano," Felton began. "There is a nigger and a kike and an Italian who decide to see who can be the biggest skin flint. They each agree to take a nickel and see who can make it go the farthest."

A black waiter came by and filled their water glasses.

"Now, the nigger takes his nickel and buys himself a big old stogie. The first night he sits down and lights up. He's got this big watermelon-eating grin on his face, because he's just sure his plan is going to win. He smokes a third of the cigar and then puts it out and saves the ashes. The second night he smokes another third of his stogie and saves the ashes. The third night he finishes it off and saves the ashes again. Then he crushes up the cigar butt and stirs it in with all the ashes and uses it to fertilize the flowers in his wife's window box."

Herman laughed. He seemed to know what was coming next.

"Meanwhile, the kike goes to his rabbi and offers his nickel to the rabbi to buy up the foreskins from all of his circumcisions. Toward the end of the month, he takes all these foreskins and makes a wallet out of them. Then the kike has to go out of town on a business trip so he takes out this wallet and starts rubbing it and rubbing it, and—presto—it turns into a suitcase. So the kike doesn't have to buy any luggage for his business trip."

The group of well-dressed men at a nearby table got up to leave amid laughter and goodbyes.

"When the three fellows get back together, the nigger is sure he will win and he can't wait to tell his story first. Then the kike tells the nigger that he's got that beat, and he tells his story. Finally, the Italian says, 'I've got you both beat all to hell.'"

The waiter brought coffee and filled their cups.

"'I went to this Kraut grocer and bought myself a nice big nickel sausage and took it home. First, I scooped all the meat out of the sausage casing and ate it for dinner. I saved the sausage casing and went out that night and bought myself a nice high yellow whore and used the sausage casing for a condom. In the morning I had to take a crap, so I relieved myself in the sausage casing, and then I took it back to the Kraut grocer and said, 'This sausage tastes like shit.' The Kraut took a taste of it and agreed and he gave me my money back.'"

Jimmy sensed that he was being watched to see how he reacted to the story. He kept up a forced laugh while the others guffawed. Then he felt an expectation to reciprocate, so he decided to tell the tale about the man who lost his coat. As Jimmy launched into his story, neither of the other men laughed. Maybe I'm not telling it right, he thought, as Felton and Herman sat in stony silence. But there was nothing for him to do but continue. When Jimmy got to the part about the pockets, Felton let out a dry little chuckle. Maybe, Jimmy thought, the story was only uproarious for Carl and Gwen and Charlie because they were all friends. He had no way to judge. Jimmy found himself wishing that he was back in Portland having dinner with those he loved, far away from this strange and unpredictable Danny Felton and this dark and hostile city.

When Jimmy finished his story, Felton and Herman exchanged looks and gave a polite little laugh. "Cute little story," Felton said. Then he turned serious. "Let's get down to business, Jimmy boy."

The same feeling of thrill and dread shot through Jimmy that he had felt the first time he met Danny Felton at the piano in the brothel.

"I'll tell you what." Felton leaned in toward Jimmy and spoke in a low, serious tone. "You can either come upstairs with me after lunch and we'll enjoy ourselves or you and your band will never work in this town again." He fixed his attention on Jimmy and studied his face.

Jimmy couldn't believe his ears. He felt like he was in a dream. He had passed through a door into a different world, and he decided he had better play by the rules of this new world if he wanted to survive. Jimmy mustered all of his courage.

"Tell me what's in it for me," Jimmy said. He was shocked by the calm, firm voice that came out of his own mouth.

Felton smiled in amusement. "What do you want out of it?"

Jimmy felt like a mouse being toyed with by a cat. But he blustered forward. "First, how about the piano playing job at Pluto's Lair? Eric tells me it's mine if I want it."

"You've got it," Felton agreed. "I think having a white piano player there during the week might help attract more of a white crowd. Besides you're very good. But the Negro band plays on Friday and Saturday nights, not you."

"Okay," Jimmy agreed.

"But, you know, I sure hate to lose Eric to the Checker Club.

He's a very talented piano player, wouldn't you say?"

"You bet he is," Jimmy said.

"I believe he's going to be a big star someday, don't you agree?"

"I sure do," Jimmy said.

"I think so, too," Felton continued. "I wish there was some way I could help him out. What do you think his plans are after the Checker Club?"

"I'm not sure," Jimmy said.

"I get the impression that you've gotten to know Eric pretty well. You must have some idea what his dreams are." Felton seemed to be fishing for information.

Jimmy felt that he could put him off by tossing out an insignificant bit of gossip. "Well, I think someday he wants to go to Paris."

Felton raised his eyebrows. "An admirable ambition." He glanced at Herman. "And what are your dreams? How can I help you out?" Felton leveled his gaze at Jimmy, and Jimmy felt compelled to answer. He decided he might as well take a chance.

"I want to make enough money to take Eric to Paris," Jimmy said, looking Felton in the eye. "How much can you offer me to play piano at Pluto's?"

Jimmy was prepared to haggle over his wages, but Felton's first offer was so generous that he accepted it right away.

The waiter came by with Jimmy's dessert. How, Jimmy wondered, could the waiter serve him with such nonchalance while Jimmy felt like he was signing his life away? At the same time Jimmy felt emboldened, having taken one step in this new world.

When the waiter was gone, Jimmy said he'd like to hear more about the music business in Chicago and asked if Felton could get him and the Diggs Monroe band into the music union. While Jimmy tasted the dessert, Felton talked about the music scene in Chicago and explained that the union membership would be no problem. He could take care of it.

"Okay," Jimmy said, pushing forward. "Now, Diggs wants

the band to play a regular venue downtown in the Loop." He was amazed to find himself negotiating for the band but he remained firm. If he was going to play this game, he might as well play it for all it was worth.

"You don't ask for much," Felton said and laughed. "And what about you and the Diggs Monroe Jazz Orchestra?"

"I wanted to strike out on my own and play a little different kind of music," Jimmy said, "but I want to try to help them out."

Felton considered this. "I'll tell you what. We're planning to open a new club downtown in about a month. Top quality. The best of everything. I'll put in a word for your boy Diggs. Meanwhile, I'll give you the name and number of the man who books for the Columbia Hotel. Robert Newhall. He'll be able to fix things up for that band of yours." Felton took out one of his business cards and wrote on the back with his gold fountain pen. "That will keep Diggs in with the society music scene."

"I'm sure he'll like that," Jimmy said. "Anything to get him in closer with high society."

"Well, it pays to be seen with the upper echelon of society. Your friend Diggs has the right idea. It sounds like he's already getting pretty cozy with the high society set. I hear he got two grand for that Gold Coast tea dance you boys played." Felton's eyes were fixed on Jimmy.

Jimmy couldn't help betraying his surprise. Diggs had never discussed all of the financial arrangements with the band members, but they hadn't been paid anywhere near their share of money like that. How much had Diggs been negotiating for their other work? Had he been cheating them out of their fair share of the take all along? Jimmy looked up and realized that Felton was reading him like a book so he looked down and took a bite of the chocolate-covered banana. All at once, he had the feeling that he was out of his league, and he had a premonition that he had made a big mistake. Maybe he had already revealed far too much.

"This Diggs Monroe sounds like a real businessman," Felton said. "Maybe I can interest him in going to work for me on the side, besides just making music."

Felton passed the business card across the table.

Jimmy took the card and looked at the back. "Robt. Newhall, Columbia Hotel" and a phone number. He kept his mouth shut. He had a passing urge to jump up and bolt from the room. But where could he run to? It was too late for that. He looked down at the dessert and realized he had lost his appetite.

They finished their coffee in silence. Felton kept looking at Jimmy, and Jimmy kept trying to avoid his stare without being too obvious. The waiter brought the bill and cleared away Jimmy's half-eaten dessert. Herman signed for the bill and the waiter left them alone.

"Well, shall we head on up and make ourselves comfortable?" Felton said with a smile.

TWENTY

They stepped out of the elevator and Herman led them down the carpeted hall and unlocked a door. They entered a sunny sitting room on the corner of the building high above the street. Herman set the briefcase down on a polished coffee table next to a small statue of a nude male athlete. Removing a pile of business papers from the briefcase, Herman took a seat in a brocade chair.

With an air of military authority Felton took command. Grabbing up the briefcase, he seized Jimmy by the back of the neck and marched him through an open door into the bedroom. Once inside, Felton closed the door, and ordered Jimmy to take off his clothes and hang them in the closet. Jimmy felt like a captured prisoner. He began removing his tie. He thought it might ease his anxiety if he had some idea what to expect, and he remembered Freddy's performance in the basement room of the brothel.

"Do you want me to fuck you?" Jimmy asked, trying to make the question sound as casual as he could.

Felton shot back. "Listen, punk, you take me for a pogue? The only time anyone fucks me is when I'm paying for the service, and this time I'm doing the favors. Today you're just my whoring little lamb."

Jimmy kept his mouth shut and took off his clothes. A wave of goose bumps arose on his flesh and he shivered. Felton carried the briefcase into the bathroom and began running water in the bathtub. After hanging up his clothes, Jimmy took a seat on the bed. He felt a quiver ran through his core.

Felton appeared in the bathroom doorway wearing nothing but a white shirt and the garters holding up his stockings. He enlisted Jimmy's assistance in the bath. Felton pulled a rubber enema apparatus from his briefcase.

"Kneel down in the bathtub," Felton commanded.

Jimmy hesitated. "Is that necessary?"

"Kid, I need to know that you're clean down there, don't I?"

Jimmy followed Felton's instructions. He guessed that Freddy and Roscoe had submitted to this same procedure at the brothel.

When Felton finished administering the enema, he ordered Jimmy to clean himself up and to go into the bedroom. "I want you down on your hands and knees. Face to the wall and don't turn around," Felton ordered, drawing a small jar from the briefcase. As Jimmy left the bathroom, he saw Danny Felton readying a condom. In a short time Felton came out of the bathroom. From his position on the bedroom carpet, Jimmy heard Felton advance on his rear flank. Felton's hand fondled his buttocks. Jimmy craned his neck around, and a sharp slap stung the side of his face.

"I thought I told you not to turn around and look back," Felton snapped. Then he let out a short bark of a laugh.

"If you turn around, you might see your tail. That's what those goddamned Huns call their pricks, you know? 'The tail.'" He laughed again. "Shows you how backward the stinking Germans are. What a bunch of Neanderthals. God, I hate the Krauts."

That hatred burst forth in a violent smack on Jimmy's backside. The sound of the loud, ringing clap and the shock of the blow sent an electric charge through him.

Jimmy remembered Carl's war stories, but even Carl did not hold a grudge against the Germans.

Felton's right hand moved up Jimmy's side and grasped hold of him by the shoulder. Felton moved in to mount him from behind, and Jimmy could feel him positioning himself and aiming with the left hand. Felton rammed through the barrier of Jimmy's anal sphincter and penetrated deep inside. An involuntary cry erupted from the depths of Jimmy's body. He felt like he'd been slugged from behind. Felton's attack was merciless. He acted with none of Eric's gentleness and sensual finesse nor Carl's forbearance. Felton's hands clutched Jimmy's shoulders as he thrust violently.

Jimmy gritted his teeth against the onslaught. Go ahead, he thought to himself. Tear me apart. I surrender. If this is what I have to do to get ahead, I'm ready and open to whatever the world has to throw at me.

During Felton's assault, Jimmy felt a strange sense of detachment, as if he were an observer, not someone engaging in sex. He remembered making love to Elsa and her air of disembodiment. Had she, too, willfully blinded herself to an unacceptable reality? The awareness dawned on Jimmy that besieged women must have felt these same feelings and thought these same thoughts throughout all of history, while submitting to the unwelcome advances of powerful men with the hope of gaining some favor.

At the same time, Danny Felton seemed to be somewhere else during this incursion. All Jimmy felt was the staccato machine of his automatic movements. He heard Felton's spasmodic panting and grunting, but there was no passion there.

At last Felton began to groan as he reached his climax. Out of the corner of his eye, Jimmy glimpsed the sparkle and flash of the diamond and onyx ring on the hand that grasped his shoulder.

After Felton withdrew, he retreated into the bathroom and Jimmy heard water running. A short time later Felton reappeared, fully dressed except for his suit coat. He carried the briefcase in his left hand. He told Jimmy to go clean himself up.

When Jimmy came out of the bathroom, Felton was sitting on the edge of the bed in his shirtsleeves. On a towel beside him, next to a gold case, lay a small glass vial and two syringes.

"Can I dress now?" Jimmy asked.

"No, not yet. It's time for a little slumber party. Come over here. I need your help." Felton removed a metal cap from one of the syringes and opened the vial. Then he filled half of one syringe and laid it on the towel. He rolled up the right sleeve of his white shirt to reveal an arm discolored with yellow and purple bruises.

"Tie this around my upper arm, right here, and pull it tight," Felton said, and handed him a black silk scarf.

Jimmy fumbled with it.

"Tighter," he said.

When Jimmy was finished, Felton opened and closed his fist and examined the blue veins of his arm. He ordered Jimmy to rub the crook of his arm with an alcohol-soaked cotton. Felton took up the syringe with his left hand and pointing the needle upward, tapped the tube of the syringe with his fingernail until a drop of fluid appeared at the end of the needle. Then Felton eased the point into his vein. "Okay, remove the scarf," he said and pushed in the plunger. A quiver ran through Felton's body, and he sat for a time without moving. After a bit he stirred and pulled out the needle and laid the syringe on the towel. Again he had Jimmy rub his arm with alcohol.

"Okay, Jimmy, it's your turn."

Jimmy stepped back and said, "No…uh…thanks." He tried to laugh. "I'll pass."

"Come on now, kid, it's time for dessert. The icing on the cake. It's just a little needle prick. It'll make you feel immortal."

"No. Really. Thanks," Jimmy said backing away. He had a sudden premonition that Felton was planning to murder him.

"Herman!" Felton shouted. An unbearable tension engulfed the room. Jimmy skittered a step toward the closet where his clothes hung. The bedroom door flew open and Herman entered with a gun in his hand. Jimmy froze.

"Herman, will you convince our young friend here to cooperate?"

Herman aimed the pistol at Jimmy. The color drained from Jimmy's face and his knees nearly buckled with trembling. There was no way out. Herman waved the gun toward the bed and Jimmy walked over to Felton and sat down next to him. If he was going to die, Jimmy decided he would prefer the needle to the bullet.

Felton helped Jimmy tie the black silk scarf around his own arm this time. "Hold that tight," he said and positioned Jimmy's hand on the scarf.

Herman stood by with the gun. Felton picked up the other syringe and needle, and to Jimmy's relief, used the same vial, but this time he filled it full. Then he repeated the preparation procedure.

"Sweet dreams, Jimmy-boy," Danny Felton said. "Maybe we can make your dreams come true."

The last thing Jimmy remembered was seeing a single drop of fluid glistening over the beveled hole at the needle tip before Felton inserted it into his vein and pushed the piston of the syringe down into the cylinder of the glass tube.

Jimmy lost consciousness.

And in the sleep that followed, Morpheus, the shape-shifting god of dreams, came and appeared to Jimmy in various forms, but the vision of these guises became lost in the labyrinth of his memory.

TWENTY-ONE

Jimmy woke with a start. The room was dark. Light from the nighttime city made its way into the room through cracks in the curtains and Jimmy recognized where he was. He lay in the hotel room bed, covered with only a sheet. He felt nauseated and a vague sense of fear troubled him. A dream image of blood and dark water and a woman singing passed before his consciousness and was gone. Then he remembered a syringe. A gun. A glistening drop of fluid on the tip of a needle. Danny Felton's unsettling smile.

He tried to sit up. Connecting the will to the muscles was difficult. He felt an urgent need to escape from this place. But he fell back on the bed. Throwing off the bedsheet, he tried again and made it to his feet. He was still naked and the room was cold. Steadying himself on a bedside table, he fumbled for the switch on the lamp.

As his eyes adjusted to the blinding light, he caught sight of a red stain the size of a silver dollar in the center of the bed. He moved closer and the realization dawned on him. It was his own blood. He became aware of a soreness in his anus and reached back to rub it. When he looked down, he saw a small smear of red on his fingers.

Jimmy stumbled to the bathroom and cleaned himself up. The bleeding had stopped but he was still sore. The memory of Danny Felton's rough handling came back to him. Then he remembered the needle and examined the inside of his elbow. Only a small red pinprick.

My clothes, he thought. The clothes closet. He had to dress and get out of there. Jimmy made his way to the closet and found his things.

By the time he got to the hallway, Jimmy had remembered the whole scene with Danny Felton. I must get back to my hotel, he told himself. Find a taxi. Feeling his pockets, he remembered he was low on cash. He found an envelope in the breast pocket of his suit coat. It was the opera tickets. I have to find Eric, he thought.

Still feeling shaky, Jimmy had to concentrate to find his way to the hotel lobby. He took out his pocket watch and found it had stopped. A wall clock behind the desk clerk read 9:15. He felt relieved that it was still early in the evening. He had to get outdoors. The cold night air cleared Jimmy's head a little, but the nausea lingered. A doorman asked if Jimmy wanted a cab. Jimmy was flooded with gratitude that someone should offer to help him. Maybe the whole world was not treacherous and hostile.

Stepping into the back of a cab, Jimmy directed the driver to his hotel. He wasn't sure what day it was so he asked the cabby.

"Boy oh boy, bud. You must be on a real bender. Yeah, it's Tuesday. Tuesday night about half past 9."

Again Jimmy felt a wave of gratitude.

When Jimmy passed through the lobby of his hotel, the elderly desk clerk called him over.

"We'll need to settle your bill for last night," he said. "And if you plan to stay on, I'd like you to pay in advance for the rest of the week."

"Oh, sure thing," Jimmy said. "I've been so busy I forgot to pay up. I left my cash in the room. I'll run up and be right back."

In his room Jimmy locked the door and took off his belt to get out the extra 200 dollars Carl had hidden in it.

The money wasn't there. Jimmy inspected the belt again. He looked about the room in a panic, hoping he had removed the cash and stashed it somewhere. He opened his suitcase and rummaged through it. But he knew it wasn't there. He examined the money belt again, hoping he had missed something.

The money was gone.

Jimmy slumped down on the bed and tried to think. His mind was still clouded by the drug. Could the money have disappeared at the brothel? He had left his clothing unattended for only a couple of minutes while he was in the bathroom and Elsa was sniffing that drug when he came out. Could she have gotten into his belt in that short time? None of the fellows in the band would have taken it, would they? No. It wasn't possible. Maybe Larry didn't like him, but Jimmy didn't believe any of the band members would steal from him. Danny Felton. But, no, that didn't make any sense. Felton was a rich and powerful man. Why would he steal money from a poor musician?

Eric? No. That was inconceivable. Eric loved him. Didn't he?

Jimmy felt the earth move under him. No. Of all the people he knew in Chicago, Eric was the one person he had to trust. Jimmy denied the possibility of Eric taking the money, and he put the thought out of his mind.

It didn't matter who was to blame. He had to do something. Could he borrow some money from Eric? Eric was working and he always seemed to have plenty of cash. But that wouldn't help Jimmy at the moment.

Maybe Eric could put him up? Jimmy thought of packing up and sneaking out the back door of the hotel. He could go right to Pluto's Lair. Eric was the one person in this city Jimmy thought he could trust—hoped he could trust. Where else could he turn?

Jimmy emptied his pockets and counted up all his money. He had enough to take a taxi to Pluto's with a little to spare. There was no other choice. No streetcars ran to Pluto's part of town. There was nowhere else for him to go.

He paced about the room for a while, considering. Then he flew into action. He packed his bag and scanned the room to make sure he hadn't forgotten anything.

The gin. He went to the dresser, retrieved the bottle from the bottom drawer, and took a long swig. A wave of nausea swept over him. He remembered the syringe in Felton's hotel room. Jimmy sat down on the bed for a time until the sick feeling passed. He began to wonder if he was addicted. He recapped the gin and packed it away in his suitcase.

He left his bag on the bed and went to the door. Turning the knob, he pulled the door open and looked up and down the hall. No one was there. He hurried along the hallway to a back stairway and went down to see if he could make his way out without being seen. There was no one around, and he located an exit at the back of the building. Jimmy thanked his lucky stars.

He returned to his room, grabbed his suitcase, and slipped out.

It wasn't until he was a block away and around the corner that Jimmy felt he could relax. He shifted the suitcase to his other hand and made his way to a taxi stand down the street.

TWENTY-TWO

When his taxi pulled up in front of Pluto's, Jimmy was still feeling queasy. But unlike his first time arriving at the club, tonight he felt a great relief settle on him. He walked in through the basement door, still a bit unsteady on his feet, but the sound of the piano from the other room raised his spirits. He left his suitcase and overcoat with the coat-check clerk and went down into the dance hall. There was a much larger crowd tonight than the night before. Seeing Eric sitting at the piano across the room and hearing him playing a lively jazz tune for a laughing, dancing crowd comforted Jimmy's soul. Maybe the world had not entirely fallen apart.

He took a seat by himself at a table in the back of the room and watched as more people came into the club. Life seemed to be carrying on much as it had before. Jimmy focused his attention on that fact, while he tried to re-establish his equilibrium.

After a while, Jasper came by and Jimmy ordered a ginger ale. His eyes followed Jasper back to the bar where he saw Roscoe pouring drinks. The scene in the brothel basement flashed through Jimmy's mind. Danny Felton in that hotel room. The soreness Jimmy still felt in the base of his body. He remembered the business card with the name of the music agent. What hotel was it? Jimmy searched his pockets. He felt a small envelope in his breast pocket. Oh, yes, the opera tickets. In the side pocket of his suit he found the business card with the name and phone number on the back. Was Felton to be trusted about opening a classy new club and employing the band? Jimmy still wasn't sure himself if he wanted to help out the band. He wasn't sure about anything. He didn't know what the rules were anymore. Well, he told himself, if you don't know the rules, you have to make them up as you go along. Jasper brought the ginger ale. Jimmy sat sipping the drink, and the nausea began to ease.

As he listened to Eric play and watched the growing crowd enjoying the piano music, he calmed down. The internal order of Eric's music soothed and refreshed him. He was overcome with love and gratitude. Eric—who had helped him, who had been his friend, who had been his lover and teacher—Eric was his only hope right now. How could he ever repay Eric's kindness?

The opera tickets. Yes, the opera. Jimmy felt his breast pocket again. Eric had agreed to go see the opera with him. Jimmy would take away Eric's opera virginity. In exchange for Eric taking away Jimmy's sexual virginity. And later on, maybe the plans for Paris would work out and Jimmy could take Eric to the Paris Opera just like Eric had dreamed.

Jimmy remembered his plan to discuss the opera with Roscoe, and he tried to recall Eric's instructions about talking to him. Jimmy turned his attention back to the bar where Roscoe was serving a raucous group of colored queens, while down the bar a dark-haired bartender was busy mixing drinks for a party of giggling white fairies. Jimmy watched as Roscoe went about his work with efficient professionalism. He remembered seeing Roscoe with that girl at the Grand Ballroom. What did Diggs say her name was? Mary Lou Rawlins. Roscoe was sure a smooth operator. Jimmy considered how to approach Roscoe about the opera, as he took his time finishing his drink. Maybe there weren't any rules any more. He decided he would have to improvise.

He was feeling better now. He recalled his bold negotiations with Felton earlier, which steeled his resolve. He was doing this for Eric. Jimmy got up and walked over to the bar. He watched as

Roscoe served up drinks for a black and white couple. When they left, he got Roscoe's attention, and Roscoe made his way over to where Jimmy stood leaning at the bar.

"Hey, Roscoe. Busy night tonight."

"Yeah, for a weeknight," Roscoe said.

"I'll just have a ginger ale."

"Bring your own bottle tonight?" Roscoe asked.

"Oh, I just want to go easy tonight for a change," Jimmy said.

"You got it."

As he counted out coins for his drink, Jimmy realized he was down to his last nickel. He hoped he could stretch that nickel further than the fellows in Felton's story at lunch. He was counting on Eric to loan him some cash.

When Roscoe handed across his drink, Jimmy said, "I've got to talk to you when you have a minute."

"You can talk now," Roscoe said.

"It's kind of a private matter," Jimmy replied.

Roscoe frowned. "Wait down at the end of the bar. Things should slow down in a bit and I'll take a break."

After a while, Roscoe made his way to the end of the bar where Jimmy stood watching Eric and the audience. "What's up?" he asked.

Jimmy gestured toward the back corner of the room. They made their way to an empty table. Jimmy set down his drink and took out a pack of cigarettes and offered one to Roscoe. He lit Roscoe's cigarette, then his own.

"You remember those opera tickets that you gave to Mr. Felton Saturday night?"

Roscoe nodded.

"He told me he had to go out of town on business and couldn't go to the opera on Wednesday so he gave the tickets to me."

"Hell, that doesn't sound like Mr. Felton. He never misses an opera."

"Well, that's what he told me," Jimmy said. "He said he'll be in Milwaukee until Friday, and he gave me those two tickets to his private box tomorrow."

"So what's that got to do with me?" Roscoe asked.

"Well, I need to ask you something since you work at the opera. Mr. Felton said I should take someone with me with the other ticket. I want to take Eric to the opera."

"Eric? Halsey? The piano player?" He laughed. "No, sir. Ain't no niggers sittin' in Mr. Felton's box seat."

"Keep your shirt on, Roscoe. Mr. Felton said I could take any one I wanted to. Now, Eric's been very good to hire me on as the piano player here—and Felton says I've got the job if I want it. I just want to do Eric this little favor. It's a gentlemanly way of thanking him."

"Look, I don't think you understand, so let me explain some things to you. Mr. Felton is a prominent member of the business community in this city. He keeps his box at the opera to enhance his public image. Now, everyone in the auditorium looks to see who is sitting in those box seats. Society people go to the opera to see and be seen—with their own kind. They don't go there to be seen brushing elbows with Negroes. And Mr. Felton isn't going to want high society accusing him of opening their privileged boxes to jazzbo niggers like Eric."

Eric's piano playing closed out a tune and there was a smattering of applause.

"Listen, Roscoe. Eric has never seen an opera. He told me it's always been a dream of his to go to the opera. You can understand that. You said yourself that you've loved the opera since you were a kid. I want to help Eric make his dream come true.

"You tell Eric that if he wants to come to the opera, he can come in the back door dressed as a charwoman and watch from the wings. He seems to like wearing a dress."

Jimmy was surprised at this enmity, but he decided to ignore the remark.

"Hey, come on, Roscoe. Felton said no one will be using his box."

"If you want to bring a girl to the opera, that's different. I don't care if you bring some flapper—as long as she's white and knows how to dress. But Eric's another story."

"I just want to do him this little courtesy to pay him back, you understand? You don't even have to be the one to seat us. You could have another usher show us to the box. No one even has to know you're involved."

"Sorry, buddy. This just isn't going to work," Roscoe insisted. "There isn't an usher working there who would let a nigger sit in Mr. Felton's box."

"What if we wait till after the lights go down and the curtain goes up. No one would notice us then. All you have to do is arrange to show us into Felton's box."

"No. It's out of the question. I can't help you. Now, I've gotta get back to work."

"Roscoe, how can I make it worth your while?"

"It isn't a question of money," Roscoe said. "I'm not going to seat any Negroes in Mr. Felton's box."

"Look," Jimmy said, trying to sound firm and serious. "I played the Grand Ballroom at the Redfield. I know all about your society girlfriend, Miss Mary Lou Rawlins." Jimmy watched Roscoe expecting some reaction, but his expression didn't change. "I bet she'd be pretty disappointed to find out about your connections with Danny Felton and this outfit." Jimmy was guessing and he knew he was taking a chance.

Roscoe laughed in Jimmy's face. "You don't know nothin'."

"Yeah, I know a thing or two. I know about you and Freddy's little performance at Miss Eva's place."

Jimmy saw Roscoe stiffen but his face revealed nothing. He stared at Jimmy for a second. "You are a little joker." He put out his cigarette and added, "Look, I've gotta get back to the bar." He stood and turned to walk away.

"Hold on," Jimmy called after him, as he rose to follow. "I can make trouble for you." Roscoe stopped without turning to look back. Jimmy came up beside Roscoe and put an arm around his shoulder. Turning him back toward the table, Jimmy spoke, close and quiet, in Roscoe's ear. "Listen, I'm not asking much. You do me this little favor and I keep my mouth shut. We can arrange things so that even if someone finds Eric in Felton's box, you can say you don't know anything about it."

Jimmy waited for Roscoe to respond, but Roscoe seemed to be considering his options.

Jimmy tightened his grip on the man's shoulder, "I won't hesitate to talk to that little girlfriend of yours. It's nothing to me."

Roscoe turned to face Jimmy with an incredulous smirk.

"Come on. We can come to a nice friendly agreement and there won't be any trouble, eh, buddy? Besides, we're going to be working together here starting next week. Let's be friends." Jimmy waited. "You do me this one little favor and maybe I can do you a favor sometime. I don't want to make trouble for you, honest."

A spirited jazz number filled the air and a number of people got up to dance.

Jimmy studied Roscoe's face as the bartender seemed to come to a decision. So this is how you get what you want in Chicago, Jimmy thought, feeling proud that he was pulling off the deal. Make up your own rules as you go along.

"Okay. You win." Roscoe extended his hand, and Jimmy reached out to shake it. Without warning Roscoe twisted Jimmy's arm behind his back and held his wrist bent double. He exerted some pressure and a pain shot through Jimmy's arm.

"You little son of a bitch. I can break your wrist so bad that you'll never play the piano again." Roscoe's calm facade was gone, and the full depth of his anger was there in his voice. He applied more pressure. Before Jimmy realized what was happening an involuntary cry of pain escaped from his throat.

"Now, you listen to me, you little punk, and you listen good. No one is going to pay any attention to you because you don't know what you're talking about, and you couldn't prove it if you did. So just keep your filthy, goddamn little trap shut. You understand?" Roscoe twisted Jimmy's arm tighter.

"Okay, okay, I understand," Jimmy said, straining to speak through the pain.

"I'd break your hand clean off, right here and now, but I know the boss wouldn't like it." Roscoe relaxed his grip and gave Jimmy a little shove. Jimmy turned to face Roscoe and stepped back, rubbing his wrist. He took a deep breath that quivered as he exhaled.

Roscoe stepped in close to him and said, "Now I'll arrange for tickets for you and Eric in the second balcony, but you can forget about the box seats. Got it?"

"Okay," Jimmy said.

"You and Eric show up an hour early and I'll fix everything up and get you to your seats. But I don't want any funny business, you hear?"

"It's a deal," Jimmy said.

"If you're not there by 7, you're out of luck. I can't help you."

"We'll be on time," Jimmy said, "take my word."

Roscoe stared at Jimmy for a moment. "You ever try to blackmail me again and I'll kill you, you bastard, without giving it a second thought. I swear it."

One of the bouncers approached Roscoe and Jimmy. "Is this fellow givin' you trouble, Roscoe?" he asked.

"You tell him, Jimmy," Roscoe said. "Are you making trouble?"

"No. There's no trouble," he said.

"You remember what I told you," Roscoe said. He turned and went back to the bar.

The bouncer eyed Jimmy for a moment and walked away.

Jimmy went back to the corner table to get his glass. As he reached for his ginger ale, he noticed that his hand was shaking. He sat down and took a long drink and focused his attention on Eric's playing. He sat back and let the music wash over him. He tried not to think about Roscoe or Felton or the Diggs Monroe band or anything. He just concentrated on the music.

As Jimmy sat there listening to Eric's music, he was tortured by the feeling that he had played his cards all wrong with Roscoe. He thought he had been dealt a winning hand but now he believed he had blown it. His thoughts wandered back to his negotiations with Felton over lunch. Maybe Felton had just allowed him to believe he was winning. Maybe he had blown that deal too.

Sitting in the back of the room all alone, Jimmy rubbed his wrist to soothe the pain and he felt his hand still trembling. Roscoe had intimidated him and he now felt powerless in a bar run by Felton and staffed by people who seemed loyal to him. Eric was far away at the other end of the hall. Jimmy pulled himself up and maneuvered to the side of the room, away from the bar where Roscoe had returned to serving drinks. He wanted to keep a safe distance as he made his way up to the bandstand to be near Eric. He took an empty table by the piano. Eric saw him and smiled, lifting his head in a small gesture of greeting. Eric's smile was a small ray of sunshine in a troubled sky.

TWENTY-THREE

After a time, Eric took a break and joined Jimmy at his table. In the absence of music the clientele became more talkative.

"Say, you look like you've been through the wringer," Eric said. "How did it go? Did you get the opera tickets?"

"Yes, Felton gave me the tickets. But that's not all he gave me." Jimmy couldn't say any more. He felt a wave of nausea and steadied himself for a moment. "Shit, Eric, it's been hell. I've gotta ask your help."

"Are you all right?"

"Oh," Jimmy said, "I'm holding together."

Eric studied Jimmy's face. "Felton didn't refuse you the job here, did he?"

Jimmy wasn't sure he could tell Eric about what had happened with Danny Felton, and he wasn't yet ready to talk to Eric about his deal with Roscoe.

"No. No, Felton says I can start playing here as soon as you leave. He's being very helpful. He's lining up work for the band and…" Jimmy's voice trailed off and he looked away.

A burst of laughter arose from a nearby table.

"So why are you dragging in here looking like a storm cloud is chasing you? Besides, I thought you were through with your band."

Jimmy didn't say anything but continued to stare down at the table.

"I know about Felton. I know how he works."

Jimmy looked up at Eric, searching his eyes. Eric seemed to understand. "You mean…Did you and Felton…?"

"No," Eric said. "Lucky for me he doesn't have a taste for dark meat. But I've heard the stories."

"Does he make everybody take…the needle?"

"Jesus, did he force you? Oh, Jimmy." Eric shook his head.

"Will I become an addict? Like Monkey?"

"No, you're okay. Don't worry about that. It takes a while. Just stay away from that crap."

"Oh, hell, Eric…I don't know what's happening any more, and I don't know what to do…" Jimmy rubbed his forehead with his fingertips and steadied himself. "And when I got back to my hotel tonight, they asked me to pay up for the rest of the week and… Eric, I'm broke…so I snuck out without paying." He sighed. "Can you put me up for tonight and advance me some money? I'll pay you back as soon as I start working here at Pluto's. Honest, I'm down to my last nickel."

"You bet, jazz boy. Don't you worry about a thing." Eric reached in his pocket for a moment and then took Jimmy's hand.

When Eric drew his hand away, Jimmy found a folded twenty in his palm. He pocketed the money. How had he gotten to this point? He avoided Eric's gaze and looked down into his ginger ale.

A waiter whisked by carrying a tray of drinks.

"Thanks, Eric. I don't understand how all this happened. When I got to Chicago, I had the band and prospects and money and a place to stay. Now I have no place to go and I'm broke and I haven't got a friend in town except you. I don't understand what's going on. I don't understand anything anymore."

"Sounds to me like you've got the blues," Eric said.

"Yeah, you've got that right."

"The best thing to do when you've got the blues is to sing the blues." Eric looked at him for a moment. "Go ahead and play." He gestured toward the grand piano on the stage.

Loud voices from across the room cut through the babble

of conversation, and someone shouted, "You need another drink, Franky."

Jimmy toyed with his glass. "Naw. Not now."

"Yes. Now." Eric was dead serious. "The crowd needs some music."

Jimmy looked down at the tabletop. He knew Eric was right.

"I mean it," Eric said. "You're going to be playing piano here, and you're gonna have to play some nights when you don't feel like it. Get up there and play."

Jimmy hesitated for a moment longer, and pulled himself up from his chair and mounted the bandstand. Settling down at the keyboard, he felt a sense of coming home. When his fingers came to rest on the keys, Jimmy forgot about the events of the past two days. He forgot about Danny Felton and he forgot about Roscoe. He even forgot about Eric. Almost before he knew it, his fingers were playing the opening chords of "Gladstone Blues."

Jimmy lost himself in the music and soon he heard his own voice join in with the lyrics. He was not aware of time or his troubles or the hush that fell over the audience in the barroom. He just played. A silence lingered after he sounded the last note. A cascade of applause brought his mind back to Pluto's Lair. He glanced out at the clapping, hooting crowd. He caught sight of Eric's knowing smile and slow nod of approval. Jimmy nodded to the audience, then struck another note and let the music move through his hands. He was not sure where his fingers ended and the black and white keys started. He could no longer distinguish between himself and the music.

TWENTY-FOUR

Jimmy played until 2 when the bar closed. As the last of the crowd was leaving, some of Eric's friends came up and complimented him on his playing. They asked if Jimmy and Eric wanted to come along to an after-hours club. Eric declined but said he and Jimmy could use a lift back to his place. After picking up Jimmy's suitcase and overcoat from the coat-check stand, Eric took Jimmy home to his room.

As they got comfortable, Eric lit a muggle. When he passed it across, Jimmy declined, and Eric took another puff. Jimmy slipped out of his coat and tie.

"I saw you talking with Roscoe tonight. Did you work out something about the opera tomorrow night?"

Jimmy felt ashamed and defeated as he recalled his encounter with Roscoe. "Well, Roscoe said he would arrange for seats for us in the second balcony."

"I thought we were going to be sitting in Danny Felton's private box."

"Roscoe says there isn't an usher in the place that would seat us in that box."

"Because I'm a nigger, right?"

"I'm sorry, Eric."

"Damn, I always dreamed that when I went to the opera, I would sit in the good seats." He draped his tuxedo shirt over the foot rail of the bed.

"Roscoe says he's trying to do us a favor. He says we have to be at the theater by 7 or he can't help us."

"Do you think we can trust him?" Eric asked.

Jimmy wasn't altogether sure if he could trust anyone, and he began to fear that Roscoe might be planning some kind of revenge. Now Eric seemed to be having doubts and questions of his own.

"I don't know. You tell me. You've known Roscoe longer than I have." Jimmy looked to Eric and saw the concern in his face. So he tried to lighten the tension by making a joke. He forced a laugh and said, "Roscoe said that since you like wearing a dress, you should come to the opera dressed as a charwoman. He said you could come in the back door and watch from the wings."

Eric's face closed up like a book.

"That bastard," he said under his breath. He turned and paced across the room. "The little son of a bitch!" Eric shouted. He paced back and forth frowning and shaking his head. "I will put on a dress to sing the blues," Eric said, "but not to sneak into the opera." Eric looked away and took a puff on the muggle and then turned back to Jimmy. "What did you do, bribe him? Is that why you're broke?"

Jimmy was not feeling good about the day's underhanded negotiations and now, on top of that, he was feeling tired and insecure.

"Let's just say I hit him below the belt."

"You must really have the goods on Roscoe. What is it? Is he screwing Felton's wife?"

Jimmy glanced away. "Well, not exactly…"

"Oh," Eric said. Jimmy looked back at Eric and could tell that he'd said enough.

"So Roscoe is Felton's butt boy." He dropped the muggle in an ashtray. "Well, that all makes sense now. I should have guessed." Eric paced around the bed. "That little asshole." After a moment, Eric stopped and looked at Jimmy. "Do you think he will follow through on this?"

"I don't know, Eric. I don't know. What do you think? Do

you really want to go to the opera? We don't have to go. I was only doing this for you, because I thought you wanted to see an opera." He was fighting back tears. "I wanted to help you make your dreams come true."

Jimmy's agitation was right on the surface where Eric could see it. He sat down on the bed beside Jimmy and put his arms around him. Jimmy let out a little sob.

"Oh, honey lamb. I didn't mean to upset you. It's okay. I guess we've both been a little on edge. It's all right. Everything is going to be all right." He kissed Jimmy and held him until Jimmy became calm. They lay back onto the bed and were quiet for a time.

After a while, Jimmy said, "How long can this last?"

"How long can what last?"

"You and me."

The radiator made a clanging noise.

"Who can say? You've got to just live for today."

"But I've lived all my life aiming at the future. Planning for a career in music—a career in jazz. Now I'm not sure what to do. Don't you have a plan for the future?"

"I don't know if a black man in America can plan for the future."

"But what about you and the Checker Club?"

"Cabarets and speakeasies come and go. They don't last long. You've always got to keep an eye out for your next job."

"But you have dreams, don't you?"

"Yeah, I have dreams. I dream of getting out of here, someday. I dream of going to Paris." He kissed Jimmy again. "But there is nothing you can be sure of."

"Nothing?" Jimmy asked.

"One thing I'm sure of is that you played some blues tonight," Eric said. "And another thing I'm sure of is what the doctor says in the song."

"What's that?" Jimmy asked.

"You remember." Eric sang.

"You need some lovin' when you feel sad.
You need some lovin' to make you real glad.
You need some lovin' when you feel blue.
You need someone to talk baby talk to you."

Jimmy couldn't help feeling a twinge of longing for Carl and faraway Oregon. "Oh, that's just one more popular song," he said. "I'm beginning to doubt if music can really make any difference."

"Music makes people feel better." He touched Jimmy's face. "And lovin' makes people feel better."

"But music is different from making love."

"Is it?" Eric asked.

The question hung in the air.

Eric nuzzled Jimmy's neck and then whispered baby talk in his ear. Jimmy laughed out loud, in spite of himself.

"You'll have to teach me that piece," Jimmy said.

"Here, I'll teach you," Eric said softly.

He brought his mouth close to Jimmy's. Their lips met and their tongues communicated in a wordless song.

They finished undressing each other, exposing the vulnerable flesh, their sore spots and their emotional wounds.

Eric kissed away Jimmy's blues, soothed him with stroking hands, and Jimmy felt glad to be shielded in his embrace. Eric's caresses distracted him from his cares.

In turn, Jimmy's hands played over Eric's body. Jimmy was no longer sure where his pale fingers ended and Eric's dark skin began. They set to making music, making time, beating out the rhythm together.

After a time their duet reached a crescendo and came to a full rest. Overtones hung in the air.

Afterwards they curled up together under the covers and as the soft lullaby of slumber settled over them, Jimmy's thoughts kept drifting back to his doctor in Portland.

TWENTY-FIVE

When they got up the next day Eric was acting very coy. He told Jimmy that he had a surprise for him, but he wouldn't tell him what it was. When Jimmy pressed him, all Eric would say was, "I'm going to take you someplace special. But let's get cracking. We've got to get there by noon. We've got a busy day ahead of us getting ready for the opera."

As Jimmy cleaned up and dressed, he kept thinking about Mr. Keys at the brothel. What was it he said to me? Jimmy thought. "Music comes from out of the deep and belongs to everybody." Was that what happened last night when I was playing the blues at Pluto's? Jimmy paused in the middle of tying his tie.

"Come on," Eric said, trying to hurry Jimmy along. "Here, I'll get your overcoat. We've got a streetcar to catch."

The someplace special turned out to be a very nice apartment house on a broad tree-lined avenue in a very prosperous-looking black residential neighborhood. As they rode the elevator of the well-kept four-story building, Eric said, "This is my parents' place. They bought this building a few years after we moved to Chicago— after they saved up a bit. It's turned out to be a good investment for them. We've been invited to have lunch with my mother, but Pop is out of town on the train right now. My sister will be here though. You'll get to meet her. We always try to get together for lunch on Wednesdays." The elevator stopped on the top floor. "Oh, and please don't bring up Fisk University with my mother. My college music education is kind of a sore spot with her. I can't explain it all now."

Eric led Jimmy down the hallway and knocked on number 43. A colored maid in uniform admitted them to a large entryway. Behind her, a well-dressed young woman was waiting and she greeted Eric with a warm hug.

"How are you doing?" Eric asked.

"I'm doing tolerably well, brother dear."

Eric introduced Alicia to Jimmy. While the maid hung their coats in an entry closet, and Alicia exchanged pleasantries with them, Jimmy took in the polished wooden columns on either side of the entrance to a drawing room. White lace curtains hung in the windows and plush upholstery covered the heavy furniture. There was a quiet grace about the apartment that reminded Jimmy of the home of the old German piano teacher in Portland where his mother had taken him as a youngster.

Alicia led them inside where Jimmy was surprised to find a larger room than he expected, ample enough to accommodate the grand piano that stood at one side. Nearby, in an overstuffed chair by a large window bay, sat a stately older woman who rose as they entered the room.

She was a light-skinned woman with facial features that could have been either African or European. It depended on how you looked at her and how you set your mind when you were trying to decide which it was.

Eric went to her and greeted her with a kiss on the cheek. Then he turned to introduce her.

"Mama, I'd like you to meet Jimmy Harper. Jimmy, this is my mother, Heleena Abbott Halsey."

Jimmy was befuddled by his own surprise. He had never thought of Eric's family before, least of all his mother, and he had not expected that he might ever meet any of them. Plus, the prosperity of this building and this apartment was such a contrast with the shabby place where Eric lived, and, indeed, most of the colored parts of town that Jimmy had seen, that he did not know what to make of it all. And above all he was entranced by this woman's aristocratic manner.

"Eric, please call me Mother. Mama sounds so country. I am very pleased to meet you, Mr. Harper," Mrs. Halsey said, shaking Jimmy's hand.

The four of them sat down and talked for a while, and Jimmy learned that Eric's mother taught in a private school besides being a piano teacher. "I'm sorry that my husband can't join us," she said, "but as you probably know he works as a porter for the railroad and is away at present."

Eric asked how Alicia's work was going and she talked about her job as a secretary in the office of a colored attorney.

Jimmy was struck by something stilted in Mrs. Halsey's speech. Something in the way she formed her words carefully in her mouth showed a studied practice of good elocution. She made a disciplined effort to avoid all slang and questionable grammar, while using a vocabulary limited to the most proper and socially acceptable terms. All this gave her conversation a formal air. Yet there was a genuine politeness and warmth in her manner that saved her from seeming cold.

Soon, the maid came into the room and announced that lunch was served. They all followed Mrs. Halsey through wood-paneled doors into a sunny dining room where a long table was set with white linen and silver. Jimmy noticed that Mrs. Halsey walked with the same tall, erect stateliness and dignity that had impressed him in Eric's gait, and certain qualities in her personal style led Jimmy to wonder how much Eric had absorbed her characteristics into Erica DeChez. In fact, they were such mirrors of one another that the more Jimmy studied them, the more he could see Erica DeChez in Heleena and Heleena in Erica DeChez, so that it was difficult to say which was the masculine female and which was the feminine male.

Eric addressed the maid as Cleo and asked how her family was and when she spoke of her ill mother, Eric expressed his concern.

During lunch Eric mentioned that Jimmy's mother was also musical and it came out that Jimmy was a professional musician.

"Well, I hope you have taken up a higher caliber of music than this popular music Eric plays," Mrs. Halsey said.

Jimmy hesitated. He had heard a similar attitude from his own mother, though not so harshly judgmental. The tension in the silence that followed was palpable. Jimmy did not feel it was his place to insert himself into what was obviously a long-standing family dispute. "Well, I dabble," Jimmy said.

Then Eric came to his rescue.

"Mother, one reason I wanted you to meet Jimmy is because he has a classical music background like me—he even studied music in college—*and* he is very interested in playing jazz music."

"Eric, I forbid you to use that vulgar term in this household—and certainly not at table."

Alicia jumped in, "But, Mother, the word is even used in the newspapers. It is a common expression now."

"I agree with you that it is a common expression. Common and low."

"But, Mother," Eric protested, "we are talking about music here and that is what this kind of music is called."

"But that is where the expression comes from—from common, low bordellos and barrel houses. It is simply not fit for polite conversation. Now let us change the subject, please."

There was another silence.

"Did you know Mr. Hatcher is giving an organ recital at St. Matthew's next Sunday afternoon? He'll be playing Bach and some modern French composers."

"Modern French composers," Eric laughed. "Well, the old fellow is getting with it." Eric turned to Jimmy and explained that Mr. Hatcher was a piano teacher that his mother had taken him to when he was a child. "How is Mr. Hatcher, anyway? He must be in his 70s."

"He's in excellent health. And he still plays beautifully. You know, he asks after you whenever I speak with him. He always offers to arrange a recital for you. He is so disappointed that you are not on the concert stage."

"I could never have a career as a classical concert pianist. They don't even let colored people into the good seats at the concert halls."

"There are Negro performers who have been quite successful on the concert stage. Why, I saw Sissieretta Jones perform back in St. Louis. She was known as the black Adelina Patti. Her voice was positively thrilling."

"Sissieretta Jones retired from the stage because she could not get enough of an audience to sustain her career," Eric countered.

"She sang on the stage for a good twenty years," Mrs. Halsey said, "and she didn't retire until she was in her late 40s. That is a good long career."

"I just don't think that is the path for me," Eric said.

"Why can't you at least try to get a job with a good theater orchestra instead of those low-life establishments where you play?"

"We've had this discussion before. Why, I'd starve to death trying to make it as a classical performer. I can find more work and earn more money at those low-life establishments, as you call them. Besides, all kinds of important people attend those cabarets. You see ward aldermen, and wealthy industrialists, and journalists. Even college professors."

"And gangsters and gamblers and painted women," she added.

"Just you wait." Eric continued. "Someday I will own my own club. You'll see. I plan to have my own cabaret in Paris one day."

Jimmy glanced at Eric, surprised at the ambition and audacity of this dream, which he hadn't heard Eric express before. Now it was Jimmy's turn to come to Eric's rescue.

"Mrs. Halsey, there is definitely a career to be made in popular music," Jimmy said. "Besides the cabarets, there are the ballrooms and grand vaudeville theaters, and now there are phonograph records and the radio. If a man can build up a reputation for himself, the sky is the limit. Why, look at Jelly Roll Morton. Because of his piano rolls and phonograph records, he's selling a ton of his sheet music compositions."

"Mr. Morton should choose a moniker by which civilized people might refer to him," Mrs. Halsey replied.

Everyone ate in silence for a time.

To change the subject, Jimmy mentioned that Eric had taken him to a storefront church the other day. There was another stony silence as Eric looked down at his plate.

"To hear some wonderful gospel music," Jimmy added. "It was some of the most powerful singing I have ever heard."

Thinking that he might have given the impression that he and Eric had spent the night together, Jimmy added, "When we first met, I asked Eric if he could take me to hear some gospel singing."

"There is more to the talent of the Negro than church spirituals, Mr. Harper," Mrs. Halsey said.

The uncomfortable silence lingered and Jimmy realized he had said the wrong thing, but he wasn't sure why it was the wrong thing.

"I didn't raise you to go worship with those hollering country niggers," Mrs. Halsey said.

Alicia said, "Mother, please. Not in front of our guest."

"I beg your pardon, Mr. Harper. Country negroes," Mrs. Halsey corrected herself. "You must excuse me, my children often get me worked up into a passion. I sometimes wonder if they don't try to do it deliberately." She turned to Eric. "You know, you could go to the Episcopal Church with me."

"You know I do not attend church. Jimmy and I just happened to be passing by one of those storefront congregations and I took him in to hear the singing."

They were all silent. Finally, Eric spoke.

"Jimmy has arranged to take me to the opera. They are doing *Orphée et Eurydice* by Gluck." Jimmy remembered hearing Felton use the French title.

"What a wonderful opportunity for you, Eric. You need to listen to more music with the refinement of opera. The interplay of the orchestration and the human voice. I saw the advance notices for that in the papers. Gluck was so important in the development of modern opera."

"Yes," Eric said, "but Gluck still wrote music for the castrati. We can hardly call that modern."

"Please, let's not speak of that odious practice over lunch," Mrs. Halsey said.

"But, it is absurd to deny history. There is no reason to pretend that these practices did not exist. The Catholic Church condoned the whole castrati system for over a hundred years, while they forbade women to sing in public. Such hypocrisy. And you wonder that I am not a church-going man."

"Well, that's the Catholic Church, not the Episcopalians."

Alicia spoke up. "But isn't that an interesting example of the way European culture praises women and raises them up on a pedestal and at the same time denigrates them for being the weaker sex?"

"I think we can all be proud," said Mrs. Halsey, "that the United States has now given women the right to vote."

"But at the same time," Alicia said, "the politicians don't want women to actually use that power. They only want women to vote if they vote the way their husbands tell them to. It's no different than giving Negroes the right to vote. Look at how many still cannot access the polling places."

"I prefer the subject of opera to that of religion," Mrs. Halsey said. "You know, I have always felt that Verdi's *Aida* should be presented by an ensemble of the colored race."

"That's what it would take—a whole horde of the race—to get such a show on the stage," Eric said with a laugh. "You know, Sissieretta Jones wanted to sing the part of Selika in Meyerbeer's *L'Africaine*, but there wasn't an opera company in America that would consider the possibility."

"And Scott Joplin wrote a race opera that has never yet been performed," Jimmy interjected.

"Because even a composer as popular as he was couldn't get it produced," Eric added.

"That syphilitic saloon pianist?" Mrs. Halsey scoffed. "It's no wonder he couldn't get an opera produced."

Alicia countered, "But just because there are Negroes on the stage doesn't mean there are going to be Negroes in the audience."

"Yes," Eric said, "there are a lot of fancy white night clubs where black musicians play on the bandstand, but you won't find a single colored person on the dance floor because they are not allowed in."

"I know, I know. I was not born yesterday, children. But we must have faith that in time things will change. We must continue to believe in the uplifting of the race. We must continue to hope and dream."

Everyone fell silent again.

Jimmy felt out of place. He decided he had better keep his mouth shut. The awkward silence was broken by Alicia remarking on a new movie that was playing and the conversation turned to movies and different film personalities. Mrs. Halsey said that she wished the cinema could be put to better cultural use. Eric pointed out that Charlie Chaplin was not only popular at the box office but that he was also a great artist. Mrs. Halsey conceded the point but pointed out that Mr. Chaplin was, after all, a comedian.

Before long Cleo began clearing the plates and Mrs. Halsey glanced at the clock and said she had a pupil coming soon. They all rose and Mrs. Halsey led them toward the entry hall. Jimmy thanked her for having him to lunch and she wished him all the best with his music career.

Eric kissed his mother goodbye and gave her a hug. She held him a moment and said, "Oh, Eric, do look out for yourself. I worry about you so—in those rough clubs. I know we don't see eye to eye on so many things, but remember that I love you, son."

"I know, Mother," Eric said. "I love you, too."

"That's my mother," Eric said, once they were out in the street. Jimmy didn't know how to respond.

"I thought," Eric continued, "that if she met a white boy who was classically educated and still loved jazz, she might begin to change her mind."

"She sounds like my mother in some ways," Jimmy said. He wondered to himself if meeting a white boy who loved jazz had made Mrs. Halsey even more defensive, but he couldn't find the words to express this to Eric.

The streetcar back to Eric's place was nearly empty and they sat in silence. After a time Jimmy asked, "How did you come to know so much about the castrati?"

"My old butter and egg man was a real opera fan. He was kind of bookish and kept making references to the castrati, since I sang on stage as a woman in a dress. The subject sort of caught my fancy, and he got me interested in the Italian Renaissance and gave me some books to read. As far as I can see, it's just one more form of church-sanctioned genital mutilation."

TWENTY-SIX

When they got off the streetcar, Eric said, "We better get cracking if we're going to be ready for the opera by 6."

"How do you mean?" Jimmy asked.

"We need to arrange for proper clothes, sugar. Unless you have a white tie and tails in that suitcase of yours."

"Can't I wear my tuxedo?" Jimmy asked.

"Look, Jimmy, honey, Erica may not know much in this world, but she does know about clothes, and if you are going to sit in a box at the grand opera, a white tie and a silk hat is de rigueur."

"But Roscoe says we will be sitting in the second balcony," Jimmy reminded him.

"Well, there are standards of dress. We don't want to be mistaken for riffraff. When you can't change the color of your skin, you learn that changing your clothes is the best second."

Once again, Jimmy found himself embarrassed and out of his league. "Well, you're leading a country yokel around by the hand." Still, he wondered why they needed to be dressed up proper if Roscoe was taking pains to keep them out of the private box seats. But Jimmy deferred to Eric's judgment.

"Will you wear the formal clothes you wore at Pluto's the other night?" Jimmy asked.

"That white-tie outfit I wear at Pluto's is far too theatrical. It just wouldn't do for the opera," Eric said. "I'll need to rent a new suit of clothes too."

Jimmy hesitated. "Eric...I can't afford to rent a soup and fish."

Eric laughed. "Oh, don't worry. I'll take care of it. I know a fellow who can fix us up. He owes me a favor."

At the clothier shop, a friendly Negro tailor greeted Eric. He fitted them out with everything they needed, including silk hats, white kid gloves, white silk neck scarves, and patent leather shoes. They carried the fancy dress clothing out in large cardboard boxes tucked under their arms. Next Eric escorted Jimmy to a nearby barber shop where they both got a shave and haircut and a manicure. Jimmy felt privileged but uncomfortable to be in an all-black barbershop, but he followed Eric's lead and tried to remain observant and take everything in stride.

Around 3, Eric suggested that they have a light meal at Florence's and then go back to his place to rest for a while before they had to get dressed up.

Being familiar with Florence's place and having spent the day in this Negro community, Jimmy now felt more comfortable. Their meal was interrupted by another private retreat to the kitchen by Eric and Florence, but Eric seemed more confident and upbeat when he returned.

Back at Eric's they stripped down to their underwear and Eric served up the last of his gin in two small glasses before they lay down to rest. He set the alarm clock and they snuggled together in bed until the jangling of the bell roused them.

After freshening up, they helped each other put on their finery, and Erica checked each of them out to make sure every detail was correct. They looked resplendent. Jimmy couldn't help remembering that first night at Pluto's when Eric transformed himself from Erica DeChez into that handsome gentleman in white tie and tails. Now Erica had transformed Jimmy into a gentleman in full evening dress, and he felt like a different person. He hadn't worn white tie since the wedding reception where he met Carl.

With all the excitement of getting ready, Jimmy's nerves were acting on his bladder and he went down the hall to use the bathroom.

When Jimmy got back to Eric's door, he heard voices inside. He knocked. The voices fell silent and Eric opened the door a crack, then hurried him inside. Before he closed the door he checked to make sure no one was in the hallway. Jasper stood leaning against Eric's piano and he eyed Jimmy suspiciously.

"You remember Jimmy," Eric said. Jasper seemed to recognize him and relaxed. They exchanged greetings.

"Look, Jimmy. Something's come up. Jasper's an old friend. He has…uh…he's sort of in a jam, and I've got to take off for a little while to see if I can help him out." His worried tone was something new.

Jimmy felt confused. "But the opera…"

"Don't worry. This shouldn't take long." Eric glanced at Jasper then back at Jimmy. "I'll meet you at the front door of the opera house before 7, okay? The show doesn't start until eight. That should still be plenty early for Roscoe to seat us." Eric glanced at Jasper again, and Jasper stroked his mustache repeatedly.

"Roscoe said if we were late, he couldn't help us," Jimmy said.

"There will be time. Remind him that we have tickets. He can have one of the other ushers show us up to nigger heaven."

"Okay." Jimmy didn't know what else to say. This sudden change in plans had thrown him into confusion. But he could see Eric's concern and understood that something serious was up. He didn't know what he would tell Roscoe, but Jimmy decided he would have to make the best of it.

As Eric pulled on his overcoat, he said, "Look, Jimmy, don't say anything to Roscoe about seeing Jasper. Just tell him…tell him my mother took sick and I had to find a doctor. Tell him it was an emergency. Come on, Jasper. Let's go."

Eric opened the door as Jasper went out into the hall. Then Eric paused and reached into his pocket and took out his room keys. "Here, Jimmy, lock up when you leave. If I need to get back in, I'll ask Jewell. She has an extra set. I'll see you at the theater by 7. I promise."

Jimmy took the keys and Eric leaned in to kiss him on the lips and give his shoulder a reassuring squeeze. "It's okay. Don't worry. Oh, and here." Eric reached in his pocket. "Here's some money for cab fare."

"Wait," Jimmy said. He remembered the tickets. "Take one of the tickets so you can get into the theater—in case something happens and you can't find me." He handed a ticket to Eric.

"Thanks, jazz boy." Eric put on his silk hat and gave Jimmy that broad smile. "You're a champ."

Then the door closed and Eric was gone.

Jimmy heaved a sigh and sat down on the rumpled chaos of bed covers. He tried to compose his thoughts.

TWENTY-SEVEN

At 6:30, Jimmy's cab pulled up in front of the opera house. He made his way past the ticket booths, through an entry hall, to a stairway with a sign reading "To Grand Foyer."

Mounting the stairs into that expansive room, Jimmy removed his silk hat and stood peering upward at the soaring ceiling where massive crystal chandeliers hung high above, lighting the polished, multi-colored marble interior. He wandered out onto the intricate pattern of the floor, staring up with his mouth open.

Someone approached him from behind and said, "It is proper to leave your silk hat on until you enter the auditorium." Jimmy turned to find Roscoe standing behind him, looking sharp in an usher's uniform trimmed in gold braid.

"Hey, Roscoe," Jimmy greeted him. Then feeling awkward, and wondering if Roscoe was joking or serious, Jimmy replaced the silk hat back on his head.

"Damnation. Aren't you putting on the dog a bit for the second balcony?"

"Well," Jimmy said, "Eric insisted."

"I should have guessed. Where is Eric?"

"He'll be along. Something serious cropped up. His mother took sick and he had to go get a doctor."

"God damn that nigger. I knew this would be nothin' but trouble. I never should have agreed to it."

"Now, calm down, Roscoe. It's okay. Eric will be here before 7. I told him I'd meet him at the front door with the balcony tickets. When he shows up, we can have one of the other ushers show us to the balcony seats, if you aren't available."

With some exasperation, Roscoe said, "Okay. Wait here while I see what I can work out." Roscoe descended from the Grand Foyer toward the ticket booths below, leaving Jimmy standing alone in the cavernous room. Jimmy felt uncomfortable in his high hat and evening clothes and out of place in these elegant surroundings, as if he had entered an unfamiliar church of some exotic denomination where he didn't know the rituals.

He wandered forward to take in the sweep of the grand staircase, which flowed upward and branched out into the two wings of tiered galleries overlooking the lobby. The echoing space was empty except for a large stocky man in a tuxedo speaking with one of the ushers at the far side of the room, and a black man in a white coat moving about the room and cleaning the sand-filled ashtrays. Occasionally an usher passed through and disappeared into a doorway, but the Grand Foyer retained an expectant, reverent hush.

In a short time, Roscoe returned from the lower levels and approached Jimmy. Handing him two tickets, he said, "Since you're dressed for it, I got you tickets in the front row of the second balcony. These seats will give you a good view. You're lucky we weren't sold out tonight."

"Hey, thanks a million, buddy," Jimmy said.

"Yeah, sure. Don't mention it, pal." Roscoe's tone was thick with irony. "Just don't make any trouble, okay?"

"You bet, Roscoe. Hey, since I'm here this early, can you show me around a little bit? I'd like to see the theater."

Roscoe eyed Jimmy with suspicion.

"Look, I've never seen such a grand theater before," Jimmy said. "Can you just show me the main floor?"

"Okay, I guess I can take a couple of minutes. Come on. Hurry it up."

He led Jimmy across the foyer, past the grand staircase, and beyond. Near the far wall they passed a lighted exit sign and then approached the back corner of the entry hall. Roscoe opened a padded door with a small window in it and ushered Jimmy from the bright echoing marble of the Grand Foyer into the quiet darkness of the carpeted auditorium.

"You can remove your hat now," he said.

They passed down a side aisle beneath the ceiling under the first balcony, then emerged into the great bowl of the theater auditorium.

"Some of the greatest voices in the world have sung here," Roscoe said, leading on down toward the enormous stage where an immense golden curtain spread out before them, filling the proscenium arch. Jimmy followed, gazing up at the decorated ceiling, which fanned out above the stage in huge concentric arcs. At the front of the hall, Jimmy peered down into the orchestra pit and saw the chairs and music stands silently awaiting the arrival of the orchestra. Somewhere, off deep in the backstage area of the theater, he could hear a soprano voice singing warm-up scales. He felt an anxious anticipation of the music to come. Turning, he saw the sea of empty theater seats stretching back across the orchestra level to the tiered layers of boxes and balconies, which formed more concentric curves up and away from the stage. He stood there for a time, taking in the ornate splendor of the vast space.

"Where are our seats?" Jimmy asked.

"You'll be up there in the second balcony," Roscoe said, pointing. "They're excellent seats."

"And where is Mr. Felton's private box?" Jimmy asked.

"The box seats are all along there. Those two tiers under the first balcony. His is that one," Roscoe said, pointing toward a stall on one corner of the arc of boxes.

"Hey, can you show it to me?" Jimmy said.

"No," Roscoe said, "there isn't time."

"Aw, come on. I've never been in a private box before."

"No, I've gotta get back."

"Which box does Mary Lou Rawlins sit in?" Jimmy asked, watching Roscoe's face.

"You sure crack a lot of jokes for a son of a bitch," Roscoe said.

"Give me a break. It'll only take a minute."

Still Roscoe hesitated.

Jimmy took a couple of steps away up the aisle, looking up at the bank of private boxes. He turned back to Roscoe and asked, "Where does Freddy sit when he comes to the opera?"

Roscoe glared at him and Jimmy stared back without blinking. "Just a peek."

Roscoe's face remained emotionless, as he shifted his eyes around. He looked back at Jimmy. "Listen, buster, if you want to stay healthy you'll remember what I said and keep your trap shut."

"We understand each other," Jimmy said.

Roscoe acquiesced. "Follow me, then. But make it snappy."

They returned to the Grand Foyer and crossed to the lighted exit sign.

"Come on, we'll take the shortcut," Roscoe said and opened the stairwell door. "Hurry up. I've got to get back to work."

Jimmy followed Roscoe into the narrow stairwell and on up the echoing iron stairs, zigzagging back and forth as they wound their way up several flights. Jimmy peered over the railing down to what must have been basement levels below, and then he looked up into the higher stories of the theater. Roscoe stopped at a door marked "First Gallery" and opened it for Jimmy.

They came out into a wide, high-ceilinged corridor that curved around the outside of the auditorium. In one direction, the corridor gave access to the grand staircase and Jimmy could see the balustrade of the gallery overlooking the Grand Foyer. In the other direction, the corridor led to the side aisles and a marble staircase leading toward the front of the auditorium against a side wall. Roscoe ushered Jimmy under a lighted sign that read "To Private Boxes" and on up the side staircase.

It appeared to Jimmy that the staircase had been laid out to separate access to the box seats from the rest of the house, keeping them exclusive. He followed on to the top of the stairs where a carpeted passageway curved along a wood-paneled wall, lined with doorways, each numbered for a separate box stall. Leading Jimmy straight across from the top of the stairs to a door labeled #8, Roscoe hurried him inside. There was a small anteroom with an area for cloaks and hats, and a heavy velvet curtain that Roscoe pulled aside to reveal the private stall. The box opened onto an impressive view of the huge stage, and Jimmy descended to the front of the stall to look out over the rows of seats on the main floor and the expanse of the great hall.

"I'll bet you can hear every word they sing from here," Jimmy said.

"You can hear perfectly from all the seats," Roscoe said. "This hall has great acoustics. It's one of the best in the world."

Jimmy turned to look about the box. He noticed that from the back corner of the stall, one could not be seen from the rest of the auditorium.

"Okay, the tour's over," Roscoe said. "I've got to get the programs distributed."

"Okay," Jimmy said. He took a last look all around the box and moved toward the door. "Boy, I've never seen one of these before. Thanks, Roscoe."

"Yeah, forget it, pal," Roscoe said, pulling closed the anteroom curtain. He escorted Jimmy out and shut the door behind them. They walked across the carpeted passageway and down the marble staircase.

"If you play your cards right and keep your nose clean, Mr. Felton will probably bring you to the opera another time. He's a very generous person to his friends."

Roscoe led the way from the bottom of the staircase across to the fire exit doorway and then back down to the Grand Foyer.

"Now, I've got stuff to do," Roscoe said. He motioned across the foyer toward the stairs where Jimmy had come in. "The street entrance is that direction if you're going to wait for Eric out front."

"Yes, I remember," Jimmy said. "Thanks again, Roscoe."

They parted and walked away from each other in different directions across the Grand Foyer.

Jimmy stood on the sidewalk near the front of the theater smoking a cigarette while he kept an eye out for Eric. It was dark now and the street was full of the headlamps of passing traffic. People passed by on the sidewalk under the streetlights. Jimmy checked his watch. It was 6:55. Still too early for the crowd to be arriving for the performance. None of the pedestrians paused to enter the theater. Jimmy put out his cigarette and was contemplating another, when a taxicab pulled up to the curb nearby. The cabby held the door, obscuring Jimmy's view, as a woman in a hooded opera cloak paid the fare and turned toward the theater. She was a tall, attractive colored woman in a dark blue full-length dress that showed below her black velvet cloak. Her gloved hands reached up and folded back her hood and she glanced around the theater entrance before her attention came to rest on Jimmy. It was Erica DeChez.

Jimmy's confusion must have been evident as Erica walked toward him, holding herself erect and dignified. She kept her gaze fastened on him. There was the slightest smile on her lips, but a full-fledged twinkle in her eye. She reached out her hand and said, "Jimmy, dear, I thought I'd never get here. The traffic has been just beastly."

Jimmy didn't know how to respond, but he took her hand, and, before he could think, said, "Eric, I..."

"Darling, you can call me Erica." She released Jimmy's hand, and took him by the elbow, as she turned to observe the building. "My, what a grand facade. Do show me into the lobby. I've heard it is fabulous."

Erica DeChez was beautiful and her illusion was complete. If she attracted any stares from passersby, it was because of the color of her skin, Jimmy was sure, not because she was a man wearing a dress. Jimmy took a deep breath and led off into the theater with Erica on his arm.

Erica took in the interior of the building as they slowly climbed the stairs to the Grand Foyer. She raised the hem of her gown with one hand while she gripped Jimmy's elbow with the other. Jimmy could feel a trembling in her hand. Already, the adrenaline of stage fright was coursing through Jimmy's veins and churning up his stomach.

"Roscoe's going to have a fit," Jimmy muttered out of the side of his mouth.

"Never mind. I'll handle Roscoe. Don't worry about it."

They ascended into the Grand Foyer. At the top of the stairs she exclaimed, "My, what beautiful marble work!"

Strolling across the inlaid floor, Erica surveyed the space, not gawking as Jimmy had done when he entered that room, but with the composure of a monarch overseeing her realm.

Jimmy was looking around for Roscoe. Even before Jimmy spotted him, Roscoe came scurrying across the foyer, barely able to repress his urge to break into a full sprint.

"What the hell do you..."

"Hush," Erica said in a sharp whisper. "If you will calm down and treat me like a lady, you won't cause a scene. Now, if you will please show us to our seats..."

"There's no way in hell..." Roscoe shot back matching Erica's whisper.

"If you don't want every usher in this hall to know that you are Danny Felton's butt boy, you will quiet down and escort us to our seats." Erica's tone was quiet but cold as steel.

Roscoe turned to Jimmy and said under his breath, "Why, you little son of a bitch..."

"I didn't tell him. He figured it out all on his own."

"Maybe one of the other ushers would be so kind as to show us the way," Erica said turning slowly toward the grand staircase and pulling Jimmy along.

Roscoe was left standing there, all but sputtering, as Erica and

Jimmy moved toward the staircase. They were halfway to the first step when Roscoe said, "Wait," and rushed over to their side. "Let me show you up the short-cut. This way." He headed toward the fire exit.

Erica stood firm. "Usher," she called out to him.

Roscoe stopped and turned. "I believe we can get there by this staircase," Erica pronounced with regal confidence and gave Roscoe a look that left no room for questions.

Roscoe returned toward the grand staircase and led the way up. At the level of the first gallery, another uniformed usher turned to stare at the threesome as they came onto the landing.

"It's okay, Barton," Roscoe said. "I'm showing these folks up to the second balcony."

Erica slowed her pace and nudged Jimmy toward the balustrade. Still holding herself tall, she peered over into the Grand Foyer as they moved along.

"Come on, folks, we haven't got all day," Roscoe said.

Barton stared after them. Jimmy was certain it was the fact that they appeared to be a white man together with a black woman that held Barton's attention. Eric was supremely confident and Erica's guise was perfect.

When they reached the second gallery, Erica again approached the balustrade and looked out at the chandeliers.

"Wouldn't I love to have a pair of earrings like that," she said in Jimmy's ear. He noticed the cluster of pearls with a dangling strand that hung from her earlobe.

They reached the second balcony and Roscoe paused at one of the doorways. "I'll need to have your ticket stubs," he said. Jimmy took out the balcony tickets and handed them over. Roscoe tore off the stubs and returned the tickets to Jimmy along with two opera programs from a stack by the entrance. Then he opened the door to the auditorium for Erica and Jimmy to pass through into the darkened interior. Jimmy removed his silk hat.

Roscoe ushered them down the aisle beneath the overhanging tier of the top balcony, past the empty rows of seats, toward the front. As they emerged from beneath the upper tier, their view of the dim, cavernous hall opened out to reveal the whole sweep of the ornate ceiling and down to the immense stage with its glittering gold curtain.

Erica gasped and paused for a moment to drink in the panorama. "Oh, my, what a gorgeous theater."

Roscoe waited in the aisle at the front row of the balcony, indicating their places. As they passed by him making their way into the row of seats, Roscoe said, "Now, you two stay put here. I don't want any trouble." He turned and walked up the aisle.

Before taking her seat, Erica said, "Jimmy, darling, would you help me remove my cloak, please." Jimmy held the back of the black velvet cape as Erica slipped out and turned to reveal several strands of white pearls that stood out against the dark skin of her neck and the dark blue satin at the neckline of her gown.

"You look beautiful this evening," Jimmy said.

"Oh, thank you, sugar," Erica said as she sat down. "I was afraid you'd be angry."

"No, I couldn't be angry with you, baby," Jimmy said leaning in close as he took his seat beside her. He caught the scent of an expensive perfume. "But I am surprised not to see you in your white tie and tails. What happened?"

"Oh, I ran into Anabella along the way and told her I was going to the opera. She started in about all the beautiful gowns I would see on the ladies in the audience, and before I knew it, she had me convinced that I had to dress up for the occasion. I think we did a pretty good job, don't you? This is her dress."

"Well, it's stunning on you. Here's your program." Jimmy held his top hat and looked around wondering where he could set it down.

"You can collapse your hat and stow it in the rack under your seat," Erica said. Jimmy collapsed the hat and standing up, he was surprised to find that Erica was correct. He settled back into the chair and scanned the introduction in the program before looking up.

There in the distance before them, behind that golden curtain, awaited all the best that European history and culture had to offer—an ancient Greek story sung in Italian poetry with music by a German composer from the 18th century. They leaned forward and looked out over the ocean of the auditorium to the distant shore of the stage. It was as wide as the Atlantic separating America from Europe, and Jimmy felt the intimidation of every inch of that distance, being not only an American but a middle-class Westerner as well. And to Erica it must have seemed an even greater gulf, deeper and wider by far, than the Mediterranean Sea separating Africa from Europe. But to her the gulf was not one of cultural inferiority, as it was for Jimmy, but of an ocean of racial prejudice, for Eric Halsey already understood the rich and profound secrets that Africa had to offer the European World.

Jimmy began perusing the program. "Hey," he said, "it's just like Felton said, all the principal roles are sung by women."

"Yes," Erica replied with a laugh, "back in the old days in Italy they would have had castrati playing all these lead parts, and wearing dresses for the female roles. Nowadays, Orpheus is a trouser role, sung by a woman in pants."

"Felton mentioned that. Interesting reversal," Jimmy said.

Erica surveyed the hall. "Well, we sure got here early enough. There isn't a soul here."

Jimmy looked up from his program and glanced around. Across the second balcony all the seats were empty. On the far side of the balcony an exit sign caught his eye and he calculated that it led down the same stairwell that Roscoe had used earlier to show him to the box seats.

Erica peered up around behind them, toward the top balcony.

"Well, it's not quite up in nigger heaven," she said.

"You've got the heaven part right, anyway," Jimmy said, peering down from the perilous height, over the balcony's front railing. Erica looked down too.

"That must be the first balcony," she said, surveying the lower auditorium. "Where are the box seats? I thought we'd be able to see them from this high up."

"They're just under the first balcony. Way up front there on the sides you can just make out the ones closest to the stage. I talked Roscoe into showing me Danny Felton's box, since I got here so early."

"Oh, really?" Erica said. "So you know where it's located?"

"It's just beneath that section of the first balcony," Jimmy said pointing.

Erica was quiet for a moment studying the hall. "You know, I still have my ticket for the box seat," she said, turning to look at Jimmy. She paused, and then added, "Won't you show it to me?"

"You're not afraid we'll get caught?" Jimmy asked.

"Afraid? I'm terrified. But I've gone so far as to put on a dress for the occasion. Why not go all the way? After all, this is a performance. Just as surely as the opera singers are performing, so are you and I, jazz boy. And I think we're up to the task."

"You know, Erica, the private box has a little anteroom, hidden behind a curtain. No one would know we were there if we stayed back until the lights go down."

"Really?"

"And there are seats in the back corner of the box, where no one from the auditorium could see us, even during the performance."

"Oh, let's do it. Look there's no one in the hall yet."

Jimmy stared at Erica for a moment. "No wonder I'm so fascinated by you."

Erica said, "Let's." Her eyes sparkled with mischief.

He took a deep breath and said, "Okay. I'm game if you are."

"Well, what can they do besides throw us out?" Erica said, rising to her feet. "Here, help me with my cape. I'll even wear the hood, so they will be less likely to see my black face."

Jimmy helped her with the cape. "Over on the far side of the balcony there is an exit sign. I'll bet you anything that's the same stairway that Roscoe used to show me to Felton's box earlier." He retrieved his silk hat. "Come on. Follow me."

They crossed the balcony to the exit sign and entered the iron stairwell. Jimmy was sure it was the right one. They descended as quietly as they could on the echoing stairs to the door marked "First Gallery."

Jimmy paused and whispered to Erica, "There is a marble staircase to the right of this door. All we need to do is go up that one flight and Felton's box is just across from the top of the staircase. Number eight. I'll lead the way."

He opened the door a crack and peeked out. There was no one around, and Jimmy slipped out motioning for Erica to follow.

Jimmy dashed across the hallway, keeping close to the side wall. He passed beneath the lighted sign that read "To Private Boxes," and trotted on up the staircase. He expected Erica to be right behind him. But Jimmy couldn't hear anyone following him. In a panic, he turned back to look behind him.

On the floor below, Jimmy saw Erica strolling in her dignified manner toward the staircase. She held her head up proudly and took in the splendor of the marble lobby as she passed. For a moment Jimmy saw the same stately presence that came on stage in that white beaded gown at Pluto's. She looked positively regal. Erica DeChez was in her element. It went unspoken, but it was clear to Jimmy that there was a contest of wills at play in Erica's refusal to be hurried. Jimmy began to feel ashamed of his furtive scampering along. In that moment, he understood that what attracted him to Eric was that dignity and confidence. It was a self-assuredness that was the product of fully accepting himself, and it was a quality that Jimmy both envied and hoped to emulate.

All at once the usher named Barton appeared from around the corner. The hooded woman took him by surprise.

"Oh, hello, miss," he said, "may I help you find your seat?"

Erica paused at the bottom step and turned. "No, thank you, I know the way."

Barton stopped in his tracks. He was speechless. Erica turned and began to climb the marble staircase.

"Those are all box seats on that level." Barton found his tongue.

"Yes, I'm holding a ticket for a box seat," Erica said, turning.

"I'm sorry, but all the box seats are filled. We still have good seats in the second balcony." He paused. "Wait a minute, didn't I see Roscoe showing you to your seats up there?"

"Yes, I believe there was a mistake. I have a ticket for a box seat for this evening's performance." Erica turned away and continued to climb the stairs.

"I'll have to ask you to show me your ticket, miss," Barton said, approaching her. Erica stood her ground on the third step, but she turned to face the usher. She folded back the hood of her opera cloak and opened the front of the cape to show off the strands of pearls. She took out the ticket from inside her cloak and held it out to the usher. Jimmy descended the stairs to stand behind her.

Barton approached, reached up to take the ticket, and examined it. "I'm sorry. There must have been a mix up. We can seat you on the second balcony."

Jimmy fumbled in his breast pocket and took out his box seat ticket. A large man in a tuxedo appeared from the direction of the grand staircase. He was the tall, stocky fellow whom Jimmy had seen in the Grand Foyer earlier, and he looked like he knew how to handle himself.

"What seems to be the trouble here, Barton?"

"I would like to speak with the manager," Erica said, descending to the foot of the stairs.

The large man eyed Erica with curiosity. "I am the manager."

"I wish to be seated where my ticket says I am to be seated, and this usher refuses to accommodate me."

Barton handed the ticket to the large man in the tuxedo and they exchanged glances. The manager studied the ticket and looked over at Erica, then up to Jimmy. He descended holding up his ticket and said, "I have a ticket to the same box. We are together."

"I know who has this private box," the manager said, "and I know he doesn't want any niggers sitting there."

"I have come to see the opera performance this evening and I will sit in the seat for which I hold a ticket," Erica insisted.

"Where did you get these tickets?" the manager said turning

on Erica with rising anger. "They were stolen, weren't they?"

"Mr. Danny Felton gave me these tickets personally," Jimmy said, stepping forward. "He told me to bring a guest of my choice."

"Where did you come by these tickets?" The manager's voice was more forceful. He began making little shoving motions against Erica's shoulders. "You stole these tickets, didn't you?"

"Leave her alone. Nobody stole these tickets," Jimmy insisted.

"Monsieur, my friend here is telling you the truth. These tickets were a gift from Mr. Felton."

Another usher hurried from the gallery accompanied by Roscoe.

"I have a gift for you, you mouthy bitch," the manager said, and he slapped Erica hard across the cheek, knocking her backwards. She stumbled and caught her balance by reaching out her gloved hand for the wall. Her cloak fell off, and her wig was knocked askew.

"Jesus Christ, it's a man in a dress!" the manager cried, taking a step backwards.

"Damn it! Leave her alone!" Jimmy cried. "Danny Felton gave me these tickets."

The manager pushed Jimmy to one side and said, "Come on. Let's get this…thing…out of here."

Before Erica could recover, Barton and the other usher each grabbed one of her arms. Erica looked over at Jimmy, and Jimmy rushed at the manager. But Roscoe grabbed Jimmy, pulling him away and slamming him up against the wall. Jimmy's silk hat tumbled to the floor.

"Let her go," Jimmy called. "We have tickets. We have tickets."

Roscoe covered Jimmy's mouth with one hand and held the front of his tailcoat with the other as he banged Jimmy's head against the wall. "Shut up! Shut your trap, you fool!"

"Come on, dinge, get your black ass out of here," the other usher barked as they pulled Erica toward the fire exit door.

Erica struggled and said, "Let go of me. I can walk out on my own, thank you."

The manager punched Erica in the stomach with such force that she was knocked backwards onto the floor and her wig came off, leaving her skull cap exposed.

"Let's go," the manager said to the ushers. "I don't care if we have to carry him out. Let's get moving." Eric tried to get up. The manager held the door open, while the ushers grabbed Eric by his arms and dragged him backwards into the stairwell. Then the door closed and Eric was gone.

Roscoe raised a fist in Jimmy's face. His breath burst out in harsh staccato puffs. "I ought to smash you in the puss."

He felt Roscoe's tense body pressed up against him. Jimmy was silent and didn't move. He sensed that if Roscoe waited a moment longer before hitting him, the heat of his anger would pass.

Roscoe loosened his grip and gave a little shove. Then he stepped back and said, "You're lucky you're not a dead man." He stood up straight and pulled the coat of his uniform down smooth.

"What the hell did you think..." Roscoe glared at Jimmy for a moment. Then he said, "Get the hell out of here—while you can still walk."

Jimmy stepped away from the wall and adjusted his tailcoat. He walked over to Erica's wig and cloak and picked them up. He tucked the wig into the hood of the cape and folded the garment over his arm. Then he returned and picked up his silk hat, ignoring the box seat ticket that had fluttered to the floor. He placed the hat squarely on his head, and without looking at Roscoe, he turned and walked along the gallery and down the grand staircase. His knees were shaking and he was afraid that they would give way under him, but he thought of Erica DeChez and concentrated on holding his head up and carrying himself, like her, erect and tall. He reached the bottom of the staircase, then crossed the inlaid floor of the Grand Foyer without looking back.

Outside, Jimmy walked on, keeping close to the side of the theater building. He couldn't think. His mind was numb. He saw no sign of Eric or the ushers, and he just kept walking. By the time he could collect his thoughts, he had circled the block and was back at the theater entrance. People were beginning to enter the building from the street. Jimmy turned and circled back around the building, still looking for any evidence of Eric. There wasn't a trace of him.

Jimmy felt dazed, but the cool night air fortified him. As he walked, he became aware of a salty taste in his mouth and a stinging on his lower lip. He pressed a knuckle against his lip and pulled it away. A spot of blood stained his white kid glove. He took out his handkerchief and held it to his mouth.

The only thing to do was to head back to Eric's and hope to meet up with him there. He felt the need to put some distance between himself and the scene of the disaster. Jimmy turned and crossed the street, looking for a taxi. Along the way he passed a couple of well-dressed men, somewhat tipsy, coming out of a doorway. Must be a speakeasy, Jimmy thought, and a drink would sure quiet my nerves.

As he entered the establishment, Jimmy passed the restrooms, and he decided he should use the bathroom mirror to examine the cut on his lip. It was worse than he thought. A trickle of blood ran down his chin, and spots of blood stood out on the white tie and the front of his starched shirt. Jimmy set down his silk hat and Erica's things and removed his gloves. He wet a towel at the sink and wiped away the blood from his chin. The cut was on the edge of his lower lip and it did not show except for a slight swelling. A drink would disinfect the cut and stop the bleeding, he thought. He wanted to cover up the blood on his shirt front, and he found that if he wrapped his white silk neck scarf across his throat and over the opposite shoulder, it hid the stains. He didn't care if it looked affected.

Jimmy made his way to the bar and had a quick gin. But he found his nerves were not settled after one drink so he had two more. By then he felt strong enough to hunt down a taxi.

TWENTY-EIGHT

When he got to Eric's door, Jimmy found the padlock and the door lock both fast.

In a panic, he thought that maybe Eric had returned and, not having his keys, had gone somewhere else. But where? He'd said that Jewell had an extra set of keys to his place. Maybe he was downstairs at her flat.

Jimmy went down to Jewell's door. He thought he heard voices inside and he knocked. After a few moments the door opened a crack and Jewell peered out.

"Say, Jewell, I'm Eric's friend, Jimmy. I met you at the rent party, remember? I'm trying to find Eric. Have you seen him?"

"No, he isn't here."

"Let him in," said a voice behind her. She hesitated and then opened the door.

Eric sat slumped back in an upholstered chair across the room. He was dressed in corduroy trousers and a blue jersey pullover, and he held an ice pack against his eye.

"Oh, God," Jimmy said, hovering in the doorway.

Jewell took his arm and pulled him inside. "Don't just stand there in the doorway like a gaping fool," she said and slammed the door behind him. It was steamy and warm in the room and the smell of cooking filled the air.

"I'll go fetch some more ice. We're almost out." Jewell said, taking her coat from the rack by the door. "Is there anything else you want?"

"You have any booze?" Eric asked.

"No, we drank it all last night."

Eric reached into his pocket and groaned. He pulled out a wad of bills and peeled off a few.

"Here, pick up anything you can find."

Jewell finished buttoning her coat and came over and took the cash. "Anything else?"

"Naw, thanks," Eric said. He and Jewell looked at each other for a moment, and he added, "Don't worry, baby. I'll still be here when you get back."

Jewell shot a look at Jimmy, then went to the door and left them alone. A wind came up outside and the windows rattled.

Jimmy went to the chair where Eric sat and sank down on his knees in front of him. "Oh, Eric…I'm sorry." Jimmy fought back the tears, but still his voice choked. He reached out and placed his hand on Eric's knee. "Oh, God, this is all my fault." The words stuck in his throat.

Eric raised his head a bit, took the ice pack away from his face so he could see. "Aw, Jimmy, Jimmy." He reached out his other hand and placed it on top of Jimmy's. Eric's face was bruised and puffy, and he had a terrific shiner on his right eye. "There's no one to blame," he said. "It isn't your fault the world is the way it is." He noticed the blood on Jimmy's shirt. "Are you hurt? Did they beat you up too?"

"No, it's nothing," Jimmy said. "It's just a little cut on my lip."

"That should be my blood on your collar, not yours," Eric said. He let out a little chuckle, and recited:

"Is thy collar held closed by a ruby stud,
Or is thy silken shirt graced with a drop of my blood?"

Jimmy buried his head in Eric's lap and tried to stifle his tears. "The opera didn't have such a happy ending after all, did it?"

Eric said and laughed again. "I always imagined that when I went to the opera, I would sit in the best seats. Well, when I go to Paris, things are going to be different."

Jimmy looked up and said, "I hope I can help you get there, Eric."

Eric reached out his hand to touch Jimmy's face and started to lean forward. Then he groaned and fell back against the chair. He put the ice pack back up to his face and sighed. They were silent a moment.

"Say, could you do something for me?"

"How can I help?"

"Take this towel and put some more ice in it?"

In the kitchen, Jimmy found an ice pick on the counter and chipped some ice from the depleted block in Jewell's ice box. Returning, he handed the ice pack to Eric.

"Thanks," Eric said. "Hey, isn't there some gin left in that bottle in my room?"

"No, we finished it off this afternoon, remember?"

Eric adjusted the ice pack on his eye.

"But," Jimmy said, "I've got a little left in a bottle in my suitcase. I'll run up and get it. Stay put."

"I don't think I could move if I wanted to. I feel like one of the dead. I ache all over."

Jimmy returned shortly with the gin bottle.

"You want a glass?" he asked.

"Naw, the bottle is more direct." Eric took the bottle and drank. "You want some?"

"No, you drink it. I stopped at a speak on the way here. I had three drinks and could hardly even feel it."

Eric drank again, then put down the bottle, and adjusted the ice pack.

Jimmy pulled up a chair next to Eric. There was a long silence before Jimmy spoke. "Tell me what happened."

"Nothing really…There isn't much to tell. They dragged me down the stairwell and roughed me up a bit. The worst of it was they kicked me in the balls. I thought I was going to join the castrati. My stomach still aches." He took another drink.

"Oh, God, Eric, I—"

"Never mind, it doesn't matter. Society eventually emasculates everyone." He took another swig of gin. "They start by cutting off part of your cock. Then, if you're a he-man, they cut you off from your feelings by telling you that you have to behave like a refined gentleman. And if you're a pansy, they try to cut you off from your emotions by telling you that you can't show your feelings. They cut you off from knowing who you really are, deep down inside, because you are so busy measuring up to what they say a man ought to be."

He readjusted the ice pack.

"Then later, they cut you off from the rest of society because your skin isn't the right color, and they use that as an excuse to cut you off from a good education, to cut you off from financial opportunities, to cut you off from the body politic. Society tries to turn us all into castrati."

He paused. "Well, at least they can't accuse me of raping their women. If I wore pants instead of a dress, they would probably try to pin that one on me too. I guess, along with Erica, I've lost my balls already."

"No, don't say that," Jimmy said. "Erica DeChez is braver than any man I know."

Eric glanced at Jimmy and looked away. "I don't know," he said and took another swig from the bottle. He was silent a moment. Then he continued.

"Well, anyway, they threw me out a back exit and left me lying there on the sidewalk. After a while I was able to stand up and make my way to an alley. There was a colored dishwasher out smoking at the back door of a restaurant. He wasn't any too anxious to help out a man in a dress, but when he realized I was hurt, he took me inside. He cleaned me up the best he could and helped me get a cab back here."

"Eric, I'm sorry. I should never have suggested going to the opera."

"No. Don't apologize. I had to go and push it." Eric paused and took another drink. "But there's more I have to tell you about."

"What do you mean?"

Eric took a deep breath. "Do you trust me?"

"Hell, yes. You're the one person here that I can trust."

"Listen. I've got to confess something. I've been lying to you."

"What?" Jimmy said. "How? How do you mean?"

"I've been lying about myself all along. I didn't graduate from Fisk. I never even went to college. I spent some time in Memphis playing jazz and I passed through Nashville on a trip to Atlanta, once. But that's as close as I ever got to Fisk University. My mama wanted me to go there, 'cause she graduated from Fisk. But I just didn't have it in me. All I ever wanted to do was play music."

"I don't give a damn about your education. It doesn't matter to me if you've been to college or not."

"But I've always felt like I should have gone. I should have taken advantage of the opportunity."

"But you've educated yourself. You know all about the castrati, and the Mogul Empire, and you're teaching yourself French. Educating yourself is a thousand times harder than having it all spoon-fed to you by a bunch of arrogant profs."

"I figured you'd think less of me."

"No. I think the world of you. I respect you even more for all the things you've done and learned by yourself. More than if you'd gone to...to Harvard."

Eric shifted his weight in the chair and groaned.

"There's something else."

"What?"

"You know how I feel about you. Believe me, I care about you, honey lamb. I never want to hurt you. Understand? But I have something else to confess." He took the ice pack down and looked straight at Jimmy. "I took your money."

Jimmy looked back at Eric, bewildered.

"Let me explain. That first night you came to my room, I got up in the middle of the night and went through your pockets. I didn't mean any harm. I just had to know that you were who you said you were. In the process, I noticed your belt and looked it over and discovered the cash. But I didn't take it that night." He repositioned the ice on his eye.

"Remember I sent you home in that cab on Sunday night because of some business? Well, the business that night was that I got together with a bunch of fellas and we decided to go in with the Irish gang to get Pluto's out of Felton's control. An Irish gang member named O'Halloran wanted five grand from us to prove our loyalty and to pay the cops to look the other way. Ten of us agreed to put in five hundred each. I needed a couple hundred bucks more to get in, but I didn't have it. So I decided I'd borrow your two hundred. I took it Monday night, when you were asleep. I thought I could replace it before you knew it was gone." He smiled but Jimmy could see it was a sad smile.

"See, you've got to understand how things started out at Pluto's, especially if you're going to keep working there. You know it's an out-of-the-way location. It's even in a different ward of the city than the Black Belt, but it's on the edge. The clubs in the Black Belt all get their booze from Felton's gang. But Pluto's Lair has always been in the Irish gang's territory—until about a year ago."

Footsteps and voices came in from the hall outside. Eric paused to listen but the sounds moved away up the stairs.

"The way things started out at Pluto's, a bunch of us queens and faggots used to hang out at Big Joe's. When we found out about the basement room there, we started having parties and drags and dances downstairs. Well, one thing led to another and we eventually decided to open Pluto's Lair. We tried to get a bank loan and couldn't get financing from any white-owned banks. That's when the Irishmen got involved. A gang member named O'Halloran wanted to supply the booze and get a cut of the take. So they fronted us some money and we did all the work, cleaning the place up and making it look nice. We even bought that upright piano and had it tuned. But then business at Pluto's kept growing and growing and the place became so popular that Felton's gang took notice."

"I've seen the news headlines about the gang wars," Jimmy said.

"It's been going on for a while. See, Felton found out that a traction company wanted to put in a trolley line through the neighborhood where Pluto's is located. I suspect he might even have helped engineer the decision. That would mean a lot more people could get to the neighborhood and there'd be a lot more business for Pluto's. Felton decided he wanted to annex the neighborhood and take over Pluto's and then develop a vice resort across the street."

The radiator began to hiss.

"Well, there were a lot of threats and fighting and a couple of Irish fellas got killed, and finally, Felton took over and things quieted down. Then, a few weeks ago, I think Felton got suspicious of me and decided he wanted me out of Pluto's, so he offered me the job at the Checker Club. I didn't want to leave Pluto's, but I didn't want to make waves, so I went along with it." He paused and sighed.

"Then this plan to throw our hats in with the Micks started brewing. My bunch agreed to act as eyes and ears for the Irishmen to keep them informed about Felton's gang. Then, like I said, they wanted proof of our loyalty—five grand. In return, they agreed to give us better quality liquor at a lower price and a better cut of Pluto's profits when they took over. That's what I meant when I talked about my ship coming in."

A clang from the radiator made them both jump. Eric settled back with a grunt.

"When you told me that Felton was going to be out of town until Friday, it sounded too good to be true. The reason I wanted to go to the opera and sit in Felton's box was to see if he would show up. I knew he rarely missed an opera. If he didn't show up, I could pass that information on, and we'd know Felton didn't have wind of our plan. Well, we blew that one, and I still don't know if Felton actually left town or if he just put out that story to throw us off."

"When he told me that," Jimmy said, "I thought it sounded odd."

"Now the plan is for the Micks to hijack the booze delivery to Pluto's early tomorrow morning. But this morning one of their boys turned up dead. That's why Jasper came by my place before the opera this afternoon. Jasper wanted me and Anabella to go talk things over with O'Halloran."

When Jimmy looked up with surprise, Eric gave a little laugh. "Yes, Anabella is mixed up in this. She was the first one to come up with the 500 bucks."

Jimmy let out a whistle.

"O'Halloran told us the killing was just a fight over a gambling debt and everything got smoothed over. Nothing to do with Felton's gang. So we're right on track. Tomorrow night should be a whole different ballgame at Pluto's."

Once again Jimmy felt like a country bumpkin. All these machinations were going on right under his nose and he knew nothing about it. At the same time he felt an intoxicating excitement at the prospect of being in the midst of such intrigues, and he was proud of Eric for his initiative and courage. Jimmy even felt proud that he himself had been able to play a small role in this scheme against Danny Felton by contributing his paltry 200. Yet he began to understand the danger to Eric and to himself. A dark apprehension took hold in the pit of his stomach.

"Eric, are you in danger?"

"No one but the Irish fellas know we're mixed up in this. They've paid off the cops so the law won't get involved. This gang is tight, and they're tough. They can beat Felton at his own game. I think they've got this thing all sewed up."

"You're a brave fellow, Eric Halsey," Jimmy said.

"Aw, hell, I don't know. This is a crazy world." Eric reached for the bottle. "Maybe we'll make it to Paris after all." He raised the bottle to Jimmy in a toast. He took a drink and held it out to Jimmy.

"Okay, I'll have a swig for Paris." He raised the bottle.

"Now, look, Jimmy, I've got to ask you something."

"Anything," Jimmy said, passing the bottle back to Eric.

"I think I'd better stay down here tonight. There's an ice box and a cookstove. Jewell will look after me. I think she'd feel better if you were gone when she gets back. Maybe you better head back upstairs to my place."

On the heels of his growing admiration for Eric, Jimmy felt crushed. "Oh," he said trying to hide his disappointment. But he saw the situation and he didn't want to cause any trouble. "All right...I...I understand."

Eric saw the disappointment and reluctance on Jimmy's face. "Honest, don't take it personally. It's just that Jewell is mixed up in this deal, too. She put up her own 500. That's why she threw the rent party. I feel like I owe it to her to keep her company." Eric reached out and took Jimmy's hand to reassure him. "We'll get together tomorrow. And we'll play together at Pluto's tomorrow night—to celebrate the takeover by the new Irish management."

As Jimmy was leaving Jewell's apartment, she came in the front door carrying a package. Their eyes met but neither of them spoke or made a greeting. Jewell's face was expressionless but she held Jimmy's gaze a moment. He sensed that she had won some victory and he averted his eyes and went on up the stairs.

TWENTY-NINE

Jimmy woke up in Eric's bed alone.

It was noon by Eric's alarm clock. He felt rested, but a cloud of foreboding still hung over him. He looked around the room and saw his rented evening clothes on a hanger on the closet door. The drops of blood stood out on the front of the shirt. He ran his tongue over the cut on his lip and found that it was barely swollen now. It was only then that he remembered Eric's story about the history of Pluto's Lair. The vague apprehension became a specific dread. A dread named Danny Felton.

As he lay in bed brooding, there was a knock at the door. He flinched and froze, listening. Then he heard a familiar voice. "Jimmy, are you there? It's Eric."

He got up and stood behind the door to hide his nakedness as he let Eric in. Eric closed the door and took Jimmy in his arms. They held each other close. Eric's hands moved over the smooth skin of Jimmy's back and down over the mounds of his buttocks.

"Good morning, jazz boy," Eric said.

"Hi," Jimmy said and shivered with cold.

"Here, hop back in bed," Eric said, holding up the covers. Jimmy wrapped himself back into the bed and leaned on one elbow. Eric sat down on the bed. He was still dressed in the same trousers and pullover, but his face was not so puffy and swollen. He looked well-rested.

"Your face looks better," Jimmy said. "How do you feel?"

"A lot better," Eric said. "We've got to get our glad rags back to the tailor. Then let's go have a bite to eat."

"I'm with you," Jimmy said. "I don't have any plans."

"I've just got to get cleaned up," Eric said. "You coming?" Eric handed him a robe.

While Eric ran a hot bath, Jimmy splashed cold water on his face and went back to dress.

In Eric's room, Jimmy put on his daywear. He was searching through the pockets of his suit coat when he found Danny Felton's card with the name of the hotel booking agent. "Robert Newhall. Columbia Hotel."

Jimmy tapped the card against his thumbnail as he considered.

After hearing Eric's story last night, he no longer knew what to think about Danny Felton. Freddy, the prostitute, seemed to have a trustworthy business arrangement with him. So did Roscoe. And Roscoe had said that Felton was generous with his friends. Felton seemed to like Jimmy—or at least his music. And Felton had come through with the opera tickets. He allowed Jimmy to drive his bargain at their hotel luncheon. And Jimmy had, after all, paid his price.

But Jimmy didn't trust Felton. Was Felton just using him as a pawn in a bigger game? If Jimmy never saw Felton again that would suit him fine.

Jimmy was curious about contacting Robert Newhall. What harm could it do? Besides, he might learn something more about Felton. Jimmy decided that he was going to at least telephone Newhall. But then that might involve the band. Did Jimmy honestly want to get back in touch with them? Well, even if Newhall did have something for the band, Jimmy didn't have to pass the tip along. Right now Jimmy was more concerned with Danny Felton than Diggs Monroe. So what if it turned out that he could do a good turn for the band? What harm could that do? Besides the prospect of going back in with the band was out of the question anyway.

Jimmy dug into his suitcase and found the other photo postcard in case Newhall wanted to see what the band looked like. He studied the photo for a moment with a pang of regret, then slipped it into the breast pocket of his suit and put the band out of his mind.

He sat down and started to play Eric's piano. He was trying to piece together the song Eric had played for him about going to see the doctor, when Eric came in.

"I heard you playing."

"Hey, teach me this tune."

"Sure. I'll teach you. After lunch though, I'm starved. And we've got to drop our duds off."

He dressed quickly.

"Shall we make tracks?"

They packed up the evening clothes and headed off. Jimmy told Eric he needed to use a telephone.

"There's one at the diner. Why? What's up?"

Jimmy explained about Robert Newhall at the Columbia Hotel.

"I thought you were through with your band."

"I am. I just want to check this fellow out. Think of it as reconnaissance on Danny Felton. I've just got to find out what kind of dealings Felton has with him. Maybe it will give you some information about what Felton is up to."

Eric looked at Jimmy and smiled. "Let me know what you find out."

Jimmy smiled back. They were now co-conspirators.

After they left the tailor shop, they went to Florence's diner. On the way, walking along an empty side street, Eric mentioned that Florence also put in 500 with the Irishmen. Jimmy remembered Eric going into the back room with her the morning they stopped in for breakfast. The world was beginning to take on a whole new shape in Jimmy's mind. What other unseen forces were at work that he hadn't imagined?

After taking their order, Florence showed Jimmy into the back room to use the phone. Jimmy told Newhall's secretary that Danny Felton had referred him. She said Newhall was in a meeting and Jimmy should call back in an hour.

After lunch Jimmy called back and the secretary put him through. He did his best to talk fast and he kept emphasizing that Danny Felton was recommending the band. Mr. Newhall sounded reluctant, but on Jimmy's insistence, he agreed to meet briefly around 4.

Back at Eric's, Jimmy reminded him about the doctor song. They sat down at the piano and Eric had Jimmy play the song from the sheet music, and then Eric played his own version. Jimmy came back with an improvised rendition of his own. Then they played the tune together as Eric sang the lyrics in Erica's voice.

"I went to see the doctor today
To see what he had to say.
Something must be wrong,
I'm worried all day long."

The music was a pleasing distraction, but Jimmy kept one anxious eye on the clock, and before long it was time for him to find a taxi to Newhall's office.

At a quarter to 4, Jimmy made his way from the lobby of the Columbia Hotel to the second floor. The office was busy with people coming and going and phones ringing. It was a while before Jimmy could catch the receptionist's attention between phone calls. When he gave the secretary his name and told her Mr. Newhall was expecting him, she replied, "Along with the rest of Chicago. Take a seat and I will let Mr. Newhall know you are here."

Jimmy sat down among an unusual group he assumed were other entertainers waiting for an audience. After a while, the secretary called his name and indicated the door to an inner office.

Newhall was on the phone. He smiled, gestured to a chair, then returned to his conversation. Listening to Newhall talk, Jimmy gathered that "Marty's band" was not having much luck even though Newhall was "wild about the band's style." Newhall hung up and introduced himself.

Jimmy repeated that Danny Felton had sent him and that the Diggs Monroe Jazz Orchestra had recently played the Grand Ballroom at the Redfield Hotel. This seemed to impress Newhall, who agreed the Grand Ballroom was a fine venue. "What other experience have you had in town?"

Jimmy mentioned the Gold Coast tea dance.

"Oh, you played for that affair?" Newhall sounded impressed. "I heard about that. Your band received a pretty penny for that little bit of work. Two thousand dollars for one afternoon of playing music is not bad. Strictly non-union." He laughed. "However, I can't offer you anything that pays quite that handsomely."

So Felton was telling the truth, Jimmy thought. Diggs had pulled one over on the band. That bastard.

Then Newhall cleared his throat and said, "You understand, of course, that I know Mr. Felton's name, seeing as how he is such an important member of the business community, but I don't know him personally."

"Oh. He didn't tell you I was coming to see you?" Jimmy said.

"Why, no," Newhall said. "I've never spoken with the man."
At that moment he was interrupted by the phone.

Things were not going the way Jimmy had expected. What was Felton up to?

Newhall dispatched the call and returned his attention to Jimmy. "Now, what kind of music does your band play?"

Jimmy wasn't sure how he should answer the question and found himself saying that they were very versatile and could play any kind of music that was needed. Then he added that they liked hot jazz.

"How big is the orchestra? Do you have a violin section?" Newhall asked.

Jimmy pulled out the photo and handed it to Mr. Newhall as he described the band. Newhall studied the photo and said, "A respectable looking group. Oh, so you play the piano? Say, we need a solo piano player for a reception this evening. I realize this is short notice, but I just got the call this afternoon."

Tonight. Pluto's Lair, Jimmy thought. "Oh, I'm sorry. I'm booked for the evening."

"Well, let me see what else is coming up," Newhall said, flipping through a calendar book on his desk. "Oh, now here is something. The Paulson Hotel needs a dance band for one night a week from tomorrow. They are holding auditions next Monday afternoon. Does that sound like something your band would be interested in?"

"Why, yes, indeed," Jimmy said, trying to imagine how he might use the opportunity to his advantage with the band.

"Here, I'll write down the particulars." Newhall wrote a name and address on a piece of letterhead and handed it to Jimmy. "Tell them I sent you, and if they decide they want your band, get back with me right away. I'll make all the rest of the arrangements."

"Of course," Jimmy said. "Thank you. Thank you very much."

"Well, there certainly is a great deal of talent in this city," Newhall said in a tone that indicated he was ready to wrap things up. "I'm sorry we don't have a need for your band here at the Columbia Hotel right now, but give me your telephone number and we will contact you if something else comes up."

Jimmy stammered that he did not, as yet, have a contact telephone since he was still getting settled, but he could ring Newhall up in the next day or so with a phone number.

"Yes, do that. You can leave the number with Mildred at the front desk." He stood up and extended his hand. "Nice to meet you, Mr. Harper."

Feeling defeated, Jimmy stood and shook his hand. He started to leave and got as far as the door. With his hand on the doorknob, Jimmy paused. Had Felton failed to live up to his word?

Jimmy turned back to Newhall and asked, "You're sure Mr. Felton hasn't contacted you—about the Diggs Monroe Orchestra?"

A puzzled expression came over Newhall's face. "No," he replied. "As I said, I've never met the gentleman. Good-bye now."

On his way down to the lobby, Jimmy hoped that Felton had forgotten to call Newhall or maybe he was too busy. After all, he said he was going out of town, and he was a busy man. But they had made a deal. Jimmy had paid his price. Surely, the bastard hadn't stiffed him. But what could he do if Felton didn't hold up his end of the bargain? Nothing.

Again, Jimmy felt the foreboding. He would be better off never to lay eyes on Danny Felton again. He remembered the hypodermic syringe and Herman holding the gun. Maybe he was lucky to have gotten off as easy as he did.

Jimmy thought of Diggs and Newhall's mention of the two grand for the Gold Coast tea dance. Boy, if the other fellows in the band found out about that, they'd have a thing or two to say to Diggs. Maybe he could use that information to get some money out of Diggs and then buy passage to Paris for Eric and himself. Getting out of town as fast as possible was looking more and more like the best course of action. He figured Diggs would be good for at least 500.

Jimmy wondered how much money it would take to book passage to Paris. Maybe they could manage the fare on a tramp steamer. Jimmy decided to use the audition at the Paulson Hotel as an excuse to get back in touch with Diggs and see what kind of deal he could work out.

In the lobby, Jimmy located a public telephone booth. He closed the door and fumbled through the book for the number of the Firestone Hotel. The clerk told him that Diggs had checked out. Did the clerk know where Mr. Monroe had moved to? No, he said, but Mr. Monroe had left a contact number. Jimmy used one of the hotel notepads in the phone booth to write it down.

So Diggs had moved on. On to where? Jimmy needed time to think this through. Maybe Eric could advise him. He didn't want to phone Diggs without having a number where Diggs could call him back. Maybe Jewell had a phone. Or maybe he could arrange for Florence to take a message at the diner. He decided to try calling Diggs later.

As he left the hotel, Jimmy was stopped by a picture of the Eiffel Tower in the window of a travel agency in a corner of the lobby. He went in and got some prices on cruise lines as well as some inexpensive freighters. The fare seemed within reach. Maybe he and Eric could get out of Chicago and on to the City of Light after all.

On his way home to Eric's, he realized it was Thursday. He remembered the cab ride to Miss Eva's with the boys in the band the Thursday night before. My God, that was only a week ago. I've been in Chicago a week and it seems like a lifetime, he thought.

He remembered talking to Freddy at the brothel, and Freddy saying he worked at Miss Eva's every Thursday night. The thought of Freddy kindled a fire deep inside him. "Come see me," Freddy had said. Jimmy considered. If he was not working with Eric at Pluto's tonight, would he entertain the prospect of going to Miss Eva's to seek Freddy out?

"Everyone plays Danny Felton's vice game," Freddy had said. Jimmy let the temptation linger for a moment longer and then put it out of his mind.

THIRTY

Eric was lying on his bed reading a book and eating an orange. A half-filled glass of gin sat beside him on the night stand. He had one hell of a shiner on one eye, but his face looked a lot better than the night before.

"Eric, I have a plan," Jimmy said. "I think we should be able to get out of here by the middle of next week." He proceeded to tell Eric about Diggs and the 2000 dollars and how he figured on getting some of that money—which, Jimmy added, he had a right to after all.

"Now, hold on," Eric said. "Slow down a minute."

"And I saw a travel agent at the Columbia Hotel and got some prices on passage to Paris," Jimmy continued. "I think we can swing this thing."

"So you're going to be my bright shining hero and take me away from this vale of tears?"

"If you want me to be." Jimmy sat down on the bed.

"I would let you. But you know, after a few months I can sell my stake in Pluto's Lair and we can go to Paris first class. With money to burn. I could set up a club and who knows what else."

Jimmy felt disappointed that he might not be able to play the rescuer, but Eric seemed to know the ropes and his idea sounded more practical. Jimmy knew his own plan was full of risk.

"What did you find out about Felton?"

"Well, Felton was telling the truth about the two grand. Newhall confirmed it. Boy, he sure put one over on us there. But, you know, Newhall says he's never talked with Felton. Never even met him. I don't get it."

"You don't?" Eric said and looked at Jimmy. "Felton double-crossed you."

Jimmy didn't want to admit it to himself, and he sat there for a moment and said nothing. That Felton was duping him, Jimmy had suspected, but to hear another voice saying the words, struck the point home. Eric was right.

Jimmy lay back next to Eric and stared up at the ceiling. He let out a sigh. "I know."

They were quiet.

At last, Eric leaned over and said, "I'll never double-cross you, Jimmy." Then Eric kissed him full on the lips.

"Ouch," they both cried. Each pulled back and put a hand to his mouth. They both laughed. Like battle-scarred soldiers, they had been through a skirmish together the night before. Both had been wounded and now they shared a bond.

"Well, I guess we'll have to go easy on the kissing for a while," Eric said. He stood up from the bed and picked up his empty glass from the bedside table. "I got another bottle while you were out. You want a drink?"

"Sure," Jimmy said.

"We need to start getting ready to go. I want to get to the club early. We can eat at Big Joe's when we get there." Eric found another glass and poured them each some gin. "You wear your tuxedo, too. We'll both play tonight. I want to put on a real show." He handed Jimmy a glass. "Here's to the new regime at Pluto's."

They raised their glasses and drank.

Eric set down his glass and started taking off his shoes. Jimmy slipped out of his suit coat and began removing his tie and then his shirt. Eric caught Jimmy's eye just before standing up and peeled off his pullover, exposing his smooth brown skin. Jimmy noticed that his dress shirt was soaked at the armpits from his encounter with Newhall, and he decided he needed a fresh undershirt. He stripped off the one he was wearing, and when he looked up, he saw that Eric was watching him. Eric held Jimmy's eye and unfastened his trousers then removed the last of his clothing. Jimmy did the same.

He remembered thinking of Freddy in the taxi on the way back to Eric's. The embers of that fire were rekindled and rose up in Jimmy's blood. But Jimmy's passion and affection was for Eric, this man who now stood before him beckoning with his eyes. Not for some phantom shade from Jimmy's memory of the brothel.

Standing there next to the bed, their hands began to touch and explore. Their faces were so close that they could each feel the other's breath.

"I guess we can get along without kissing," Eric said.

"Let's see your tongue," Jimmy said, and he began to lick Eric's tongue, like a hummingbird hovering near a flower. He continued licking Eric's lips, then his swollen eye lid, and the other bruises on his face. Eric's dark hands moved over Jimmy's skin. Jimmy's tongue began to wander along Eric's limbs.

They lowered onto the bed, their limbs entwining.

They had both grown erect and Eric said, "Let's see your member." He reached down and took Jimmy's cock in his hand and stroked the head.

"And your member," Jimmy said. He rolled Eric onto his back and straddled his trunk as he took hold of Eric's.

"Re-member," Eric said and laughed, taking both the stems together in his hand like a bouquet of exotic blooms.

Jimmy took hold, also, and together they began to move. Each watched the other's face watching him.

A pleasure blossomed between them until their semen flowed like milky sap.

They were silent for a long time, waiting for their breathing to return to normal. Little shudders, like breezes shivering foliage, passed through their bodies.

Then they embraced, folding closed into each other's arms,

and rested in that garden of intimacy, reluctant to let it go.

"*La petite mort*," Eric said, after a time.

"What?" Jimmy asked.

"That's what the French call it. The little death. That's what they call the orgasm."

They were quiet again for a while. Then Eric adjusted his weight. They rolled apart. Jimmy raised up on one elbow and stroked Eric's hair.

They smiled into each other's eyes.

"Well, my nuts are still working," Eric said, and laughed, pulling himself into a sitting position on the edge of the bed. He turned and reached out to stroke Jimmy's face. "We better clean up and get dressed. We've got a show to do."

Before they left, Eric rifled through the stacks of music on top of the piano and pulled out an old songbook. Leafing through it, Eric said, "I better take some Irish music for the occasion. Here. 'Danny Boy.' Now that's ironic." He laughed and closed the book. "Oh, let's take 'U Need Some Lovin'. We'll play a doctor duet."

THIRTY-ONE

While riding to Pluto's Lair, Jimmy remembered Freddy again and entertaining the thought of a sexual encounter. The idea seemed absurd now. The relationship he shared with Eric was so much more than a simple financial transaction with Freddy. Or the complicated financial arrangement with Danny Felton. They had gone through so much together. More than just sexual favors, they had exchanged a kind of closeness, even a kind of love. The glow of their recent intimacy lingered, and Jimmy felt that an abiding connection with Eric had taken root in his soul.

They arrived at Big Joe's around 7 and went into the cafe. The place was nearly empty except for a few couples sitting here and there around the room. They fell silent when Eric came in. Big Joe was wiping down the counter. Eric led Jimmy to a table at the back.

"Wait here a minute," Eric said to Jimmy and went to the counter and spoke with Joe. Jimmy took a seat and Eric was back in a minute.

"Everything's jake," he said and sat, looking calm, as he surveyed the room, but Jimmy could feel a tension in the air.

Big Joe came around with two glasses of water. Eric introduced them, and Jimmy shook Joe's big thick hand.

"You must have heard that Jimmy's going to be playing piano downstairs starting next week."

"Yeah, so they say," Big Joe said and smiled at Jimmy. "I'll try to make it down to catch your act." He took their orders and left.

A few more patrons came in while they ate in silence. Eric kept an eye on each person who entered. When they were finished eating, Eric paid the bill and they left.

As they approached the basement stairwell, Eric nodded, directing Jimmy's attention to a small panel truck and a car parked nearby. As they went down the stairway, he told Jimmy that those vehicles belonged to the Irish gang. They knocked and the doorman admitted them.

Pluto's was just getting ready to open. Eric and Jimmy walked through the maroon curtains and surveyed the room from the top of the short stairway. Roscoe and another fellow were setting up the bar, and waiters were lowering the chairs down onto the floor and wiping off the tabletops. Roscoe stared at Eric and Jimmy as they came down the stairs.

Eric walked in, erect and self-possessed, and in an affable, off-hand manner greeted Roscoe. Without stopping, he went to the upright. Jimmy followed close behind.

"Jimmy, you take this sheet music and play here," Eric said. "I'll take the big piano. Let's give this doctor song a quick run through before the place opens up. You start when you're ready. I'll join in after you play this version, just like we did this afternoon. But this first time let's do it without the singing."

Jimmy settled himself on the swivel stool and spread out the sheet music before him, while Eric climbed the stage to the grand piano.

They went through the number as planned, and the act of playing loosened them up. The sound of the music dispersed a tension that was hovering in the air.

"Let's try it one more time," Eric called over to Jimmy, "but this time I'll sing the lyrics."

Jimmy nodded and started again. This time Eric came in with the words of the song, singing with surprising verve and giving certain phrases a sly turn, à la Erica DeChez. When they finished, a couple of the waiters applauded. One of them, a short colored fellow, had drifted down toward the stage.

"Boy, that's some shiner you got there, Eric."

Eric stood up from the concert grand and, in a voice that carried across the room, said, "Yeah, Bernie, I had a disagreement with someone last night. I guess he didn't like the way I wore my hair." Eric and Bernie both laughed, and then the waiter went back to the bar where Roscoe stood staring back at Eric.

Eric hopped down from the stage and went over to Jimmy, who swiveled toward him on the stool. Eric leaned in and said, "Let me play for a while to get warmed up, then you take over for a bit. We can take turns. I think Erica DeChez will be putting in an appearance later tonight. A little makeup will help the looks of this battered-up face, don't you think?"

Jimmy laughed and stood up.

Eric went back to the concert grand and began to play. Jimmy sat at a table near the bandstand where he could watch Eric and still keep an eye on Roscoe, who busied himself with the bottles and glasses.

A few patrons began to drift in. Bernie began to circulate. Jimmy caught his eye and ordered two drinks. When the drinks arrived, Jimmy took one to the stage and left it on the piano. Eric gave him a wink.

It was not a busy night, but Jimmy still felt some tension in the room. He told himself it was just having Roscoe there after everything that happened at the opera. Maybe Roscoe had told some of the others at Pluto's about the incident. On the other hand, if someone in the Irish gang had been killed, as Eric said, couldn't word have gotten around? And what if it wasn't understood that it was only a fight over a gambling debt? Rumors could easily get out of hand. It was hard to say. Eric seemed confident that everything was under control, especially after seeing the vehicles out front. After a while, Eric took a break and sat down at Jimmy's table.

"That felt good," Eric said. He was buoyant. "You play for a while."

Jimmy took over the grand and Eric sat at the table and kept an eye on things. After he started to play, Jimmy saw a colored fellow he didn't recognize walk up and sit down at Eric's table and begin talking with him.

As the evening wore on, Jimmy grew more apprehensive. But Eric seemed even more confident that everything was fine, and he was gay and talkative. More people came in and a few began to dance. The place became quite lively for a while.

Jimmy and Eric continued to take turns at the keyboard. As it got later, the crowd dwindled and the place thinned out a bit. Eric, in his celebratory mood, had had a couple of drinks. He came down from the bandstand to Jimmy's table and, leaning into him, said, "Okay, now, you take over for a bit." He smiled. "It's time for Erica to put in an appearance. Let her start out with 'U Need Some Lovin'. When you get the word from Bernie, you can announce me and then play a long vamp while I make my entrance."

Jimmy nodded and went up again to the concert grand. He charged into "Gladstone Blues." Eric located Bernie, and the two of them hurried through the back door toward the dressing room.

In a while, Bernie approached the bandstand and told Jimmy that Erica was ready. Jimmy brought the tune he was playing to a close, then played a dramatic flourish across the keyboard.

"Ladies and gents," Jimmy announced, "now for your entertainment, we would like to introduce that favorite chanteuse, well known to denizens of Pluto's Lair, Miss Erica DeChez!"

The lights dimmed and the stage lights came on. There was applause and Jimmy played an extended intro as Erica DeChez sauntered onto the stage in her white beaded dress. She struck a pose at the side of the grand piano and Jimmy launched into the doctor song. Erica slinked around the bandstand as she sang the song to Jimmy, teasing him with the lyrics and running her fingers through his hair.

When the song came to an end, there was enthusiastic applause from the small crowd. A few folks had moved up closer to the front.

After taking her bows, Erica sat down at the piano next to Jimmy and suggested that they play a duet. Erica took the treble and Jimmy took the bass, and they improvised for a while. In high spirits Erica took chances at the keyboard, which challenged Jimmy to try new licks. Then they came together and brought the piece to a rousing close, both of them laughing with exhilaration and relief. The audience applauded their approval. Even Roscoe was clapping.

Erica stood and pulled Jimmy up and they both bowed. There was more applause, during which Erica said in Jimmy's ear, "Why don't we try a two-piano duet? I'll take the grand, you take the upright." As Jimmy made his way to the upright, Erica took her place and struck a few introductory chords.

"Since we are approaching the witching hour," she announced, "we'll try a duet on one of your favorites and mine: 'Midnight Blues.'"

Erica began to play and Jimmy joined in, entwining ornaments around Erica's melody. As Erica began to sing the lyrics, they played cat and mouse, alternating pianos with just enough notes of the melody and harmony to support the singing. The effect was simple but mesmerizing. The small crowd sat spellbound.

Bursts of machine gun fire erupted in the street outside. Pistol reports popped. The music dwindled into silence and Erica turned to face the hall, her eyes alert. The room became so quiet you could hear a hairpin drop. More sporadic gunfire could be heard outside. It continued off and on for a bit. Then a tense silence hung in the air. The sound of voices drifted into the quiet barroom from the front entry hall and then footsteps.

Danny Felton and five men with Tommy guns and pistols drawn appeared through the maroon curtains at the top of the stairs.

Erica stood up with great calm and crossed the stage. She descended the steps from the bandstand to the upright where Jimmy sat and leaned down to whisper in his ear. "Play something.

Anything. And no matter what happens, don't stop playing and don't turn around."

Jimmy swiveled to the keyboard. As he placed his fingers on the keys, the first thing that came to his mind was 'U Need Some Lovin'. Then his eyes fell upon that same sheet music that still lay open in front of him. He began to play the tune pianissimo. "I went to see the doctor today..." The lyrics sang in his mind.

Erica took a few steps away from the Jimmy and stood firm, waiting for Felton.

"That's right, we need a little music in here," Felton called out across the room. "We're going to have a little private party. And don't any of you think about rushing off. We've got the building surrounded."

Jimmy could hear Felton's voice approaching the bandstand.

"That's right," Felton went on. "Just a friendly little party with a few close friends. Right? We're all friends, here, aren't we? You're my friend, aren't you, Roscoe?"

"Yes, sir," Roscoe answered.

"You're my friend aren't you, Ronnie?"

"Yes, sir," answered another voice.

Felton walked forward to one of the seated patrons. "And what about you? Are you my friend?"

"You bet, Mr. Felton," came the reply.

"You see," Felton said, approaching the front of the room, "we're all friends here. And I don't ask much from my friends—only that they buy their liquor from me."

From the corner of his eye Jimmy saw two of the gunmen walk over to the door that led to Erica's dressing room. One of them went in with his gun drawn, while the other stood guard, blocking the exit.

Jimmy continued to play, his fingers moving mechanically over the keys.

He heard footsteps drawing close on the concrete floor.

"What about you, Jimmy Harper? Are you my friend?"

Jimmy was too frightened to answer.

"Oh, I see you're busy at the piano. Well, I'll take that piano playing as a yes. You're so eloquent at that piano. Do you think I'm your friend? Of course I am. We have a special friendship." There were other footsteps. "Do you think Erica DeChez is our friend, Jimmy?"

He continued to play.

"I don't think she is. You think she wants to follow you to Paris. But I don't think so. I don't think she wants to follow you to New York or Paris or anywhere. I think she was just using you. She just wanted your money for her little scheme."

"Don't listen to him," Erica called out. "He's just trying to trick you. Keep playing the piano." A calm firmness entered Eric's voice. "Felton, leave Jimmy out of this. I'm going to get out of this town one way or another and you're not going to stop me."

Jimmy's playing slowed and he felt the color drain from his cheeks as doubts overcame him. He turned around and looked into Erica's eyes, hoping to see that he could trust her. She stood in place, a few steps away, looking back at him with eyes that were full of affection and radiating that calm dignity and strength that he had seen in Erica at the opera. In that instant Jimmy knew that Eric loved him. At the same time, he detected a fear that Eric wasn't able to conceal. A wave of panic gripped him and before he knew it, a tear welled up and stung his eye.

Felton let out a laugh. "Don't stop the music. Keep playing."

Automatically, Jimmy turned back to the keyboard and resumed playing soft and slow. He wished more than ever that music could stop bullets. He concentrated on his playing hoping that was true. But he knew it was too late.

"And what about you, Erica DeChez?" Danny Felton continued. "Are you my friend?"

Erica said nothing.

"Hey, Herman, is Erica DeChez my friend?" Felton said.

Jimmy heard footsteps and Herman said, "No boss, I don't think so."

Still Erica said nothing.

"I don't think so either," Felton said. "I don't think friends pay your enemies to steal your business and your livelihood. Friends don't pay the cops to look the other way when you're being robbed. Does that sound like a friend to you, Herman?"

"No, sir."

"No. Friends like that deserve to be shot." Felton said and there was a loud metallic click.

Still Erica was silent.

"Well, your flannel-mouthed friends double-crossed you, Erica. O'Halloran told us the whole story. Down to your little 500 club. And I don't like it." There was a pause. "Should we let her go to Paris, Herman?"

Another metallic click came from Herman's direction.

"I don't think we can let Erica leave, can we, Herman?"

A gunshot deafened the room. Then another. Jimmy's body jolted. A spray of blood splattered across the page in front of him—scarlet musical notes scattered over the staves of the sheet music. A scream sounded from a female patron across the room. Jimmy's hands jerked on the keyboard and came down on a dissonant chord. There was the thud of a body hitting the floor right behind him. Jimmy found his fingering again and his hands kept up their automatic movements over the tiny droplets of red spattered along the piano keys. He kept his gaze just above the sheet music on the inlaid wooden pattern. He didn't dare move except for the mechanical action of his hands. The room was silent except for the sound of the piano. Somewhere behind him a man's voice said, "Jesus." Gun smoke hung in the air.

"Folks, the club is now closed for the evening," Felton said. "I expect you will all acquire a good case of Chicago amnesia if you know what's healthy for you."

Jimmy's peripheral vision caught the gunmen at the back doorway move toward the front of the club.

Footsteps sounded directly behind him, and Jimmy heard Felton's voice in his ear. "Take my advice, kid. Get out of town as fast as you can—and don't look back." Jimmy kept playing.

More footsteps sounded as Felton and his men retreated.

"Roscoe," Felton called. "See that the place gets cleared out after we leave. We'll send someone over to clean up the mess."

Then Felton and his men were gone.

Jimmy played on. "I went to see the doctor..." There was the scraping of chairs as people started to get up and make their way toward the front door. No one spoke. Waiters moved about the room and there was the clinking of glassware as they cleaned up. Jimmy couldn't move. He sat there playing the same tune over and over. His eyes were still fixed on the inlaid wood above the sheet music.

As his foot worked the pedals, it began to slide on the floor. He looked down. The concrete floor was dark and wet. It took him several moments for Jimmy to realize that it was blood.

His fingers slowed and the music came to a stop as his hands froze in place. Jimmy turned, following the trail of blood with his eyes.

Erica's body in the white beaded dress lay face down, surrounded by a pool of red.

A small sound escaped from Jimmy's throat. He jolted, pushing his hands against the keyboard, now covered with red fingerprints. He backed away from the puddle of blood, leaving red footprints. The discordant vibrations of the piano strings died away as the blood continued to spread across the floor. Jimmy stood paralyzed, staring. Then he turned away and reached for a chair to steady himself. Don't look back, he thought. Get out of town as fast as you can, and don't look back.

He felt beads of cold sweat forming on his forehead, and his mouth began watering metallic saliva. His stomach turned over, and he vomited on the floor. He held onto the chair until he could catch his breath. He spat several times, trying to clear his mouth. It took him some time to pull himself together and straighten up. He wanted water. He wanted a shot of liquor.

Jimmy steadied himself with one hand while he pulled out his handkerchief and wiped his mouth. As he took the white cloth away from his face, he noticed blood on it and began wiping at the side of his face. There was so much blood.

He made his way to the bar down to where Roscoe was putting away glasses. "Give me a glass of water and a shot of gin."

"Look, buddy, you better just beat it while you can," Roscoe said.

A hot wave of rage came over Jimmy and he stepped up on the brass rail, lunged across the bar, and grabbed Roscoe by the front of his coat and shook him. Between the anger and the adrenaline, his strength and ferocity surprised even Jimmy.

"Damn it, I said I want a glass of water and a shot of gin, you bastard!" Jimmy hissed in Roscoe's face, spraying him with saliva.

Roscoe looked at him with a trace of fear in his eye. Jimmy could feel his face twisted with anger and he held Roscoe for a moment in a long stare, then slowly released him.

"Okay," Roscoe said, taking a step back. "Okay, settle down." He set a glass of water and a bottle of gin with a shot glass in front of Jimmy, then stepped back again.

Jimmy washed his mouth out with water and spat it on the floor. Then he took a long drink from the bottle. He stood for several moments holding onto the bar. Finally he fumbled in his pockets and threw down a few bills. As he capped the bottle, he noticed that his hands were trembling.

"I'll take this with me," he said, and walked away from the bar and up to the front hallway.

He found the bathroom and went to the sink where he washed his face and rinsed his mouth again. Jimmy stared in the mirror as the water ran, but he didn't know who he was looking at. He stood there unable to move.

After a long time, he took out his handkerchief and rinsed it under the faucet. Studying the reflection, he wiped away the splattered blood from his ear and the side of his face. He saw drops of blood speckled across his shirt front and one shoulder of his tuxedo. "...a ruby stud..." Well, there was nothing to be done. All at once he realized it was Eric's blood. His hand froze in midair, holding the damp red-stained handkerchief. He stared. Eric's blood.

Eric. Who was Eric? Where was he now?

"If I have a single drop of Caucasian blood in my veins…" A shudder went through Jimmy's body and he was overcome with horror. He cast the handkerchief from him as if it were something unclean.

He turned and vigorously washed his hands. At last, he turned off the water, dried his hands, and walked out. He went to the coat check, still carrying the gin, and retrieved his overcoat. He stuffed the bottle into his coat pocket, and as he walked out of Pluto's Lair, he tried to hold the collar of his overcoat closed to hide the blood on his shirt. It didn't matter. There was no one on the street to hide it from.

THIRTY-TWO

Aimless and heedless, Jimmy walked for a long time, occasionally stopping to take a drink. Passing a puddle of water in the gutter, he remembered the blood on his shoes and sloshed his feet back and forth to wash them off. He walked on and on. He began to shiver, more from cold than from shock. He realized that he was drenched with sweat and that his shoes and socks were soaked.

He came to a busy street and flagged down a cab. "Take me to the train station," he said as he got in. When the cabby asked which station, Jimmy didn't know what to tell him. The driver asked where he wanted to end up, and when he learned that Oregon was Jimmy's destination, he said that would be the Union Pacific station.

Jimmy sat in the back corner of the cab taking swigs of gin as he watched the lights flash by outside the window.

"Say, ain't you that jazz singer from the Diggs Monroe band?" the cab driver asked. The name of the band seemed a distant memory and it dredged up a sour taste.

"Yeah, how'd you know that?" Jimmy said.

"I remember you. You and that gang sang a number for me one night about a week ago. I drove all of you to that cat house across the river."

That seemed like a hundred years ago, but between the gin and the numbness, Jimmy was unable to comprehend or care.

Out of the murky depths of his drunken thoughts, what did emerge with crystalline clarity were Danny Felton's words to Freddy in the basement of the brothel.

"You're a good boy. You deserve a special favor after that."

And something else from the past stirred in Jimmy's mind. He took another long drink.

"Hey, sing me another song," the cabby said.

The liquor had loosened Jimmy's tongue. A verse filtered up from the depths of his confused memory and he recited aloud:

"Little Jack Horner
Sat in a corner
Eating his curds and whey.
He stuck in his thumb
And pulled out a plum
And said: What a good boy am I."

Then he called out to the cabby, "Hey, Every Good Boy Deserves Favor. You know that? I'm a good boy. Don't I deserve some favor? When do I get my favor?"

"Hell, that ain't much of a song," the driver said. They drove on in silence. Jimmy took another long drink.

When he got to the station, the liquor had drowned Jimmy's pain. He got out and staggered around to the driver's window to pay him. The driver announced the fare and looked up at Jimmy in the light from the station. "Jesus, buddy, you okay?" he said. "You got blood on your shirt."

"Aw, it ain' nothin'. I got in a fight," Jimmy said. He went through all his pockets and handed all his money to the cab driver. It amounted to a handful of change. The cabby told him it didn't cover the fare. Jimmy continued searching his clothing. He found Eric's keys, glanced at them, and jammed them back in the pocket. He pulled out Felton's business card with Newhall's name on the back. He stared at it for a moment, then threw it into the gutter.

Steadying himself on the roof of the taxi he leaned down to the cab window. "That's all I got," he said.

The driver reached out of the cab and grabbed the lapel of Jimmy's tux. He saw that the tuxedo was also splattered with blood and with a little shove he released his grip. There was nothing to be done.

"You bastard," he called.

"Here," Jimmy shoved the gin bottle through the opened window of the cab. The driver took the bottle. "It's still half full," Jimmy said backing away.

"Go soak your head," the cabby grumbled and drove off.

Jimmy stood on the sidewalk in front of the station for a time. He couldn't think straight.

"Get out of town as fast as you can and don't look back." Felton's words.

Where was he to go but back to Oregon? He had to phone Carl. He had the blues and he needed to see the doctor.

He felt in his pockets knowing that he had just given his last cent to the cab driver. How was he going to get a train ticket when he didn't even have a nickel for the telephone?

Jimmy pulled out his billfold and checked it, hoping to find a forgotten dollar bill. There was no money. A business card tucked in the back of the wallet caught his attention. He pulled it out. It was Carl's card with his office and home numbers on it.

Oh, God…Carl, Jimmy thought. What can I tell him? How can I explain any of this? How did all this happen?

Jimmy put his billfold away and held Carl's card in his hand, studying it as if it might tell him what to do next. He looked around himself. A row of doorways leading into the building lined the sidewalk under a bright neon sign for the Union Pacific station. Jimmy stared up at it for a time, focusing his eyes. A few people passed in and out. Jimmy was the only person in a tuxedo. Through the glass of the doorways, Jimmy could see people scattered around the brightly lit interior. He took a few steps toward one of the doorways. He wavered a bit on his feet. A man in a fedora came out of the station, and Jimmy approached him, still holding Carl's business card in his hand.

"Say, can you help me out with change for a phone call?" Jimmy asked.

The man gave him a gruff look and brushed past him.

Jimmy walked up to one of the doors and entered the station. A young man and woman walked arm-in-arm toward the street exit. He approached them and held up the card. "I gotta make a phone call," he said.

They didn't stop to listen to him.

Jimmy stood and looked about the great hall of the station feeling lost. He wandered forward.

From across the room, a Negro couple came toward him heading for the street exit. The man was a bulky, older fellow in a bowler hat, carrying a suitcase in one hand and escorting a younger woman on his other arm. Jimmy felt drawn to them and approached.

They were laughing and the man was saying, "Love? If you find true love, then hug it to your bosom with all your might, and praise the Lord as if your life depended on it, because that's the one thing every one wishes and prays for."

Jimmy stopped. He recognized the man.

"Mr. Keys!" Jimmy called out and hurried up to the couple. They stopped and Jimmy went down on one knee and bowed his head before Mr. Keys.

The old piano player set down the suitcase and, patting the girl's hand, he said, "Wait here just a minute, Dora, darlin'."

He came forward and took Jimmy under the arm and pulled him up.

"Sweet Jesus, you hurt?" Mr. Keys said. "You got blood on you." He led Jimmy several paces away.

"Son, what's the trouble?" Mr. Keys said. "You been hurt?"

Jimmy's thoughts raced and memories of all that had happened since he arrived in Chicago flooded his mind. Where could he start? Tears welled up in his eyes. He couldn't speak.

"What can I do for you, son?" Mr. Keys asked.

Jimmy held up the card. "I've got to…" Jimmy's voice broke. He paused, struggling to control his emotions and compose his thoughts.

Jimmy took a deep breath and started again.

"You know that song…about the woman with the blues?" Jimmy sang, "and this is what the doctor said…" He paused and took a deep breath. "I've got to call this doctor."

"I see," Mr. Keys said. "It seems you been drinking. Is there someplace you can go sleep it off, son?"

"No. No, there's no place…I've gotta go to Oregon. I just have to make this phone call. You understand about the song, don't you?"

Mr. Keys glanced around at the young woman and back to Jimmy. "Look, son, I'm just an old man who don't know nothin' but how to play the piano. I just came down here to pick up my little daughter at the train. She's home from college on a visit and I've got to be gettin' her on home to her mama. Now, the telephones are over there, if that's what you're looking for. Can you find your way?"

"I don't have any money," Jimmy blurted out in desperation.

"I see." Mr. Keys reached in his pocket. "Well, here, son. Take a nickel for the phone." He held out a coin.

Jimmy took the coin and gripped Mr. Keys' hand. "Thank you. Thank you," he said, shaking Mr. Keys' hand and looking into his face.

"It's all right. Don't mention it. I've gotta go now. My daughter's waitin'. Take care of yourself." Mr. Keys smiled at Jimmy. He extracted his hand from Jimmy's grip. "You be careful," he said again and laid his hand on Jimmy's shoulder. Then he turned and walked back to the girl.

Jimmy watched them walk out of the station. He stood there for a long time. His panic and confusion subsided, and he tried to collect his thoughts. He had never been broke and on the street. He felt lost. But he had a coin. He could make that phone call.

Weaving, he made his way across the station to the phone booths. The alcohol was surging through his system, making it difficult for him to control his movements, but mercifully numbing his memories so that somehow it was easier for him to focus his attention.

When he got inside the booth, he mustered all his concentration to direct the nickel into the slot. He heard the coin drop and he held up Carl's card so he could read the home number. When the operator came on, he tried to explain that he wanted to make a collect call to Oregon but it took him a couple of tries to get his intentions across. He tried to read the number to her but again he had to try more than once. At last, the operator put the call through and it rang for a long time. While he waited for an answer, Jimmy fumbled with the card trying to put it back in his pocket and finally succeeded.

At last, Carl answered and accepted the reverse charges. His voice bridged a chasm that was wider than a continent. Jimmy's heart was flooded with relief and guilt, joy and grief, all mixed up together. For a moment, he couldn't speak.

"Hello," Carl said again.

"Carl—" he said. "Carl, this is Jimmy." He wanted to say a hundred things at once, but his voice choked with tears and he wasn't able to say anything more.

"Jimmy! I'm so glad to hear your voice. I got your postcard."

"My postcard?"

"Yes, of you and the band. Great picture. How are things going?"

Jimmy regained control of his voice. "Carl, I'm…I've had some trouble."

"Are you all right? You don't sound so good."

"I'm…I've had a little too much to drink."

"What kind of trouble? It's after midnight here. It must be… past 2 in Chicago."

"I need your help."

"Of course, I'll do anything I can. But tell me what's going on?" Jimmy could hear the concern in his voice.

"I can't explain right now. There's too much…Look, I need to get a train back to Oregon…but I'm broke. I've got to have some dough right away."

"I can wire you some money. Should I send it to your hotel? Or to Diggs?"

"No," Jimmy said with such force it surprised him. "Not Diggs. It's a long story. Jesus, so much has happened. We had a falling out."

"With Diggs? Is there someone else I can send the money to?" Carl asked.

Jimmy felt scared and alone.

"No. I don't…" He broke off, then gathered himself together. "There is no one. I've gotta get back to Oregon, Carl. It's very important. I'm just trying to get from here…to there." Again his voice broke.

"Okay, Jimmy, it's going to be all right. Try to pull yourself together. Now listen. Where are you?"

"At the train station."

"Which one?"

Jimmy thought for a moment and remembered the neon sign out front. "Union Pacific."

"Okay now there will be a Western Union counter there. Have you got that?"

"Yes, the telegram place."

"That's right. Western Union. They should have someone there all night. Tell them you are waiting for some wire funds from Oregon. Tell them my name, that the wire is coming from me. I'll send the money as soon as I can. You understand?"

"Western Union. I got it."

"Jimmy, you know I'd do anything for you," Carl's voice was confident and reassuring. "I'll wire $200. That should be enough money to get you a berth on the train to Portland, plus some extra to see you through."

"Thanks a million. I'm sorry for the trouble."

"It's no trouble if it will help you out of a jam. Now, will you be okay?"

"Yeah, thanks." But Jimmy wasn't so sure.

"It's good to hear you. I can't wait to see you again. Let me know when you'll be arriving in Portland. You can send a telegram. I'll meet your train."

"Okay. I'll be in touch."

"Do. You can call me any time."

"Well…goodbye. And hey, thanks again."

"Don't mention it. I love you." Carl hesitated, then said goodbye and hung up.

Jimmy followed Carl's instructions and found the Western Union counter. He kept his overcoat clutched tight so the clerk wouldn't see the blood stains or that he was in rumpled evening clothes. The Western Union man told him to wait on one of the nearby benches and he'd call Jimmy's name when the money came through. Jimmy sat and tried to stay awake, but he kept dozing off and on until about 4 in the morning when he heard the clerk calling his name. With the cash in his pocket, he went to the ticket counter and booked a berth on the next train to Oregon, departing at 10. Then he wired his arrival time to Carl. At last he felt secure enough to relax a bit and he let himself drift off to sleep on one of the benches.

Jimmy awoke with a start around 8. He remembered the night before as if it were a bad dream. His mind was a blur of confused thoughts and he was hung over. He went to the men's room and washed his face. The bloody handkerchief darted through his mind. Then in the mirror he saw the blood on his clothing.

He wanted to get out of his tuxedo and blood-stained shirt. It was more than an hour before his train left, so he walked the sunlit streets till he found a second-hand clothing store where he bought and changed into a set of street clothes, down to the socks and shoes. As he was gathering up his blood-splattered tuxedo, Jimmy remembered the blood on the floor at Pluto's. He examined his shoes to see if there was any blood left, a part of Eric. Jimmy felt a wave of nausea sweep over him. He closed his eyes, took a deep breath, and held onto the dressing room door, waiting for the feeling to pass. The store clerk wrapped his evening clothes in brown paper and tied it with a string.

Jimmy walked out of the store carrying his bundle and went back to the barbershop at the train station. He asked the barber where he could buy a bottle of gin, and while the barber gave him a shave, he sent the shoeshine boy out to a speak. Then Jimmy had a meal in the station coffee shop as he waited for the train. After eating, he felt better. Not long before 10, he got settled on the train, and he was ready for a long rest.

When the train pulled out of Chicago, Jimmy didn't look back. He was fast asleep.

EPILOGUE

When you live with someone for many years, you will hear about some event from out of the past, perhaps a mention here and a detail there, of which you were not aware. During dinner with friends, your companion may bring up some aspect of that distant incident that had never before been told. Another time, perhaps when you are traveling, your friend will, out of the blue, be reminded of another element that had never come to light, of that same long forgotten happening, prompting a remark from you like "I never knew that."

Over time, often without even being aware of it, you piece things together in your mind and fill in details—at times totally fabricated out of imagination. Slowly some semblance of a story takes form—a personal fiction that gives the illusion of coherence to those accounts of long-past remembrances.

But we never truly know what happened. And if someone else were to tell it, he would give you a completely different narrative.

The accuracy of parts of this account may be diminished by my failing faculties of recollection, and there is much in this tale that I have had to create where I could not reconstruct, for this retelling is obscured by the absence of any firsthand observation on my part.

While I hope to be true to Jimmy Harper's attempts to describe what had happened to him, this part of the story must remain my discoveries and revelations as I pieced together an invention of Jimmy's time in Chicago. It is made up of scraps and hints and loose threads, drawn from clues and hunches, as Jimmy shared bits of his story with me.

I have never been to Chicago. So it is a mythical Chicago where this tale unfolds, a city reflecting my memories of Jimmy's words, a city created out of my own imaginings. Whether this is truth or fiction, I am not the one to say. Perhaps it is the kind of story that should have begun, "Once upon a time…"

—Carl Holman, 1981

Esteemed Reader,

This is a self-published novel. You can help make it a success:

• Tell all your friends about this book.
• Post reviews on amazon.com and goodreads.com
• Sign up for my newsletter at medicinefortheblues.com
• Share about the book on social media networks and blogs.

Thank you for reading books.

Jeff Stookey

ACKNOWLEDGEMENTS

I must thank Merilee Karr, MD, for invaluable advice about medical details, for pointing me in the right direction in areas of medical history, and for recommending numerous resources. I thank her too for her encouragement and for implanting in my mind the dangerously liberating concept of writer's intuition.

Historians George Painter, author of *The Vice Clique: Portland's Great Sex Scandal*, and Tom Cook, founding member of the Gay and Lesbian Archives of the Pacific Northwest, have both been extremely helpful. I am grateful for their generosity with their time, their resources, and their knowledge of Pacific Northwest gay history. The Archive is now housed at the Oregon Historical Society.

I have to acknowledge the memory of Jesse Bernstein (known as Stephen J. Bernstein in print). Even though he's been dead for all these years since his suicide, I have felt him watching over my shoulder as I wrote this, and I could never have done it without his example and his encouragement. I guess you won't mind, Jesse, that I used some of your ideas.

All my dear friends who read the first draft have my undying gratitude for saving me from numerous mistakes, and my writing group from The Attic contributed invaluable feedback. This book would never have emerged into public form without the help and encouragement of my editor Jill Kelly. She reined me in and prodded me to judiciously prune countless twigs and branches.

And, it goes without saying, (but those are the things that must be said), that I am forever indebted to my partner, Ken Barker, for tolerating, and even encouraging, this peculiar obsession with writing words on paper. Thanks for your support in keeping me going, and especially for helping me to keep from losing my nerve.

THE STORY CONTINUES.

Watch for *Dangerous Medicine*, Book 3 of the trilogy
Medicine for the Blues. Available Fall 2018.

Please visit the website:
www.medicinefortheblues.com

ABOUT THE AUTHOR:

Growing up in a small town in rural Washington State, Jeff Stookey enjoyed writing stories. He studied literature, history, and cinema at Occidental College, and then got a BFA in Theater from Fort Wright College. In his 40s he retrained in the medical field and worked for many years with pathologists, trauma surgeons, and emergency room reports.

Jeff lives in Portland, Oregon, with his longtime partner, Ken, and their unruly garden. *Acquaintance*, Book 1 of the trilogy *Medicine for the Blues* was his first novel. Contact Jeff at **medicinefortheblues.com**.

www.ingramcontent.com/pod-product-compliance
Lightning Source LLC
Chambersburg PA
CBHW071457110726
47908CB00003B/645